Jordan's Return

SAMANTHA
CHASE

sourcebooks
casablanca

Published by Sourcebooks Casablanca, an imprint of Sourcebooks, Inc.
P.O. Box 4410, Naperville, Illinois 60567-4410
(630) 961-3900
Fax: (630) 961-2168
www.sourcebooks.com

Originally self-published in ebook format in 2011.

Printed and bound in Canada.
MBP 10 9 8 7 6 5 4 3 2 1

This book is dedicated to my wonderful husband of twenty-five years. Without your encouragement and understanding, I never would have sat down and taken the time to pursue my dream. You mean the world to me; you are my Knight in Shining Armor, and without you, there would be no laughter in my life.

Prologue

THE SLEEK MERCEDES PICKED UP SPEED AS IT MADE ITS WAY along the interstate. The driver kept one hand carelessly on the wheel while tormenting his passenger.

"You are such a disappointment to me, Jordan," he sneered. "I mean, I had such high hopes for you, and you just let me down time and time again."

With a white-knuckle grip on the door handle, Jordan prayed her ex-husband would drop her on the side of the road; she would gladly walk the entire thirty miles back to her home if it got her out of this hell.

Eric removed his sunglasses and gave her a lecherous grin. "When I married you, I thought you understood what I wanted, what I *needed*, in a wife." He reached over and touched Jordan's face with his cold hand, laughing when she flinched. "If you had put *my* needs first, we would have been fine. But you wanted to stay home and take care of those brats. Did you really think a man like me would find that attractive?"

"Eric, please," Jordan began, fearful of the way the car was starting to swerve between the lanes.

"I love it when you beg, Jordan, I really do, but unfortunately it won't do you any good. I am finally free of you and have what I've always wanted. Marcy understands me; her father's firm is practically salivating to have me join them."

"I'm happy for you, Eric, I truly am. Could we just please—"

"*Happy?* Ha! That's laughable, sweetheart. You're just anxious to get more of my hard-earned money for those whiny kids you forced on me! Well, let me tell you something, you'll get nothing more from me! *Nothing!* You won't see a dime more than what the judge ordered."

Eric's voice was piercing, and as he threw his head back and laughed, Jordan looked around for a way to escape. This wasn't going to end well. The erratic driving was getting worse, and Jordan had no doubt Eric had been drinking.

"By the time the ink is dry on the divorce papers, I'll have everything I want, everything I deserve. You held me back, Jordan. We could have had it all, but you wanted something out of a friggin' outdated Hallmark movie. Why couldn't you just do what I wanted? You ruined *everything*!" On the last word, his right hand swung out and hit Jordan hard on the side of her face, and she cracked her head against the window.

"Don't ruin my damn car, too. It cost me almost a hundred grand!" With his focus on Jordan and a feral smile creeping across his face at the pain he had caused, he missed how the car had swerved dangerously toward the median. When his attention turned back to driving, Eric couldn't bring the car out of the course it was taking.

As the car bounced and rocked over the grassy divide, he cut the wheel sharply, his actions jerky and lacking coordination due to the alcohol he'd consumed at lunch. Hysterical laughter bubbled out of him as the full impact of an oncoming car hit the passenger-side door.

And Jordan.

Chapter 1

OPEN ROAD. THERE WAS SOMETHING VERY PEACEFUL ABOUT driving down a deserted highway, particularly when the passengers in the backseat stopped arguing. She glanced at them through the rearview mirror and smiled. They were finally asleep and there was silence in the car. Ever since they were babies, the car had been the magic sleeping place, and when all else had failed to lull them, a ride in the car would bring peace and tranquility. It was funny how twelve years later, it still had that effect.

Chancing any repercussions, Jordan Manning slipped a CD in the player and let her head relax back on the headrest. Yes, this was exactly what she needed to be doing: taking a long trip with her boys to recuperate and get focused on the future. Her sons had been less than thrilled at the prospect of spending a month away from their friends. They had been downright surly when they found out it was a month on the beach at the end of the season.

Jordan couldn't help the timing. The off-season was the least expensive time to travel. Raising and homeschooling two boys alone didn't allow for many luxuries. They may not view this trip as a luxury, but Jordan sure did. At thirty-two, her life was very different than she had imagined. But looking in the rearview mirror again at her sons, Joseph and Jacob, Jordan knew she wouldn't change a thing.

Checking the GPS one last time for her own reassurance, she knew she was heading in the right direction and relaxed even more, enjoying the scenery and listening to Matchbox Twenty on the stereo. While singing softly, she let her mind wander to the things she hoped to accomplish over this break.

Besides letting her body heal from the injuries she'd sustained in the near-fatal car accident at the hands of her psychotic ex-husband, she hoped to bond with the boys. Without conscious thought, she lowered her hand from the steering wheel and rubbed it along her ribs on the right side of her body, stretching a little to keep from stiffening up.

A frown creased her brow at the memory of waking up in the hospital three days after the accident with fractured ribs, a broken leg and arm, as well as internal injuries. Her recovery had been long, its progress slowed by her anger at the fact that Eric had walked away with very superficial injuries. Apparently, the man was unbreakable. He had come to visit her once and had laughed at her appearance. Mentally, she had conceded defeat, unable to battle with him any longer. But the sight of her children had jolted her out of her pity party and forced her to recover.

Life had been chaotic for all of them lately, and she knew if she didn't do something about it now, the results could be irreversible.

Joseph was twelve and already starting to rebel against everything. Jake, however, at only eight, was her "fixer." He wanted nothing more than to keep the peace and make everyone happy. Neither of them seemed very happy lately, however. Jordan frowned. It was hard to understand what it took to make little boys happy, having had only sisters growing up, and now she had no help from her ex-husband to give her boys a father, a role model, and the male perspective on things.

Smiling weakly, she thought how particularly relentless her own mother had been lately, saying the boys needed a positive role model in their lives. A positive *male* role model. Well, it wasn't so easy to find one, and if it were, Jordan wouldn't have minded having one in her life either. She had been alone for a long time and missed having a man around. Single moms weren't high on the dating food chain, and she hadn't wanted to get into all that in front of her children. Plus, being an invalid for the last six months hadn't put her out on the singles scene much either.

No, her children had to be her top priority right now, and if that meant being alone and desperately miserable, then so be it. Well, maybe desperately miserable was a bit of an overstatement. Desperate for affection, maybe? Yes, Jordan definitely missed that. Eric had left their life together without so much as a backward glance. He'd had a new life waiting for him, which he had been orchestrating while he and Jordan still looked happily married.

What a fool she'd been! Looking back, she saw all the signs, but during it all, she had been ignorant. Well, not anymore! She was here to get her head together and a month on the Virginia coast was exactly what the doctor ordered.

One hour later, Jordan pulled her silver Explorer to a stop in front of an adorable bungalow a mere two blocks from the beach. It was a cheery yellow, with a white picket fence around it and a wide front porch with wicker furniture and flower boxes filled with red and purple pansies. Her real estate agent had told her the place was furnished but she would need to bring a lot of her own necessities such as bed linens and towels. It had made packing a bit more complicated, but the results would be well worth it.

She woke the boys, popped open the tailgate, and began the process of unloading the vehicle. They were still sleepy from the drive and showed no excitement whatsoever about having reached their destination. Jordan unlocked the bungalow's front door and stepped inside. It was perfect. Bright white walls were covered in framed pastel prints, and natural wicker furniture adorned the front living area while more solid, sturdy furnishings filled the den near the back of the house.

The house was small with one large area for the living room, kitchen, and den, and a short, wide hallway that led to the two bedrooms in the back.

The boys had begged Jordan to find a house that would allow them to have their own rooms, the way they did at home, but she had to stay within a budget and that meant they had to share a room for the month. It added to their already disheartened view of this vacation.

Neither boy spoke while they unloaded the vehicle, and it wasn't until everything was in the house that anyone uttered a word.

"Well?" Jordan smiled at them expectantly, arms spread wide to indicate their surroundings.

Joseph spoke first. "This stinks. I knew I should have packed my Xbox!" He skulked over to the sofa and crashed down on it, pouting.

"You have your Nintendo DS with you," Jake offered, ready to right all the wrongs of the world.

"C'mon, boys," Jordan said cheerily. "Let's get your room set up and then we'll see what we can do about some dinner." Slowly, she lifted the box marked "linens" and headed down the hall. Moments later, she heard footsteps behind her.

They worked together and had the room looking as if they'd always lived there in a matter of minutes. "We make a good team," she commented as she looked around the room with satisfaction. The boys were starting to relax, and Jordan held on to the hope that they were off to a good start. The boys went on to help her get her own bedroom set up and unpacked. It was near seven in the evening when they all collapsed on her bed complaining of hunger.

"Okay, let's tackle the kitchen!" she cheered in hopes of motivating them.

"Aw, Mom!" both boys cried out.

"Can't we go get some burgers or something?" Joseph asked wearily. Much as Jordan hated to admit it, the idea sounded wonderful. The thought of cooking after a long day of driving, with so much still to be done around the house, was really unappealing. Besides, her body was protesting all the activity—not that she had let on.

She stood still in a dramatic thinking pose, pretending to contemplate the possibilities.

"Please, Mom!" they pleaded with the biggest, saddest eyes they could muster. She caved in.

Before she knew it, they were back in the car and on their way into town. She had been sure to make a mental

note of all the fast food places to eat as she drove past
them on the way to the house. They drove through the
first place they came upon and then headed back to the
house with a bag of burgers and a mountain of fries.

Jordan stood and watched as Jake went about setting
the table. His mop of dark brown hair looked as if it
had yet to meet a brush and could definitely use a cut.
A pair of crystal-blue eyes peered out from beneath
the bangs.

"Almost ready." He smiled.

Joseph set the food out. Where Jake looked scruffy
and mussed, Joseph was neat as a pin, his own dark hair
short and trim. He had inherited Jordan's dark brown
eyes, but his seemed full of sadness. His expression was
serious as he went about his task and Jordan couldn't
suppress a sigh. They were as opposite as night and day
and they were all hers. They made a good team, the three
of them, and it filled Jordan with pride.

Since the accident, the boys had matured a lot, going
out of their way to help her. It wasn't always with the
most cheerful demeanors, but they did what they could.

Jordan had her family to thank for that. Her mother
had spent three weeks with them while Jordan was in
the hospital, and then her sisters had alternated staying
with her once she had come home. It had taken almost
three months before Jordan had felt confident being
home alone with her sons, and she'd still had a physical
therapist or a nurse's aide there to help her.

The thought of her sisters made Jordan smile. They
had been like a lovable military while they lived with
her during her recovery. Being mothers themselves, they
knew how to keep both boys in line and help them learn

what they would need to do to help their mother if she needed them. The fact that her children had been forced to deal with such a big responsibility added fuel to her anger toward Eric.

Everyone was silent as they ate dinner. It wasn't so much that the food was good as that they were all starving. Jordan couldn't help but smile as she watched the boys inhale their food. As soon as the meal was done, both stood and cleared the table and took out the trash. *Damn, they're good*, she thought to herself.

"Okay, guys," she said as she stood. "Showers, pj's, and bed. Jake, you go first." Her younger son nodded, running off to do as he was told after stopping to plant a loud, smacking kiss on her cheek.

Jordan looked around to assess what needed to be unpacked next. As if reading her mind, as he was prone to do, Joseph grabbed the box marked "kitchen" and carried it over to her.

"We'll probably need this stuff in the morning," he stated as he opened the box and started putting its contents away with her approval.

"We'll go shopping in the morning to stock up," she told him with a smile. "Why don't you think about some of the things you want me to get, and then we'll make a list, okay?" The boy nodded and went back to his work.

"I think there's still some stuff in the cooler we can have for breakfast," she said, and in the blink of an eye, Joseph unloaded the cooler without being asked.

Again Jordan couldn't help but sit back and observe her son. He seemed so different from the boy he had been six months ago. Much as she wanted to attribute it to the fact that he was almost a teenager, the sad truth was he had taken on the role of man of the house. Judging by the look on his face, he took the job seriously.

Therein lay the problem: he was way too serious for such a young boy. She hated that all this responsibility had been thrust upon him. Joseph certainly did his share of complaining, and he was entitled to it, but it still made her heart ache for him. Her sons deserved better than this, and she was going to do something, anything, to make their lives better.

Jordan heard the bathroom door open and knew Jake had finished in there. Joseph finished his work in the kitchen and then walked down to his room to get ready for bed. When she at last heard the door to the bathroom close and the water for the shower turn on, she walked down to the boys' room and checked on Jake. He was lying in bed, reading a book.

"Hey, bud," Jordan said as she sat down next to him on the bed. His dark, wavy hair was still wet and he hadn't bothered, yet again, to brush it. She combed her fingers through it, hoping to tame it a little. "This will be a wild mess come morning." He looked up at her with his big blue eyes and smiled his most cherubic smile.

"It's always a mess in the morning, Mommy." He laughed, wrinkling his nose when she bent down and kissed him. "Will you read this to me?" he asked sweetly, barely stifling a yawn.

Taking the book from his hands, Jordan sat and read with him until Joseph came in. She smiled at Joseph as he climbed into his own bed wearing a pair of crisp cotton pajamas. They both smelled so clean and wonderful that she wanted to hold them close to her.

"Why don't you join us over here, Joe?" she asked

as she held out her arm to him. "We're halfway through with the book."

Joseph let out a loud sigh, climbed back out of his bed, and walked over to her. He rolled his eyes as he came to sit down. "This one again?" he whined.

"Oh, hush," Jordan playfully scolded. "This was one of your favorites too when you were Jake's age."

Joseph sat there silently while Jordan finished the story.

"The end!" Jake said as Jordan placed it on his nightstand. She grabbed Joseph in a bear hug before he scampered back to his own bed on the opposite side of the room.

"You know," she began, "this room isn't so bad." It was actually quite nice—pale blue walls, crisp white trim, and natural hardwood floors. The tailored midnight-blue curtains matched the small throw rug in the center of the room; combined with all the blue bedding the boys had brought from home, it was most definitely male territory in here.

Jordan smiled down at them both as she came to stand in the middle of the room, observing the complete picture they made.

"We're going to have a great time this month, I promise," she said lovingly. "We'll finish unpacking in the morning and stock up the kitchen, and maybe even do some exploring around town when we're done." The boys looked up at her, lacking the enthusiasm that she felt. She leaned down at their bedsides and kissed them both.

"Really, it's going to be fine, you'll see." She wished them a final good night as she shut off the lights and closed their door. "It's going to be fine," she whispered reassuringly to herself.

The morning came way too soon. The boys were bouncing around her bed, and Jordan was sure it couldn't possibly be the sun she saw peeking from behind the window shades. It seemed she had just fallen asleep, and now here they were.

"C'mon! We're hungry!" Jake said as he bounced on the king-size mattress. "Can we make pancakes?"

Jordan shook her head to get her bearings and looked at the clock. "Six forty-five!" she scolded them. "Do you wake me up this early at home?"

The boys seemed not to hear her.

"Can we, Mom?" Jake asked again with boundless energy.

"Can we what, baby?" she asked with confusion, pushing her chestnut hair away from her face.

"Pancakes," Joseph answered. "He wants pancakes. I told him no but he didn't believe me." He stuck his tongue out at his little brother, who in turn mimicked the action.

"Sorry. No pancakes today, guys," she said around a yawn. "We only have what was in the cooler. We'll go shopping after breakfast, okay?" That seemed to satisfy them and they left the room. Jordan thought about possibly going back to sleep, but after hearing the beginning of yet another argument, she knew she'd never have the opportunity.

Reluctantly, she kicked the blankets off her bare legs and rose from the bed. The wood floor felt cold against her feet as she walked toward the lone bathroom to take a shower and prepare for her day. By the time she emerged from the steamy room, the boys were quietly watching television, happily eating some of the fruit, bagels, and juice she'd packed in the cooler the previous morning. Without letting her presence be known, she smiled to herself and went back to her bedroom to get dressed.

Leaning against the door, Jordan took a moment to look at her own environment. In all the commotion yesterday, she hadn't had the time to appreciate her personal surroundings. The room was very feminine, quite the opposite of the boys' room. Her walls were painted a cheery sunflower yellow, and the window treatments were done in a sheer, gossamer fabric that pooled on the hardwood floor. There was a large burgundy chaise lounge in the corner of the room with a dressing screen behind it for effect. Small pieces of bleached oak furniture finished off the room, and there was an enormous walk-in closet with mirrored doors Jordan adored.

She was already beginning to feel at home in this place. It was peaceful and quaint and exactly what she had always wanted. Eric had always wanted a large house with large, ornate furniture. He had dictated what kind of decor they had and never let Jordan pick anything for herself. In this little house, with its bright colors and simple furnishings, she felt herself start to heal right down to her very soul.

She was, of course, thankful for that fact because she had paid for the house in advance and it would definitely have been a disaster if she'd had to stay in a place she hated. She'd had enough of that back at home—the home she had shared with Eric.

Checking her reflection in the mirror, she felt mildly encouraged. She didn't seem to look as tired as she'd felt lately; her brown eyes looked brighter and her long hair had been recently cut in a more stylish manner that accentuated her high cheekbones. Heck, even her smile seemed more relaxed than it had been in a long time. She was beginning to feel like her old self again, now that she had something to look forward to.

After applying a little makeup—just a touch of mascara and lipstick—she went to check on the boys, who were still engrossed in an episode of *SpongeBob*.

"Okay, who's ready to food shop?" she challenged in a playful tone. Both boys gave her a quick glance, then returned their attention to the TV.

Feeling a little of the wind go out of her sails, she repeated herself. The boys got the hint and went about getting dressed and ready to go.

While she waited, Jordan prepared herself half a bagel and a cup of orange juice. Once the boys returned to the kitchen, they helped their mother make the shopping list before heading out the door.

As she climbed into the car, Jordan racked her brain to remember where the local grocery store was located. She couldn't recall having seen one during their brief drive through town. Not feeling too bothered by the notion, she started the vehicle and headed for town.

It was very early in the morning—not even eight thirty—and the town looked a little deserted.

"Man," Joseph groaned, "there is *no one* in this town."

"It's still early, Joe," Jordan reminded.

"That and the fact that the season is over," he mumbled under his breath, hoping his mother hadn't heard him.

Driving slowly down the main street, Jordan spotted a figure up ahead. Deciding she had no choice but to ask for directions, she pulled over next to the man and rolled down her window. "Excuse me," she said. "Could you please tell me where the nearest grocery store is?"

The man had his back to her, momentarily bent over retrieving a newspaper from the ground. Once he stood up and turned around, however, Jordan felt all the color drain from her face.

He was tall, clearly over six feet, wearing a pair of well-worn, form-fitting jeans. His broad chest and shoulders were covered in an indigo-blue button-down shirt, the sleeves rolled up to his elbows, exposing an enticing length of tanned, muscled arms. Jordan's mouth went dry as she took in his sun-kissed, playfully mussed, sandy-brown hair. But it was his eyes that captivated her, chocolate-brown eyes that sparked with recognition.

"What was it you were looking for?" he asked casually, taking a sip from the travel-style coffee cup he held in his large, tanned hand.

"I was, um, I was looking for the nearest..." She paused to clear her throat. "We need to go to the grocery store," she croaked.

"Uh-huh," he replied as he slowly approached her vehicle. His steps were even, measured, and when he was finally close enough to the door to put a hand on it, he glanced inside. He noticed the boys sitting in the backseat, watching him warily.

His lips fought against a grin as he noticed the pulse in her neck beating erratically.

"So, what brings you to the Virginia coast, Jordan?"

Chapter 2

BEFORE JORDAN COULD FORM AN ANSWER TO HIS OH-so-nonchalant question, Jake asked, "Do you know him, Mommy?"

"Yes, sweetheart," she replied as she turned to give her sons a reassuring look before turning back to the man in the window. "This is Mr. Tyler. We went to school together." She nervously looked up and met his smiling eyes.

"Hi, boys," he said, relieved that they stopped looking at him as if he were an ax murderer. "You can call me Rob." The boys, in turn, introduced themselves and said hello.

Rob Tyler. Of all the people Jordan could have run into today, who would have thought it would be her first love? She hadn't seen him in years, hadn't even thought about him, but now, watching him stand there before her, the years just melted away.

He was still as handsome as she remembered, and her heart still beat erratically at his closeness.

Rob turned his attention back to the woman sitting before him. You could have knocked him over with a feather when he heard her voice. He hadn't even needed to turn around to know it was Jordan. He'd know her honeyed voice anywhere. "So, you were saying…" he prompted her.

"We're here on a family trip and needed to get some

groceries," she stated. "Is there a supermarket nearby?" Her voice shook a little and she hoped it didn't sound as obvious to Rob as it did to her. It was a little unnerving being this close to him after so many years. He had been her first love, her first everything.

Rob leaned in close to Jordan. "Did you leave your husband home in bed?" he asked quietly.

"Our dad isn't here with us," Joseph supplied, and Jordan shot him a look in the rearview mirror.

"He doesn't live with us anymore," Jake chimed in. Jordan's head hit the headrest and she shut her eyes, unable to believe her children chose now to come out of their shells.

Taking a deep breath, she tilted her head to the side and looked at Rob with mild embarrassment. "About that grocery store?" He didn't respond, but instead walked around to the passenger side of her SUV and let himself in. Jordan stared at him incredulously as he made himself comfortable.

"It's just easier to show you," he said as if it were the most natural thing in the world for him to be there with her.

It wasn't natural, however. He made the entire interior of the SUV shrink, and Jordan could feel her whole body tense with awareness. Rather than make a scene in front of the boys, she snapped her mouth shut and listened for what she was sure would be long and confusing directions.

Less than five minutes and one right-hand turn later, they were parked in front of a huge supermarket. Jordan silently glared at Rob.

"What?" he asked innocently with a smirk. "It seemed

farther away in my head, I guess." When she continued to glare, he added, "Besides, I needed some things too. Lucky for me you came along when you did."

They all climbed out of the car and Jordan walked away to retrieve a shopping cart. She wasn't surprised when Rob came up behind her.

"You don't mind if I share, do you?" he asked close to her ear. He didn't wait for her to answer. He was walking ahead of her now, her sons clamoring around him.

Jordan paused for a minute to compose herself. *What the heck just happened?*

"C'mon, Mom!" Joseph prompted. Shaking her head, she met up with them at the store entrance.

To any observer, they were a family out doing their shopping. To Jordan's thundering heart, they were a disaster waiting to happen. How had she gone from single mom on a family vacation with her boys to grocery shopping with her ex-boyfriend? With a panicked look at the three males, it hit her that they *could* pass for a family. The boys had always favored her looks more than Eric's and at this moment, they even seemed to resemble Rob. It was almost as if... *Oh, never mind!*

Her sons asked Rob nonstop questions about the town and he very patiently answered all of them. He told them about the best spots on the beach, where to find a playground, where the movie theater was, all the hot spots for kids. The boys listened in rapt attention.

"Do you have any kids?" Jake asked, and Jordan found herself suddenly very interested in the conversation. She strained a little while pretending to look for fresh green beans.

Without looking her way, Rob answered the boy.

"No, I don't have any children. Sorry," he said lightly. Jordan let out a breath she hadn't realized she'd been holding and noticed she had collected enough green beans to feed a small army.

Just because there are no children doesn't mean there isn't a wife waiting at home.

Staying a few feet away from wherever Rob went, Jordan's memory of him and the food he liked all came back. It amused her to be able to predict what foods he was going to pick next. Jeez, what did that say for her life if fourteen years later she could still remember how much he loved grapes? *Pathetic, Jordan. Truly pathetic.*

They made their way through the store, filling up the cart. Rob let the boys go on ahead, giving them each an item to find. Jordan was sure it was a ploy to stop the endless barrage of questions. Before she knew it, they were alone in the aisle and Rob got in step with Jordan.

"So, how long are you in town for?" he asked as he placed a package of Oreos in the cart.

For a brief moment, her mind whizzed back to when she was seventeen and she and Rob would take picnics out to the local park. He would always feed her Oreos because he knew they were her favorite. Had he put those in the cart deliberately? *Down, girl.* Just because she was able to remember some of his favorites did not mean that Rob had that same ability. Didn't everyone like Oreos?

"Not long," she said evasively. She was still reeling from the fact that he was here with her, and had a hard time speaking over her rapidly beating heart that seemed determined to break through her chest.

"Humph," he breathed beside her. He stopped and

watched as she made her way up the aisle. She looked exactly the same. He never would have thought it possible, but Jordan looked exactly as she had at the age of eighteen. She wore her hair a little shorter, but her figure would never let on that she'd had two children. He admired how she looked in a pair of faded blue jeans that hugged her rear nicely, as well as the form-fitting teal knit top that kept drawing his eyes to the full swell of her breasts.

Jordan looked back at him with whiskey-colored eyes, showing how uncomfortable she was. He felt like some creepy stalker for staring.

"What?" she asked as she watched the amused expression on his face.

"I guess I still can't get over the fact that you're here," he stated honestly. "How've you been?"

"Fine." She reached for a box of cereal and started to walk away from him. Rob stood where he was, holding the coffee cup he had been nursing since he'd climbed into her SUV. "What?" she asked again with irritation when she turned and noticed he hadn't moved.

"Are you going to give me an inch or what?" he asked as he stood looking helpless in the middle of the aisle.

"What are you talking about, Rob?"

"You haven't given me one straight or honest answer to anything I've asked you. It's been all one-word answers. And for the record, 'fine' doesn't really describe how someone's been for fourteen years. I mean, I got you here to the grocery store to help you out and—"

"Got me here? I may not have graduated with honors but I think I could've understood 'go to the corner and turn right.' You're crazy," she muttered and continued to walk away.

He caught up with her in the next aisle. "Fine, I'm crazy," he began, but before he could continue, the boys were back, having succeeded in getting the items he had assigned them. "Great job!" he enthused. "So, boys, how long are you in town for?" Rob's eyes clashed with Jordan's and a smile tugged at his lips.

"We're here for a whole month!" Jake said proudly.

"Wow!" Rob whistled. "That's a long stay."

"I'll say," Joseph added with a mumble.

"You don't want to be here, Joe?"

"No," he replied flatly.

"Why not?" Rob's curiosity was piqued.

"None of my friends are here, I don't like the beach, I couldn't bring my Xbox, and it's gonna be boring just hanging around taking care of Mom and—"

"*Joseph!*" Jordan cut in. "That is enough," she said in a hushed tone. She looked up at Rob's questioning eyes. "Twelve is such a fun age." She shrugged and moved along up the aisle as she continued shopping.

The three males fell in step behind her, and together they finished finding everything on her list as well as Rob's and headed for the checkout. Jordan hesitated a minute, having realized that Rob's stuff was mixed up in the cart with hers. He watched her and, as if reading her mind, stepped forward and handed the cashier his Visa card. Without even a glance in Jordan's direction, he began bagging up their order.

She stood and silently fumed at him. Jake and Joseph, however, were back at his side, chatting Rob's ear off. They really were starved for male attention.

Maybe they were the key to making *this* particular male go away.

Perhaps if they annoyed him enough with their endless chatter, he'd stay clear of them from now on. Maybe. Jordan knew they could be a handful, but they were hers and she loved them. To someone who didn't have children, they could be just a tad bit overwhelming.

Rob did seem to enjoy talking to her sons, but maybe he was just being polite. Maybe by the time they were done with the groceries and she dropped him back off where she'd found him, he'd be glad to be left alone.

Taking the receipt from the cashier, Rob turned and waved good-bye to the store manager and pushed the shopping cart back out to Jordan's car. He had Jake standing behind the handlebar, his back against Rob's chest, and Joseph standing on the front of the wagon as they flew across the parking lot, whooping it up with laughter. Their sounds of pure joy filled the air and Jordan suddenly felt like an outsider. It had been a long time since the three of them had acted silly and carefree with each other, but she shook her head to clear those thoughts and reminded herself that Rob was the outsider—these were her kids and Rob would be gone in a matter of minutes.

Feeling better after her little inner pep talk, she caught up with them at the car and popped open the hatch while instructing the boys on how to place the groceries in the back. Rob stood back and watched the boys work.

"You've got some good helpers here, Jordan," he said encouragingly.

"I sure do," she agreed. When they were done,

Joseph took the cart and placed it back with the others. When he approached the car, Rob clasped him on the shoulder.

"Good job, Joe."

"Thank you, sir." The boy beamed. "I always help my mom, especially since the accident." Having said that, Joseph climbed into the backseat of the car and shut the door.

Jordan looked away to avoid Rob's inquiring eyes.

"Listen, Rob, I didn't expect you to pay for our food. Let me write you a check and—"

"Don't worry about it, Jordan," he said nonchalantly and turned away. Jordan stood there dumbfounded for a moment and then walked around to the driver's side. Rob climbed into the passenger seat and watched as Jordan stiffly settled in and started the car.

"Everybody buckled?" she asked. They all answered in unison and she put the car in gear and drove back to where she had first seen Rob. She parked the car next to the curb and turned to him.

"This is where you needed to be, right?"

"Yes. Thanks," he replied, but he wasn't ready to get out of the car. He had a million questions for her, but one look in her eyes and he read their meaning: "No questions, please." He would respect that silent plea.

Hell, he had no choice. He was in no position to make any demands of her, especially here in front of her children.

Picking up the grocery bags he had kept with him up front, he turned around to face Joseph and Jake. "Thanks for shopping with me, boys," he said brightly and was met with two smiling faces in response. "It was really nice meeting you both. I hope you have a good time here on the coast."

"Hey, Rob," Jake started, "do you think maybe you can come over and show me how to build a sand castle sometime?"

Rob turned to Jordan and shrugged. "It was one of my selling points to them on the benefits of living near the beach," he confessed with a sheepish grin.

Jordan couldn't help but smile. He really had helped the boys focus on how much fun this vacation could be, something she had been unable to do in the long weeks of planning before they'd arrived here.

"Maybe sometime, sport," he replied, and noticed how the young boy's face fell. He silently turned to Jordan for help.

"Jake?" she queried. "What's the matter, sweetheart?"

"That's what Dad always says when he doesn't mean it," he responded sadly, looking down at his hands twisting in his lap.

Jordan's heart ached at the sight of her son. When would the hurt of Eric's leaving end? Bracing herself, Jordan turned to Rob.

"So, do you have any plans for dinner?"

Rob pulled up in front of Jordan's bungalow a little after five that evening. He had readily accepted Jordan's invitation to dinner and felt like it was a gift from above. He wasn't foolish enough to believe she had actually *wanted* to invite him over, but he was not above being thankful for sad little boys, either.

He sat in his truck for a long moment and thought

about the events of the morning. During their time in the grocery store, Jordan's sons had shared a wealth of information. For instance, he knew Jordan and Eric had divorced several years earlier and Eric was now splitting his time between New York and Los Angeles. He also dated a *lot*. At least according to Joseph.

He also learned their father rarely came to see them since he'd moved out, and during his last visit he had forced Jordan to go out with him and they had been involved in a near-fatal accident due to Eric's driving drunk. Rob had wanted to push for more details, but there wasn't time. Plus, since it was clearly such a traumatic incident, perhaps the supermarket was not the best place to get into it. There was no doubt in his mind the boys would have told him everything, but he was sensitive enough not to force them to relive all the details. Rob remembered Eric from high school and had never understood how Jordan could have married him—or how she could have left *him* for Eric. He could admit his own actions had caused the breakup between him and Jordan, but the fact that she'd chosen to date Eric so quickly—and stayed with him—threw him for a loop.

Eric was the class president, full of charm and charisma. He had always irritated Rob. Eric had the type of personality that seemed sincere but once you got to know him, you came to realize it was all just a smooth, pretty-boy facade. How could the woman he had known and loved so dearly marry someone like Eric?

Joseph had gone on to tell him how badly Jordan had been injured in the accident: broken ribs, internal injuries, a broken leg—her entire right side had basically been crushed. Rob hadn't noticed any outward signs of the accident. Jordan still looked perfect to him. But then again, Jordan had always looked perfect to him.

From the very first time he had seen her in second period biology class, he was lost. They had dated for two years in high school, and Rob had thought they would eventually get married. But, being a foolish eighteen-year-old partying hard at a keg party or two, he had been caught kissing another girl in a moment of pure stupidity, and he had lost her. He wasn't even attracted to the other girl; he had just been all puffed up on himself and thought, "Why not?" It just goes to show where thinking south of the border got you.

Jordan had rebounded quickly with Eric and had never given Rob a second look. She hadn't spoken a word to him since that fateful night. Rob had hoped, foolishly, that Jordan would go off and have her "payback fling" with Eric and come back to him. But she never had. He had wanted to go to her so many times and beg for forgiveness, but she had turned to stone where he was concerned. It had been hard to accept that, after all they had shared and how much they had loved each other, she could just walk away from him.

Of course, he had no one to blame but himself. Looking back at that time in his life, he could kick himself. No one had ever attracted him or turned him on as Jordan had. Not that he'd been living the life of a monk all these years. He'd just become more selective in the women he slept with, in hopes there would be a spark like he'd had with Jordan. It had never happened and he'd come to accept that you just didn't have that kind of chemistry twice in a lifetime. It didn't thrill him, but he'd come to live with it. Only Jordan had ever had the ability to turn him on just by being near him.

And she still did. Just spending time doing something as mundane as food shopping with her today had been enough to make him hard. Time had been kind to Jordan Manning, and although Rob knew he was here to appease her children, he secretly hoped that in time she'd be as happy about seeing him as he was about seeing her again.

Now, standing on her doorstep, he felt extremely self-conscious and nervous. He knew he would need to put her at ease. Rob wanted the chance to get to know Jordan again, and her kids. But if after all she had been through, she let it be known that tonight was all he would be given, then he would be fine with it.

Yeah, right.

Taking a deep breath and feeling more nervous than a man his age should, Rob rang the doorbell. Dinner, conversation, a casual evening. No harm, no foul. He could do this. No problem. Her children, however, had a completely different game plan in mind, one in which they were oblivious to the underlying feelings of the adults around them.

—◦◦◦—

Jordan nearly jumped out of her skin when she heard the doorbell. Before she could move to answer it, she was nearly plowed down by the boys in their excitement to get there first. It sounded like a tiny stampede in their rush to the door. Feeling that they had it all under control, Jordan went back to the kitchen and the dinner preparations.

Rob called out a casual greeting to her and she watched him get dragged right back out the door by her sons. Chuckling to herself, she went about filleting the chicken. Once she had that simmering and the salad prepared, Jordan looked up and stared in fascination at the scene in the yard.

Rob was tossing a football back and forth with her boys. Both Jake and Joseph looked very animated and she could hear their laughter. The sound tugged at her heart. It had been too long since she'd heard them laugh with such pure joy, and twice today Rob had been the cause of the wonderful noise.

Jordan stood and watched the man responsible for the laughter in complete awe. He hadn't changed much in all these years. His sandy-brown hair was still wild; he never did brush it properly and so it had a constant "just out of bed" look to it. She loved that. He was still in excellent physical condition, and even though he was dressed casually in jeans and a polo shirt, she could see the muscles of his upper body straining against the fabric of his clothes. His skin was nicely bronzed; beach life, she supposed.

Earlier, when they were shopping, she had tried to avoid looking into his chocolate-brown eyes. In her youth, she'd told him he most definitely had bedroom eyes. He still did and they were still very sexy. The few times she had allowed herself to meet those eyes, her tummy had fluttered nervously.

Looking at his profile, she realized he was quite a perfect specimen of a man. His features weren't so outrageous, but the straightness of his nose and the squareness of his jaw and, hell, cheekbones a model would kill for... *Stop it!* she mentally yelled at herself. *He's just a man, for goodness sake!* Sure, he was a beautiful man, with broad shoulders; a wide chest; big, muscular arms... *Oh.* She groaned out loud. It was going to be a long night! She grabbed a glass of cold iced tea she had poured for herself earlier and took a healthy drink.

Forcing her attention back to the dinner she had to get on the table, she turned and took the biscuits out of the oven and placed them in a basket. Jordan turned again to the window and raised it to alert them all that dinner was ready. Within seconds, they filed in and the boys went directly to the bathroom to wash up. Rob sauntered toward the kitchen. She watched his approach with a dry mouth.

Damn, he looks good.

For the briefest of moments, she envisioned Rob coming up to her and kissing her senseless, her with oven mitts on her hands and an apron around her waist. Sure it was a boring, very domesticated fantasy, but man, oh man, did she itch for it to be real.

Shaking herself out of her reverie, she slipped off the oven mitts and faced Rob as casually as she could. "Having fun yet?"

"Absolutely," he replied as he walked over to the sink to wash his hands. "What can I help you with?"

You could rip this apron off me and kiss me like you've missed me all these years.

"Nothing. Everything's ready, just have a seat." She motioned toward the table and he sat down and turned to watch her work. Jordan hoped he didn't notice the slight tremble of her hands under his watchful gaze.

"Oh, before I forget." Jordan reached into her front

denim pocket. "Here." She handed him money for the groceries he had purchased.

"You don't need to do that, Jordan. It wasn't that big a deal." He tried to put the money back in her hands, but she refused. He held her hand in his for just the barest of seconds, heat beginning to build in his veins.

"I appreciate the offer, but feeding the three of us costs a small fortune and it's not your responsibility." Her tone was light and cheery but Rob still slightly resented the fact that she wouldn't let him help her. "I can take care of my family without any help from anyone." Her tone turned slightly sharp on that last note and Rob raised an eyebrow. Clearly he had struck a nerve.

"I wasn't implying you couldn't—"

Jordan cut him off with the shake of a hand and a nervous laugh. "Sorry. I didn't mean to get so defensive. I get a lot of sympathy from people who are just so sorry I'm a single mom. But single mom or not, I can take care of my boys just fine. I have no worries about it."

"If you're sure…"

"Yes. Thank you." She turned to finish getting their meal on the table.

The boys came scampering down the hallway and into the kitchen, where they began to help serve the meal. Jordan prepared all their plates, directing Jake as to whose plate was whose and instructing Joseph on the salad and dressing placement.

When they were all seated and had said grace, the chatter started up immediately.

"Rob used to play football… Rob said he had a baseball mitt I could use… Rob said he has a boat that we could fish off of… Rob said there was a video store nearby…" On and on it went, and the snarkier side of Jordan was having a field day inside her own head.

Rob said he could walk on water, her inner self mocked and she chuckled. Snapping out of her own wayward thoughts, she forced her attention back on Rob and the kids.

"Easy, guys," she scolded gently. "It was very nice of Rob to come by tonight, but he is not here to entertain you. He has a life of his own and we are here to have fun together, just the three of us, remember?" As soon as the words were out, she felt like the wicked witch of the west. The smiles on their faces disappeared and they became very quiet.

Jordan put her fork down in resignation. Rob didn't want to interfere and put his two cents in, but he truly felt Jordan could use a helping hand in this situation.

"Hey, you guys, come on. Give your mom a break," he addressed them in a firm yet loving tone. "She has planned this great trip for you and she's right. I have a job and commitments of my own." That hadn't helped much; if anything, the boys looked even a little more devastated. "I can come by once in a while and hang out with you, but ease up on your mom, okay?"

"Yes, sir." As far as pep talks went, it stunk, but both Jake and Joseph pushed on, a little of their cheer returning.

Rob looked over at Jordan and she mouthed, "Thank you." He nodded and turned his attention back to his dinner.

"When you said dinner, Jordan, I figured you'd make some burgers or something. This is way more than I expected. I hope you didn't go to too much trouble." Rob helped himself to some salad. "This has been a real treat."

Jordan wasn't deliberately trying to show off; she enjoyed cooking and this really was a standard meal for them: sautéed chicken, angel hair pasta with peas and cherry tomatoes in a creamy herb sauce, biscuits, and a salad. Well, maybe it was a little more than their standard meal, but Rob didn't need to know that.

"Amazingly enough, the boys prefer this kind of cooking," she told him. He looked at the boys in disbelief. "They're not that interested in fast food."

"It's true," Joseph confirmed. "Mom's a great cook. Whenever I eat at a friend's house, I always come home and tell Mom how thankful I am that she can cook!" They all laughed at that. "Really, you wouldn't believe how many moms out there can't cook. That's why most kids want fast food. But not me. I want my mom's homemade pizza or her chicken cutlet parmesan. *Yummm…*" The boy was obviously lost in the thought of·it all because his big brown eyes sort of glazed over.

Jordan rubbed the top of his precious head and smiled.

"That's quite a compliment," Rob commented as he placed his napkin on the table next to his plate. "That was fabulous, Jordan. Thank you."

"My pleasure," she said, and meant it. Jordan glanced around the table. "Time for cleanup," she prompted, and the boys sprang into action.

Rob rose as well and began to help but Jordan swatted him away. "This is part of their chores. Please, just sit and relax."

Rob sat back and enjoyed the sight of Jordan and her sons working together in the kitchen. She ran a very tight ship. A single mom would have to do such things, he realized. In a matter of minutes, the room was immaculate. He was amazed the boys didn't complain about having to help out so much, but maybe it was just because they had company. He smiled as Jordan placed a kiss on each of the boy's heads.

His smile turned to a frown when he realized this could very well signify an end to their night and he wasn't ready to leave this family yet. He was enjoying himself and had hoped to have more time to talk with Jordan alone. Thinking quickly, Rob rose from his chair and clapped his hands together.

"Who's up for ice cream?" he asked. He risked a look at Jordan and mentally kicked himself. Maybe she didn't allow for such things. He was mildly surprised when he got a positive response from all three Mannings. The boys ran off to their room to grab their jackets and waited anxiously by the front door while Jordan went to her room to get one for herself.

As they walked out the front door, Rob said, "There's a great place down by the beach."

"We're already by the beach, Rob," Jake reminded him. Rob chuckled and patted the boy on the head.

"I meant it's within walking distance," he said to Jordan. "If you don't mind the walk." Though she showed no outward signs of difficulty from her accident, Rob wasn't sure if she was fully up to walking around town.

"That sounds nice," she replied as she slipped a black cardigan sweater on.

Rob held the picket gate open for them and as Jordan walked past him, she caught a hint of his aftershave. Without conscious thought, she said the name of it out loud. She smiled at the thought that the simple woodsy scent was still his.

"Excuse me?" he chirped from behind her.

Jordan blushed furiously and ducked her head. "Nothing," she said as she walked as fast as her still-sore body would allow to catch up with her sons, thoroughly embarrassed.

Real smooth, Jordan, she chided herself. *He probably thinks you've been pining away for him all these years.*

Soon they were all heading down the few short blocks to the beach. The thought of seeing the sun set on the ocean had Jordan picking up her pace a little. She breathed in the salty air. The smells of the beach filled her senses, and she inhaled deeply and smiled. It was early September and the nights hadn't cooled much yet, but there was still a hint of a breeze coming from the ocean. Once they reached the sand, Jordan stopped and kicked off her shoes. She turned when she heard Rob's soft laughter.

"What's so funny?"

"Still hate to wear shoes on the beach, I see," he observed.

Jordan found herself laughing, too. "Honestly, who likes to wear shoes in the sand?"

His eyes were watching her intently and Jordan felt very aware of him at the moment. It was getting hard to force her gaze away, but the sound of Jake and Joseph taking off down the sand forced her to straighten and stare after them.

"Boundless energy, those two," she muttered with mental exhaustion.

"I'll handle it. You take your time," he said and took off, sprinting after them.

Jordan watched him run. No one had the right to

look that good in motion. He had a confident air about him, and rightfully so. It had always been that way. Rob looked good in everything he did, particularly when he was involved in physical activities.

Great, now there was a mental picture that was going to stick around for a while. She chuckled lightly when Rob finally caught up with her sons, scooping one up in each arm and swinging them around. That was no small feat considering Joseph had just had a growth spurt. She could hear their laughter. Eric had never roughhoused with the boys. He always said he didn't want them messing up his clothes or his hair. It still was hard to swallow that she had actually married such a man. The more time passed, the less she could explain what she had ever even liked about him or what had attracted her enough to make her believe she had loved him and wanted to marry him.

Sighing, she walked slowly, making her way to catch up with them while enjoying the feel of the sand between her toes. The slowness of her gait wasn't only because of the pleasurable feel of the silky-soft sand; it was all part and parcel of her recovery. Walking long distances still caused some discomfort, but after the scene she had just witnessed, she'd gladly deal with the muscle aches.

By the time she met up with the three of them, her boys were already sitting down in the sand enjoying their ice cream cones. She smiled at them as they waved and just then, Rob turned and handed her a cone. She nearly cried when she saw it. He had remembered all her favorites: chocolate ice cream, wafer cone, and chocolate sprinkles.

Reading her thoughts, Rob leaned in close to her and

whispered, "I always think of you when I have chocolate ice cream." His voice was so deep, so masculine, Jordan had shivers of delight running down her spine.

Memories of other picnics, picnics shared under the stars after making love when he'd fed her chocolate ice cream, swam in Jordan's brain. The playfulness of young love, the laughter, the plans… Being with Rob back then had been a full-sensory experience. Everything had been new and exciting, and their whole future had loomed brightly ahead of them. It had been a long time since she'd allowed herself to look back on that time in her life and remember all that was good, all that was right, and how much she had loved Rob.

Tingling all over, Jordan moved away quickly to the safety of her children. Rob joined them moments later on the sand, and they all ate in silence, enjoying the cool breeze coming off the water and the sweet ice cream.

"Thank you so much," Jordan said finally as she bit into her cone. "It's been a long time since we've indulged like this, right, guys?" The sight of her boys nearly made her cry out with laughter. There seemed to be ice cream everywhere. Rob, noticing the same thing, jumped up to grab some extra napkins to assist in the cleanup.

He'd make a great father. Jordan blushed at the thought. "Thank you," the boys said in unison when he came back and handed them each a stack of napkins. Once they were done and cleaned up, they stood and asked Jordan if they could go down near the water and look for shells.

"Oh, I don't know, guys." She hesitated. "I'm sure the water is very cold now and—"

"We'll walk down with you while you check it out,"

Rob interrupted. He was getting awfully cocky with her and he knew he was pushing some buttons that he probably shouldn't, but he couldn't seem to help himself. The look on her face when he spoke had been priceless. He chose to ignore her wide-eyed response to him and instead stood up, brushed off the excess sand, and held out a hand to her.

Instead of arguing, Jordan reached up and accepted his hand. The contact was electric and as soon as she was steady on her feet, she quickly removed her hand from his and turned to look out to where the boys had run off to. Without a word, she and Rob walked side by side toward the water.

The loud shrieks confirmed what Jordan had thought: very cold water. The boys didn't seem to mind, and after she finished her cone, she sat back down in the sand next to Rob and watched them frolicking around, splashing one another. Rob was sitting so close that she could feel the heat emanating from his body and thought that he could surely hear her heart racing.

"They're great kids, Jordan," he said matter-of-factly.

"Thank you," she whispered.

"You're very lucky to have them." He sighed. He was watching them closely when she turned to look at him.

"I know it's not any of my business and I hope you don't mind my asking, but why haven't you settled down and started a family?" She would understand if he didn't reply, but inside she was dying to know. Was she hoping for an ego boost by hearing him say he'd never gotten over her? She groaned inwardly, hoping she wasn't that shallow.

Without taking his eyes off her sons, he said, "I got

close to it once. But she was a career woman and the thought of living in a small town, raising a family and doing the soccer-mom thing wasn't appealing to her."

Jordan felt a pang of jealousy she had no right to have, then chastised herself for being ridiculous.

"It's funny; it was the exact opposite with Eric. He was the one who didn't want the whole family thing. He resented my getting pregnant with Joseph because it meant I wouldn't be able to work any longer. He eventually gave in and accepted the idea of me being a stay-at-home mom, but he never liked it. In his eyes, I should have been content with a career and should never have wanted to be a mother. I couldn't help it; that's the life I always wanted to live."

Rob sat in stony silence for a moment, remembering all the times he and Jordan had discussed their future and how they would have a bunch of kids and grow old together. Their plans had always included having kids right away, Jordan staying home with them while Rob got his architecture career off the ground.

"I guess it never occurred to me that anyone *wouldn't* want to live that life," he said with a sigh. Did Jordan remember all those plans? Did she ever regret giving their dream up? Not sure he wanted the answer, he switched gears. "So, I live vicariously through my sister with her kids. I get to be their favorite uncle and spoil them rotten with none of the real responsibility."

"Claudia?" Jordan said as she suddenly remembered. "Oh my gosh! How is she? Does she live here now, too?"

"Yeah, Claude's great," he said with affection. "She's been married forever and has four kids now." At Jordan's shocked expression, he nodded. "I know, hard to believe that my party-hearty sister settled down to be the ultimate domestic wife and mother, but she did and she loves it."

"Good for her! Do you see them often?"

"I have dinner with them at least once a week. She has three daughters and a son. I love my nieces, but I find I favor my nephew; he needs all the help he can get with that many females around!"

Jordan laughed. "I'm sure he does." She watched her sons as they dug in the sand before turning back to Rob and sighing. "Sometimes I feel that outnumbered."

She hadn't meant to share that much about her life with him or with anyone—at least not yet. She loved her sons more than life itself, but there were times when the responsibility of being both mother and father to them was overwhelming. Her family didn't seem to understand, and she was sure Rob wouldn't either. Suddenly Jordan felt very self-conscious that she had spoken her feelings out loud. She ducked her head and tried to think of something else to say to change the subject.

Rob could hold back no longer. The need to touch her became too strong to resist. He reached over and gently placed a hand on top of hers where it rested on her knee and then squeezed. Jordan's eyes widened at the contact. His hand was large and warm and callused, and it felt wonderful. Without conscious thought, she turned her own over in his and let their fingers mesh together.

"I'm sure you do," he whispered. There was no condemnation in his words, and for the briefest of moments, Jordan believed he really did understand how she felt. She looked up at him with gratitude as he began to lean into her, hoping to feel her warm breath on his face before he kissed her.

"Hey, Mom, check out these great shells! I'm going to keep them and start a huge collection for when we go home. Aren't they cool? Hey, are we going to be able to find our way home in the dark?" Jake had cluelessly bounded over to ask the questions, unaware of what he was interrupting.

Jordan forced herself to move away from Rob's warmth. "We should go," she said with a ragged voice. Rob nodded, not trusting himself to speak just yet. They stood and told the boys to go on ahead but to stay close as they made their way slowly back up the sand and to the road.

During the walk back to the house, the kids commented on how much fun they'd had and thanked Rob and over and over for the ice cream. He smiled and took it all in. They were such a sweet little family, and Rob found himself wishing they were his. His split with Amy had been amicable and he had eventually convinced himself he could live without fulfilling his dream of a wife and kids. But now as he walked with Jordan, he knew it wasn't possible. He wanted the dream. He wanted the original dream he and Jordan had shared.

Once back at the house, while the boys each took their turn in the bathroom showering off all the sand and ice cream, Jordan and Rob sat and made small talk in the den.

"So, where are you living now?" he asked.

"We have a house down in Raleigh, but I'm planning on selling it. It's too big for just the three of us and it's a lot to take care of." He nodded. "What about you? How long have you been here on the coast?"

"I moved down here after college. My grandparents were living here at the time, and it just seemed like the perfect place. I had vacationed here as a kid and it had always been a secret dream of mine to move here." He shrugged. "So, I got my degree and lived with my grandparents for a year while I got my architectural firm up and running and now…here we are."

"I had no idea you wanted to live here. I remember you talking about your trips here but I didn't think—"

"It's no big deal," he interrupted. "I never told anyone about wanting to live here. It all just sort of fell into place that way. I don't think it was a conscious decision to move here but I don't regret for a moment doing it. I've always loved it here." Looking back, Jordan thought it seemed odd that Rob had never shared that part of his dream with her. "Anyway, I'm very fortunate that I'm living part of my dream. Not too many people can say that." Jordan nodded sadly and they both grew silent.

Rob hung out until both boys were clean and ready for bed. Jake had insisted on showing him the room he was sharing with his brother and then sharing in great detail all about their rooms at home. Joseph told him about trophies he had won that were proudly displayed in his room as well as his dreams of a more grown-up room—since he was getting to be almost a teenager. For all the hard times they'd suffered lately, they still seemed content. He only wished he felt the same about his own life.

When Joseph and Jake walked back to the living room to kiss their mom good night, Rob wished them both a good night and told them he'd be back when he could, not wanting to step on Jordan's toes. Both of the boys were too worn out to argue the point and thanked him again. The excitement of the evening had worn them out, and Jordan kissed them both and told them she'd see them in the morning as they headed sleepily off to their room.

Now, alone in the living room, she was a jumble of nerves. Alone with Rob. What would she do? If she were honest with herself, she'd like to lean in close to him on the sofa and have that moment from the beach back.

"I had a lot of fun tonight, Jordan," Rob said from his standing position in the living room.

"Yeah, me too," she replied a little breathlessly. Jordan walked slowly toward him, hoping he'd join her on the sofa.

"Thanks again for dinner," he said as he walked over to the front door. Jordan watched him quizzically. Was he leaving?

"Oh, sure. No problem. The boys really appreciated everything you did with them today." *So did I. Please don't go.*

"I guess I'll see you around." He waved and was out the door, his eyes never quite meeting hers. At the sound of the door clicking closed, Jordan should have felt relief.

Instead, she felt a little angry.

"That was it?" she asked herself out loud. She stood, dumbfounded, rooted to the spot. Secretly, she had hoped he would at least try to kiss her or ask to see her again, but instead he had retreated as soon as he had the chance. She heard his car pull away. This was what she had wanted, wasn't it? She didn't want him hanging around, letting her kids get attached to him.

Why, then, did she feel so rejected and alone?

Chapter 3

THREE DAYS LATER, THE BOYS WERE *STILL* TALKING about Rob. His name was the first thing she heard when she woke up, the last thing she heard when she put them to bed, and *damn* if he wasn't all that she saw in her dreams! Placing her face in her hands, Jordan had to stop and count to ten to get through yet another Rob story.

"Hey, Mom!" Jake called from the kitchen. "Can we go to a movie today?"

Yes! she thought, *a movie. A good movie.*

A movie of *their* choosing! A movie that would erase all conversations about anything else in the world for at least a day. It was such a simple plan that Jordan had to stifle a giggle.

"What a great idea, Jake!" she gushed. "Why don't you guys pick the movie, okay?" This was exactly what was needed. Normally, she picked the movie, but in her desperation to clear their minds of Rob and move on to another subject, *any subject,* she'd sit through just about anything. Jordan found herself almost frantically doing a Google search of the local theater and movie times. The sooner the boys were engrossed in the quest for a movie, the sooner her mind would be cleared of all things Rob.

They decided on a matinee of the latest action flick that involved robots and the end of the world. *Fun.* Jordan cringed a little at the thought of it, but in the end, it would all be worth it. If her boys thought it odd that their mother suddenly had no problem with action movies filled with violence, they chose to keep that observation to themselves. Smart children.

The drive through town was uneventful, and Jordan found herself straining her field of vision a little as they drove past the place where they had first seen Rob. Was that possibly his office he had been standing outside of that day? She had never asked. Either way, she saw no signs of him. Just a glimpse would have been nice. With any luck, the darn movie would clear *her* mind as well. Luckily, the boys hadn't noticed where they were driving past, too wrapped up in conversation about the upcoming movie and all the blood they were going to see. A couple of times Jordan actually felt her stomach roll at the vivid pictures they were describing, and she hoped against hope they were exaggerating.

After parking the car a block away from the theater, but several blocks from Rob's office, they climbed out and got in line for tickets. Since the tourist season was over, the line wasn't too long—just long enough for her boys to take note of the man walking on the opposite side of the street.

"Hey, look! There's Rob!" Joseph yelled. Jordan rolled her eyes.

This cannot be happening! she thought, frustrated.

Looking amazing in faded blue jeans and a snug red T-shirt, Rob smiled brightly as he spotted them and jogged over. Her sons were jumping up and down, waving him over.

"Hey, you guys!" he said, beaming at both boys. "Doin' a movie today, huh?"

"Yeah! Mom let us pick the movie and we're gonna see explosions and blood and everything!" Jake said excitedly.

Rob looked at Jordan with amusement and she shrugged. "Wow!" he said with exaggerated enthusiasm. "She *is* a great mom!" Rob had to suppress a laugh because he remembered well how much Jordan hated violence in any form. If she was willing to sit through this particular action flick, she had to be truly desperate.

The boys dragged Jordan forward with the line, barely able to stand still for all their excitement.

"Can you come with us, Rob?" Joseph asked.

Rob looked at the boy, who seemed to have a trace of desperation in his eyes. "Well, that's up to your mom," he said diplomatically, firmly placing the ball in her court, although secretly hoping she'd think it was a good idea.

"I'm sure Rob is working right now and far too busy to take the afternoon off to go to a movie," she said with confidence. "Aren't you?" she urged, hoping he'd get the hint.

But Rob decided to have some fun with her. "You're in luck!" he said with a huge grin. "Today's my day off and I had been hoping to see this movie. I hear it is especially bloody." He watched Jordan pale. The boys jumped up and down, cheering with glee, and Rob nearly choked when he looked back at Jordan, who was shooting daggers at him with her eyes. This probably wasn't the best way to get in her good graces, he realized a little too late.

For days, Rob had been trying to come up with a believable excuse to see Jordan and her boys but could come up with none. It was just a coincidence that he had seen them here today and he was thrilled.

It had taken every ounce of strength he possessed to leave Jordan's house days earlier. His original plan had been to stay after the boys had gone to bed and try to rekindle some of those old feelings they'd once shared. He'd longed to take her in his arms and kiss her senseless. At some point while they had sat and talked, sanity had returned and he'd realized he would need to proceed slowly and with caution. They weren't kids anymore and Jordan had kids of her own to consider. Plus, she had been put through the wringer with Eric. She might not be feeling too kindly toward the male sex as a whole right now.

No, he couldn't act impulsively. He would have to earn her trust and respect, as well as the respect of her sons. Somehow, he felt he'd achieved that part already as he looked down and saw Jake standing close to him, looking up at him with a wide, bright smile on his young face.

"You excited, sport?"

"Yes, sir," Jake said, clearly pleased with the nickname. "Mom never lets us see these kinds of movies. This is going to be so cool! I'm real glad you're here to see it with us."

"Me too," Rob said as he placed his hand on Jake's shoulder. Once the tickets were purchased, they went inside and lined up at the concession stand to pick out snacks.

"Remember what I told you on the way here, guys," she reminded them as they pressed their faces up to the glass. She was only allowing for popcorn and a shared soda. Each boy whined at the reminder. Rob, meanwhile, decided on several different boxes of candy, nachos, and the jumbo-size soft drink.

Jake and Joseph stared at him in awe. "Is all that for you?" Jake asked in amazement.

"Nah," Rob said as he tried to balance his bounty of junk food, "it's for all of us to share."

Jordan wanted to slap him. Didn't he hear what she *just* said? These were her kids, for crying out loud! Did he have any idea how consumption of all that junk food would affect her small children? They'd either get tummy aches or be bouncing off the wall by the time they got home! Either way, she'd end up being miserable.

She'd have to have a talk with him about this after the movie. There was no way that she would sit back and let him make her look like a wet rag while he portrayed the cool hero. Clearly he had no idea what it was like to be a parent and the importance of not letting your children overindulge on junk food. Sure, it didn't make you popular, but as the adult, you sometimes had to make decisions based on practicality, not popularity.

Sometimes being an adult really sucked.

Once inside the darkened theater, Jordan went first into a row near the middle of the theater. She'd expected one of her children to follow, but they shoved Rob in after her. Oh, they were sneaky, these kids of hers. They knew that with Rob between them, she wouldn't be able to see all the junk food they were going to consume. *Fine*. Let them eat junk. One less meal for her to cook later. But the mom in her couldn't help but also imagine the mess she'd have to clean up if they got sick from it all. Just the thought of it all was beginning to make Jordan sick.

After they were all settled into their seats, Jordan turned to talk to Rob about his indulgence of her kids and his lack of respect for her rules, but as soon as she tried to speak, he held up a hand and shushed her!

"I love coming attractions," he whispered, his eyes never leaving the screen.

Well, of all the… She was furious! How dare he shush her!

Jordan sat back in her seat none too gently and huffed. She didn't even have her popcorn! She had let Jake carry it and now she had nothing to do with her hands. To show her mood, she sat ramrod straight in her seat and folded her arms stiffly across her chest. No one even noticed.

Joseph and Jake were excitedly sharing snacks, drinks, and awed expressions with Rob. As the movie got into gear, Jordan tried to force herself to relax. As soon as she eased into a more comfortable position, Rob placed an arm around her and handed her the bucket of popcorn—all without looking at her.

The man was infuriating! She grudgingly took the popcorn and thought of shoving his arm off her, but wouldn't give him the satisfaction of knowing he was getting to her. So she let him keep it there during the whole movie, but she sat stock-still, not leaning into it, not accepting its strength, warmth. It was harder to do than she'd thought.

Back when they had dated in high school, they'd sit like this as they watched a movie, but Jordan would lean her head on his shoulder and eventually, the movie would be forgotten and his mouth would be on hers. Jordan had to stifle a groan at that kind of memory. Her mind toyed with the question of whether Rob was thinking the same thing. Would their kisses be all that she remembered, or was she just over-romanticizing the experience of first love?

Of course she was over-romanticizing. If things had been as wonderful as she thought they had been, they would never have broken up. Rob had broken her heart all those years ago. The very last thing she should have been doing right now was thinking of that time of her life with anything but anger. If Rob had been faithful, her heart never would have been broken. She never would have dated Eric and she… Jordan stopped herself and sighed. If all those things had never happened, she'd never have had her boys.

Before she could examine that thought any further or figure out what was going on in the movie, the lights came back up and it was time to go. As soon as they were out of their seats, the nonstop chatter started up again. Her sons were beside themselves with the whole movie experience.

"Did you see when that plane blew up?"

"Wasn't it cool, Rob?"

"It was *so* awesome when that guy fell out the window…"

"Did you like it, Rob?"

"I can't believe he shot all those robots…"

"Can I finish the soda, Rob?"

Jordan groaned. Now she'd have to sit and listen to the reenactments of the movie *and* more stories of Rob the Great! Would she never catch a break? How had the day gotten so out of control? This had been a foolproof plan! Okay, it was time for some damage control. With a couple of firm words to Rob and those traitorous kids, she'd be the one back in charge.

As they stepped back out into the afternoon sunshine, the brightness of the sun struck with full force and Jordan swayed. It took a minute to adjust, but luckily Rob was right there to put an arm tightly around her waist and steady her.

"Are you okay, Mom?" Joseph stepped forward and asked nervously.

"I'm fine, sweetheart," she reassured him. "The light just got to me, that's all. Don't worry." The boy didn't look too sure and Rob made a mental note to talk to him about that when they had some time alone.

Walking them to their car, Rob watched as the boys climbed into the backseat; Joseph was still eyeing Jordan cautiously. Rob wanted an answer; he wanted to find out what would cause a young boy to be filled with the kind of anxiety Joseph was exhibiting right now. If he didn't do something quick and make definitive plans with Jordan, he wasn't sure he'd ever get the chance.

"What are you doing for dinner tonight?" he asked when the boys were out of earshot. Rob hoped he sounded casual, that his desperation to be with them again wasn't too obvious.

"Look, Rob," she began with as much enthusiasm as a funeral procession, "I appreciate all you did today, and I know the boys loved that you went to the movies with them, but I have certain rules with my kids and I don't appreciate you ignoring them." She couldn't quite remember why she was so angry, though. So he'd treated her boys to some snacks. Wasn't that really part of the whole moviegoing experience?

"I'm sorry," he said seriously, knowing full well he had gone overboard today. He couldn't seem to help it;

these kids looked like they needed some fun and extra attention, and if he could see to it, then why shouldn't he? *Because it's not your place. These aren't your kids. Remember that.*

"Maybe Claudia doesn't mind you spoiling her kids, but I don't want you getting involved here because it will be that much harder when we leave."

Harder on who, Jordan? You or them?

Suddenly the thought of leaving this place and never seeing Rob again filled Jordan with great sadness. It had only been a week, and yet she knew for sure that walking away from Rob Tyler a second time would kill her. Both she and the boys would feel his absence for a long, long time. Oh, sure, she was complaining about it now—the constant mentioning of his name, his insinuating himself into their family outings—but truth be told, Jordan was enjoying her time with him.

Rob reached out and traced a line down the side of her face with the tips of his fingers. He stared deeply into her eyes, and Jordan found herself unable to look away. His touch was whisper soft and yet it touched Jordan to her very soul, making her long for things that had been denied her for way too long.

"I don't want to do anything you don't want me to do," he murmured as he moved a little closer. "I'm sorry if I offended you today. That was never my intention." His words were spoken softly and Jordan just let them wash over her. They were almost touching from head to toe, and Jordan closed her eyes as he continued to stroke her face.

He could smell the faint scent of strawberries and suddenly remembered how she'd always favored a strawberry-scented shampoo when they were in school. He inhaled deeply and leaned in closer. It was odd how after all these years, he could still remember every small detail about her. He'd kill to know if she'd still melt into him when he kissed her. "What about dinner?" he said softly into her hair. "I know a great place where we can go. The boys will love it."

Without conscious thought, Jordan reached up and placed a hand on his forearm. She squeezed it gently, relishing the feel of his muscles bunching under her hand. Before she knew it, she was responding. "We have no plans."

"Good," Rob said as he slowly removed his hand from her face and stepped back a little. Jordan opened her eyes and let her hand drop from his arm, suddenly feeling very alone even though he was still so close.

"I'll pick you all up around six. Is that too late?"

"No," she whispered. He smiled at her, said his good-byes to the boys, and walked away.

Jordan watched as he walked down the sidewalk back toward his office until he was out of sight. The sound of Jake and Joseph chattering about the movie brought her back to reality. She drove home but waited to tell them who they were having dinner with. Jordan knew they would burst if things went any better today and thought they needed time to calm down before she told them.

She'd be wise to take the afternoon to calm herself down as well. Her body tingled with the thought of all the possibilities.

Chapter 4

SHE WASN'T READY. IT WAS FIVE MINUTES TO SIX AND Jordan was still throwing clothes all over her bedroom. She didn't think she *needed* to look special, but she wanted to make sure she looked…nice. It had been a long time since she'd felt the need to look nice for anyone.

But this wasn't just *anyone;* this was Rob she was dressing for. She wanted to look nice without looking as if she was *trying* to look nice.

Standing in front of the full-length mirror, she held up one outfit after another, finding fault with them all.

Too dressy, too casual, makes my hips look big… On and on it went until she heard the knock at the front door. She froze.

"Okay." She sighed and dove into the closet one last time. "Stop being such a ninny and just *pick* something!" she said to herself. When she'd packed for this trip, the thought of going out with anyone other than her sons had never crossed her mind. Next time, she'd be prepared. *Next time*? Jordan just prayed she survived *this* vacation!

Off in the distance, she heard the boys let Rob in, then a mass of conversation. She was sure her sons were talking Rob's ear off about the movie today. Jordan relaxed, knowing it would all be okay out in the other room for another five minutes and returned to the task at hand—finding something to freakin' wear!

Back in the living room, Rob was sitting on the sofa with the boys on the floor, watching TV. Having nieces and a nephew made him familiar with kid TV. Nickelodeon was a staple at his sister's house. In minutes he found himself laughing along with the boys at an episode of *iCarly*. As much as he hated to interrupt the episode—that Carly always managed to get into a crazy scenario—Rob knew this was his opportunity to get some answers from Joseph. He cleared his throat.

"Hey, Joe, can I ask you something?" he began casually, and Joseph turned to him, eager to tell him anything he wanted to know.

"Sure, Rob."

"You were really concerned today for your mom when we came out of the movie theater. Was everything all right?"

"Well," Joseph began, "she gets dizzy sometimes since the accident for almost no reason. It's weird. One minute she's fine; the next she's grabbing a piece of furniture until the room stops whizzing by. She fainted a couple of times when she first came home, but one of my aunts was always there to help her." The boy frowned. "I just want Mom to get better, you know?"

Rob nodded in understanding and Joseph continued, obviously grateful for the opportunity to talk to someone about how he felt.

"I know Mom's tired of feeling bad and all, and that's why we came here: so she could get some rest and get better. It's been a long time since she's felt good and I hate that for her." His tone was serious and Rob didn't doubt for a minute that Joseph loved and cared for his mom very much. He seemed much more mature than the average twelve-year-old, and Rob hated the fact that this boy had to take on so much grown-up responsibility because of his deadbeat father. Rage built up in Rob like he had never known before. If he ever had the opportunity to see Eric again, surely he would kill him. How dare he neglect this family! Eric didn't deserve them. As his fists clenched, Rob realized Joseph was still talking.

"I know it's a big help when Grandma or my aunts come around, but I just want our lives to go back to normal." He smiled weakly at Rob before he added, "But I don't even know if I remember what normal is anymore."

Rob reached down and placed a hand reassuringly on Joseph's shoulder and gave it a squeeze.

"It was hard when Dad moved out, but we got used to it being just the three of us. Jake was playing little league and I was playing soccer. We were starting to have fun again. And just when we were doing okay, there was the accident. Jake and me, well, we've spent more time sleeping at other people's houses than we have at our own. We had to drop out of the sports because it was too much for Grandma and Aunt Laura to drive us around and take care of Mom. I'm tired of not being in my own house, my own room." He looked up at Rob sheepishly. "I must sound like a baby to you."

"Not at all, Joe. You've been through some rough stuff and I know your mom's lucky to have you." He hoped his words were of some comfort. "If anything happens while you're here and you need help, I want you to call me, okay?" Rob handed Joseph his business card with his phone number on it. "I'm not saying you have to call me, but if you need help or even if you just want to talk, I want you to know that you can."

"Yes, sir. Thank you." The boy was polite to a fault. He stood and placed the business card in his pocket.

Rob patted him on the back and was about to turn his attention back to the TV when he heard Jordan's footsteps coming toward them from the hallway. He looked up to see her enter the room. His chest tightened at the sight of her.

She was dressed in a pair of black capri pants with a lightweight lavender sweater that molded beautifully to the curve and swell of her breasts. Rob swallowed hard. She looked fabulous. Her chestnut hair shined as it flowed around her shoulders and framed her heart-shaped face; her lips were glossed to kissable perfection and it almost made him bold enough to walk over to her and claim those lips with his. For the moment, he didn't have the right. But if tonight went as he hoped, he'd be able to kiss Jordan freely in the very near future.

Jordan noticed Rob's stare and suddenly felt very self-conscious. "Sorry to keep everyone waiting." She blushed. The boys ran over and hugged her and then immediately started pushing her toward the door.

"We're hungry!" they began to chant. "Sheesh, Mom, it took you, like, *forever* to get ready!" Jordan looked over at Rob and saw he was shaking his head and chuckling.

"Are you wearing makeup?" Jake asked in utter confusion. "You *never* wear makeup anymore!" Joseph made a similar comment about her perfume and Jordan felt herself blushing clear through to her roots with embarrassment. Clearly her boys thought she normally looked like some sort of troll.

"Never a dull moment," she heard Rob say as they walked out the door.

Jordan stopped short at the sight of his vehicle parked in front of her house. Why hadn't she noticed it when he came for dinner the other night? It was a brand-new, limited-edition Lexus SUV. It made her own older vehicle look, well…old. The boys were, of course, in awe of the shiny new truck and made all kinds of "manly" comments about it. Rob had a captive audience to give all the details of the wonders of his truck. Jordan knew her boys didn't understand half of what Rob was saying, but they *oohed* and *aahed* in all the right places. Listening to them made her smile.

"Men," Jordan sighed as she climbed into the front passenger seat where she waited many long moments before all the males joined her.

Once everyone was seated and buckled, Rob looked at them all and smiled. *This must be what being part of a family feels like*, he thought to himself. He'd taken his sister's kids out often enough, but it never felt quite like this. He needed to be careful. Rob was beginning to feel himself getting drawn into this little family and it felt too good. Too right. Of course, he was the one drawing himself in, and if it all came to an end in three weeks and he was left alone and deserted, he'd have no one to blame but himself.

Shaking that depressing thought from his mind, he called out, "Who likes pizza?" The response from the rear of the vehicle was a loud chorus of "me" and "I do." He laughed, put the truck in gear, and pulled away from the tiny bungalow.

"Now, I know your mom is an awesome cook, so I

can't guarantee that it's better than your mom's," he told the kids, "but I think you'll like it."

Jordan took in the sights of the town on the short drive to dinner. It was a cozy, picturesque place to live. Rob sporadically threw out an interesting fact or two about places they were passing. It was so different from their city life, and she found herself unable to stop wondering what it would be like to live here all the time. Could this be where she and the boys were meant to be?

She looked at the man sitting beside her. His eyes were fixed on the road, and she allowed herself just to stare for a moment. He was so handsome, so sexy, and she had to hold on to her hands to keep from reaching out and touching him. Would he be part of their lives if they moved here? Would he *want* to be part of their lives if they moved here?

This was crazy. They hadn't even been there a full week and she was already entertaining thoughts of moving here and being with Rob! What was next, "and they lived happily ever after"? *Get a grip, Jordan!* she scolded herself. *There are no happily ever afters for you, haven't you learned that yet?*

The sound of voices arguing woke her from her reverie.

They weren't really fighting. They were simply having a "heated discussion" over who could eat the most pizza. But the discussion was getting a bit old.

"That's enough, boys," she warned lightly as Rob pulled the truck to a stop in front of a quaint-looking Italian restaurant. There were bistro sets outside for dining lit with large candles in glass globes. The brick-and-stone facade gave it a warm feel—one would never know you were dining off a main road with this kind of ambience. For a brief moment, she considered asking Rob if they could eat out here, but he gently took her hand and led her through the glass front door.

Once they stepped inside, Jordan realized the front hadn't done the place justice. The restaurant was huge on the inside and yet had a very cozy feel to it. There were tons of tables covered in red-and-white checkered cloths, and each one had a wine bottle with a candle in it. It was like every Italian restaurant Jordan had ever seen, but nicer.

The boys weren't too impressed until Rob handed each of them a roll of quarters and pointed them in the direction of the arcade tucked away in the back. Once they were on their way amid shouts of joy, Rob led Jordan to a table near the back, next to a stone wall. It was very intimate: dimly lit by both a candle and a small wall sconce.

Rob held out a chair for her, and once she was seated, he asked, "So? What do you think of the place?"

"I love the authentic decor and it smells absolutely wonderful in here. I bet there's not a bad thing on the menu!"

"This was my grandfather's place," he stated with pride as he sat down opposite her.

"Really? I didn't know your grandfather was in the restaurant business."

"He left it to me several years ago when he died. Now I have this as well as my architecture firm to keep me busy."

"Wow, that's unbelievable." Jordan looked around the place. "How do you have time for both?"

"Well, the staff here is great and we have a manager who runs the place. I'm just a figurehead to them, you know? My office is right up the street, so it's not that hard for me to keep an eye on everything."

"Wouldn't it have been easier on you to sell it?"

Rob smiled. "I couldn't sell this place. It was my grandfather's dream. He loved this place. I know it's not something I ever thought to be a part of, but he entrusted it to me. It was important to him that I have it." Rob paused and looked around. "Besides, the place practically runs itself, it's been here for so long."

As if on cue, a petite brunette dressed in black slacks, white tuxedo shirt, and red apron appeared. "Good evening, Mr. Tyler." She smiled, handing menus to them both. "Can I get you both something to drink?"

Jordan placed the drink order for her and the boys. Rob inquired if she would like a glass of wine but Jordan declined. Rob ordered a soft drink as well, and then listened attentively as their server listed the specials for the evening. When she stepped away to let them decide, Rob put his menu down and asked, "Anything sound good to you?"

She nodded as she handed him her menu.

"I think it all sounded wonderful. I'm tempted to ask for a sample of all of it!" Jordan smiled and Rob felt a tightness in his chest. It was nice to see Jordan finally relaxing around him. In that moment, he was glad he had taken the chance to ask her out tonight. The waitress reappeared with their drinks and handed Jordan hers. She placed it on the table and then turned to Rob. "You order for us."

Rob looked at her in stunned silence. "What?"

"This is your place, so you know what's good. Surprise us. We'll trust you to do the ordering." The look on his face was priceless. If she didn't know any better, she'd swear he was scared. "Don't worry; they're not as picky as you think." With a surge of confidence, Rob rose from the table without a word and headed for the kitchen.

Jordan watched him walk off and admired his form. He was dressed casually, too, in black jeans and a gray T-shirt. The man filled out his clothes extremely well, with his lean hips and sexy walk. He oozed confidence.

She rolled her eyes. She was doing it again and wanted nothing more than to slap herself.

Sure, it had been a long time since she'd been with a man, but she had to stop ogling Rob and mentally categorizing all of his body parts. Besides, it wasn't as if he'd shown any *real* interest in her. He was just being nice to her boys because he felt sorry for them. Nothing more to it. This was all going to go nowhere.

So he caressed her face in the middle of the street. No big deal. He was simply treating her like an old friend. Although Jordan couldn't remember the last time she'd caressed the face of an old friend, it still didn't mean anything, did it? *It's all no big deal*, she reminded herself.

Nope. Not a big deal at all.

Rob came back to the table and took his seat opposite Jordan again. One look at those big brown eyes of his and Jordan realized what the big deal was: she wanted him to caress her again. Here. Now. All over.

Naked.

Now there was an image to get people talking— *Out-of-Towner Naked in Local Restaurant*. With her children present! Jordan grabbed her water and took a quick drink.

Taking a deep breath, she started a conversation about the restaurant business that kept them going until their food arrived and the kids were seated at the table with them. It was a safe topic and it kept her mind off her wayward, sexually charged thoughts. Whenever she found her mind wandering to places it shouldn't, she'd force herself to ask a question about keeping inventory.

Rob had ordered them two pizzas—one with extra cheese, the other with everything on it. The boys dug right in and raved about how great it was, especially after learning that Rob owned the place. Jordan found herself relaxing deeply, enjoying her meal and the company. She could not even remember the last time they had sat down to dinner with a man. Eric had been gone for a long time, and if she was honest with herself, Jordan would have to admit she missed the simple things of family life, like sitting around the dinner table together.

Jordan couldn't believe how animated her boys were being. It had been so long since they had socialized with anyone other than her family, and yet here they were, chatting with Rob as if they'd known him their entire lives.

Each boy took a turn telling Rob about school and what his favorite subjects were. Rob patiently listened to all the details of their video game collection and which games they had mastered. Jordan couldn't help but mentally note how good Rob was with her kids—he would make a great father someday. Maybe not to her kids, but to kids of his own. He deserved that.

It was still early when they finished dinner and Jake asked if they could go to the video store to rent a movie.

"Didn't we already see a movie today?" Jordan asked her younger son.

"Yes, ma'am," he said pitifully, playing with the pizza crust left on his plate.

Feeling like the wicked witch yet again, Jordan conceded. They were on vacation. Why were her first reactions to squash any fun the boys wanted to have? Too regimented, that was her problem. Way too regimented. "Where's the local video store?" she asked Rob wearily.

They were rising to leave when an attractive blond walked over to their table. "Hey, Rob!" she said cheerily as she wrapped her arms around him and placed a kiss on his cheek.

"Hey, Kelly. Kelly, this is Jordan Manning." He motioned toward Jordan, and Kelly reached out to shake her hand. "And these are her sons, Joseph and Jake."

"Hi, boys!" Each boy smiled and greeted her politely. "I see you had some pizza tonight. Did Rob let you toss the dough?"

The boys looked at her with wide eyes. "Do you really let people do that, Rob?" Joe asked.

"Sure do. I just thought you were having fun with the video games so I didn't want to disturb you. But I promise the next time we come here, the shape of our pizza is completely up to you." He grinned broadly as both boys gasped with certain glee. He could tell they were already planning their next visit.

Kelly turned her attention back to Rob. "So, are we still on for this weekend? I can pick you up tomorrow around four if that will work for you?"

"Absolutely," he responded, his hand resting on the small of her back, and Jordan felt her spine stiffen at the sight. With his free hand, he reached into his pocket and fished out his car keys. "Here are the keys, Jordan," he said as he handed them to her. They were being dismissed. "Why don't you and the boys go on out to the car? I just need to speak with the manager before we go. I'll be out in a minute."

"Oh, sure," she said quietly and looked away. "Come on, boys. It was nice to meet you," she mumbled as she ushered the boys out the door and to the car as quick as she could.

"Who was that, Mommy?" Jake asked as Jordan unlocked the truck.

"I don't know, sweetheart. Maybe she's Rob's girlfriend," Jordan said sadly. Glancing back into the restaurant, Jordan saw Rob was still talking to Kelly. She couldn't seem to tear her gaze away and almost let out a cry when the woman wrapped her arms around Rob's neck as she hugged and kissed him again. Jordan climbed into the truck testily, and the boys noticed.

"What's wrong?" Joseph asked as he got comfortable in the backseat.

"It's nothing, baby." She couldn't let them know she was jealous of this woman, this blond-haired nightmare who had ruined what was promising to be a perfect night.

The sad fact was she really didn't expect that Rob was living the celibate life, waiting for her to come back and find him, right? She had to accept that, as she had told her children, Rob was not here just for their entertainment. He had a life of his own. Jordan simply hadn't expected that life to tear at her heart so badly.

Forcing her gaze away from the restaurant, she turned to the boys. "So, what movie are we getting?"

Rob joined them a few minutes later and asked the same exact question. Joseph told him of a comedy he had wanted to see, and without any input from Jordan, they took off driving in the direction of the video store. If Rob noticed Jordan's cool demeanor or the way she was staring out the window ignoring him, he chose to say nothing.

Once in the video store, Rob joked with the boys by picking up "chick flicks" and asking if any of them were the movies they had in mind. Jake laughed hysterically every time. By the fifth movie, the joke had gotten a little stale and they all finally headed over to the comedy section.

Within minutes they decided on a movie and Rob very respectfully asked Jordan if it was all right for them to get some microwave popcorn to eat while watching the movie. After his behavior earlier in the day at the movie theater, he certainly didn't want to take a chance on offending her again. The boys had eaten quite a bit of junk food in the afternoon and had just consumed a ton of pizza. He wanted to be certain Jordan was okay with the plans before he plowed on through with them. She mumbled her response, but the boys were so busy chattering at him that Rob didn't notice her disinterest.

Once they were back at the house with movie in hand, Joseph asked Rob if he was going to stay and watch it with them and he readily agreed to. Jordan excused herself and went to the sanctuary of her bedroom to calm her nerves and change her clothes. She could have told them all her plans but their conversations at this point clearly did not include her.

As she closed the door behind her and flipped on a

small lamp, questions flooded her mind. Why would he be hanging out here with them when he had a girlfriend waiting for him? Wouldn't this Kelly person be peeved at all the time Rob was spending with Jordan and her kids? It made no sense.

Stepping into her large closet, she kicked off her sandals rather aggressively before grabbing a change of clothes: yoga pants and an oversized T-shirt. She looked at her reflection in the mirror and, feeling even more pitiful, pulled her hair up into a ponytail. Hell, there was no point in *trying* to look nice now. Jordan even considered going into the bathroom and washing off all traces of makeup, too. Might as well go back to looking like that troll she envisioned earlier. Clearly even with the effort, she couldn't attract a man. Even one who used to be attracted to her. How pathetic was that? With a deep sigh, she padded back out to the living room and found they had left the couch empty for her.

"Wow, you look ready for bed already," Jake said as he briefly took his attention away from the giant bowl of popcorn in front of him.

"We know how you like to lie down on the couch and watch TV," Joseph said as he started up the movie. Rob was sitting in the large chair next to the sofa while the boys sat on the floor. Jordan didn't even spare Rob a glance but she could feel his eyes on her.

"Hey, Mom? Want some popcorn?"

"No thanks," she replied flatly while trying to get herself comfortable on the sofa and avoid Rob's watchful eyes. Damn him for making her think all kinds of silly, romantic thoughts of him when all the while he had a girlfriend! When would she ever learn?

Leave it to Rob to omit that little tidbit of information. Who would have thought that at the age of thirty-two, the old hurts of eighteen could come back with such a vengeance?

Dammit!

If it hadn't been for that woman showing up tonight, she'd be sharing the couch with Rob, comfortably leaning into him the way she'd longed to this afternoon in the movie theater. But now, if it weren't for the fact that it would upset the boys, she'd actually be asking him to leave. With any luck, the movie would be short and he'd leave immediately after it was over.

But then when had luck been with her today?

It was sometime later, maybe halfway through the movie, when Jordan felt she could no longer hold her eyes open. The day had been emotionally draining and had finally caught up with her, and the boys were wrapped up in the slapstick comedy. She couldn't even see Rob because she had slouched down as far as she could into the sofa so she wouldn't have to see him.

Finding it too hard to stay awake, she decided to give in and just rest her eyes for a little while. No one would notice and the couch was oh-so-comfy. Her last thought was that wherever they ended up moving to, she had to purchase a couch just like this one because it was pure heaven to relax on.

When the movie was over, the boys turned expectantly toward Rob. "What did you think?" Jake asked.

"It was a good movie." He stood and stretched. He glanced at his watch and saw it was almost eleven o'clock, then he looked down at Jordan, fast asleep on the couch. Rob looked from her to the boys.

"She does that a lot," Jake supplied. "Sometimes we can't even get her to wake up so we have to leave her on the couch all night. That makes her real cranky the next morning."

Rob almost grinned. "Why don't you guys go on and get into pj's and get in bed? I'll straighten up in here so you won't have to do it in the morning." The eyes that stared back at him were full of gratitude. "I'll take care of your mom, too."

"Thanks, Rob," Joe said around a yawn. Clearly the events of the day had worn him out.

"Will you come over tomorrow?" Jake asked, himself stifling a large yawn.

"I can't, guys. Sorry. I'll be away over the weekend but I promise to come by and see you when I get back, okay?" At their sad faces, he repeated himself. "I promise." That was all they needed to hear before they headed off to bed.

Rob went about cleaning up the popcorn mess and straightening up the room. When there was nothing left to do, he stopped and watched Jordan sleeping on the couch. He crouched down beside her and gently swept her hair that had escaped her ponytail away from her face. God, she was beautiful. He didn't want to leave. Without thinking, he bent forward and placed a soft kiss on her temple. Jordan sighed deeply and shifted slightly. Lost in the moment, he carefully scooped her up in his arms and carried her to her bedroom. Lord, but she felt good curled up against him!

She had barely stirred as he carried her and he held her close while he turned down her bed. Placing her gently down on the mattress, he felt suddenly protective of her. She seemed so tiny and fragile, like the young girl of sixteen he remembered.

But she wasn't a young girl anymore. No, this was no girl lying on the bed with her soft lips slightly parted. This was a woman—a woman who still had the ability to stir his blood.

She had been quiet tonight after they'd left the restaurant and he had no idea what had caused the change in her attitude. He had thought they were having a good time. A really good time. They were talking comfortably just like they used to and he had felt a glimmer of hope. It seemed somehow they had finally crossed that invisible barrier and Jordan had let down her guard around him. He was seeing hints of the woman he used to know.

When they'd returned from the video store, Rob had hoped they'd share a spot on the sofa during the movie and he'd finally have the chance to touch her freely. Well, as freely as being surrounded by her children would allow. While carrying her had felt good, it wasn't what he had been hoping for. By the time they'd gotten back here, she was barely speaking to anyone at all. What could have happened to make her whole demeanor change? Did she feel okay? Was she in pain and reluctant to draw attention to it, lest she upset her sons?

Rob watched as Jordan snuggled deeper into her pillow. He hated that she was raising her sons alone, and felt terrible for all she had gone through because of her ex-husband. His hands clenched at his sides at the thought of how hard her life had become because of Eric. Rob had a share in that blame. If he hadn't screwed up so long ago, Jordan never would have married Eric. They never would have broken up and he would have had all these years to show Jordan how much he loved her.

Not knowing what else to do, he placed another lingering kiss on her cheek and wished her a good night. She whispered "good night" back to him in her sleep and he smiled warmly. He wanted nothing more than to climb into that bed beside her and hold her close all night. In truth, he wanted to climb into bed beside her every night and hear her sweet voice wish him a good night every night for the rest of his life. He sighed wistfully and forced himself to look away. It was no use standing there and wishing for things that might never happen.

He tiptoed out of the room and then went to check on Jake and Joseph to make sure they were both asleep. Rob stood in the doorway to their bedroom just watching them sleep. He had always known he wanted to have kids but hadn't really felt the void of not having them until now. It had been nice to go out tonight with Jordan and the boys. He'd thoroughly enjoyed coming home together, getting comfortable, and watching a movie. Even cleaning up and putting everyone to bed had felt good. Felt right. In one short night, Rob Tyler came to realize all that was missing in his life.

Once he was sure they were asleep and secure, he locked up and left, feeling like he had just left a little piece of his heart inside the little beachside bungalow.

Chapter 5

JORDAN WOKE THE FOLLOWING MORNING, NOT QUITE remembering going to bed the night before. As she lay there, the morning light filtering into her room through the window shades, it dawned on her how she must have gotten there and felt herself flush with embarrassment. The only upside to it was that she hadn't had to face Rob again last night. She knew the hurt she was feeling over finding out about Kelly would surely have been obvious in her eyes. Rob had always said her eyes betrayed her every thought.

She stretched, rose slowly from the bed, and left the room to go find the boys. They were in the den watching TV and eating bowls of cereal. Jordan took a moment to observe them before letting her presence be known.

"Good morning," she said as she sat down on the sofa with them. "Sorry I fell asleep on you last night."

"It's okay, Mom," Jake said around a spoonful of Frosted Flakes. "Rob took care of us." That thought warmed Jordan for a brief moment, and then she remembered Kelly.

Pushing all thoughts of Rob to the back of her mind, she asked, "So, how was the rest of the movie?"

"It was great. Thanks for letting us rent it," Joseph said, his eyes on the TV the whole time, milk dribbling down his chin. He wiped it away with the back of his hand, never breaking stride.

Jordan went into the kitchen to pour herself something to drink and announced she had a surprise. With eager anticipation, the boys jumped up from the floor, leaving their bowls and spoons where they lay. Jordan took them each by the hand and led them back to her room, where she pulled out two large, wrapped boxes from her closet.

"Wow, how'd you get these in here without us seeing them?" Joseph asked.

"It's a special gift moms have," she replied with a mischievous smile.

The boys tore into their gifts and shrieked with delight when they found model airplanes that they could build and then fly on the beach with remote controls. They were totally psyched at the prospect.

"Cool! Thanks, Mom!" they shouted and ran to make room at the kitchen table to begin their tasks.

All day Friday was spent working on the planes. Jordan tried to help where she could, but found the boys enjoyed doing the craft by themselves. She wasn't offended. In truth, she had no idea how to put a model airplane together and would probably end up messing it up or gluing her own fingers together in the process. It was times like this that Jordan felt most inadequate as a parent; this was a time a dad would come in handy. She didn't let herself dwell on that fact for too long. It was too depressing. Besides, the only one who seemed to be struggling with that right now was her.

While the boys worked together on their planes, Jordan took the time to enjoy the peacefulness of being on vacation and pulled out a book. Curling up into the corner of the sofa, she let herself get lost in the story, only stopping when it was time to fix a meal or stretch her stiff body. Who needed distractions? This was what the vacation was supposed to be about—time alone with the boys, a time to get reacquainted with one another and figure out what they wanted to do with their lives and their future.

Returning to her novel, Jordan lost herself in the story and forgot the worries of what was, what could be, and what might have been.

After breakfast on Saturday morning, they were out on the beach enjoying the fruits of their labor and Jordan was able to go for more than a few minutes without thinking about or looking for Rob. It was strange how much of an impact he had made on their lives in the short time they'd been on the coast.

"Hey, Mom! Look at this!" Jordan looked up in the sky to where the planes were flying and all thoughts of Rob were forgotten for the day.

While they were out on the sand, Jordan took advantage of another task she wanted to accomplish on this trip—taking pictures of her family. This was an important time in their lives and scrapbooking had always been a favorite pastime of hers.

Snapping one digital shot after another, Jordan knew they were making memories here that would last a lifetime.

Just then, Jake let out a laugh of pure glee and Jordan quickly aimed the camera and captured it. Smiling, she realized it would make the perfect cover shot for her scrapbook.

The remainder of the weekend flew by and by Sunday afternoon, one plane was demolished, she had taken close to a hundred pictures, and Joseph had a touch of sunburn. Jordan had convinced herself it was a good thing Rob had gone away with his blond. She and her boys did not need him around to have a good time. They were having fun together and were bonding for the first time in a long time. She would do well to remember that if they ever saw him again.

That was the million-dollar question: Would they see Rob again? Jordan knew she had behaved childishly when they had come back to the house after dinner the other night. You'd think that at this stage in her life she would have matured a little and moved on from being so easily hurt.

Her marriage had taught her a lot about being hurt, and even after everything Eric had done to her and her children, Jordan realized the emotion she felt most strongly was anger. Rob's betrayal had left her broken when they were younger, and here she was hurting again. When would she ever learn?

That train of thought had to stop; Rob was not betraying her and really, what had happened between them was ancient history, and it was time she stopped carrying it around with her every time she and Rob were together. It was time to let the past stay in the past and to focus on the present. Jordan had no idea what was even going on between her and Rob, but maybe this time around they could be friends.

Yes, she thought, that would be the answer to all the questions swirling around in her head. They would be friends. There was no reason to feel betrayed by—or jealous of—Rob going away with this Kelly person if they were just friends. She would welcome him back into her home for her sons' sakes and they would all be friends.

It made sense, and if there was one thing that Jordan prided herself on at this point in her life, it was that she was doing things that made sense. She was proud of herself for finally coming to this point.

Jordan was enjoying the peace and quiet after the boys had gone to bed Sunday night. The phone call from her sister was a welcome interruption.

"Listen," Laura began, "Mark is coming up that way for a conference tomorrow and wants to come by and say hello." Mark was Laura's husband and a favorite uncle to Joseph and Jake. "Is there anything from home that he can bring you?"

"Oh, Laura, that would be great!" The women spoke on the phone for the next hour. Jordan had a list of items she had forgotten to bring with her but didn't want to go out and buy, as well as foods the boys liked that she hadn't found at the local grocery store.

After jotting down all Jordan needed, Laura wanted to get down to the real reason for her call, to check on Jordan's progress. After months of looking after Jordan and the boys, Laura had been hesitant to give her blessing for this trip. As the older sibling, she had always been protective of Jordan, and after witnessing all that her sister had been through, not only during her marriage and divorce but the physical recovery process as well, Laura had been unsure Jordan was ready to be so far from home.

Of course, Jordan would have been furious if Laura

had voiced that opinion. Lord knew Jordan was ready to have control of her life once again, and even though her family was only looking out for her and wanted what was best for her, Laura was sure on some level they were smothering her.

"Okay, you've had some fun with the boys, the house is lovely, your scrapbook is going to be fabulous, blah, blah, blah," Laura said. "Now tell me how you're really feeling."

"Physically? I feel okay. I'm getting plenty of rest and it's so peaceful here that I'm finally getting my head together."

"That's good. I knew some time away would work wonders," she lied. "Now tell me how you managed to get Joseph to relax! He was totally against this trip from the get-go. What changed his mind?"

Jordan took a deep breath and forced herself to talk about the one person she had avoided talking about all weekend. "Well, do you remember Rob Tyler?"

"Rob Tyler? Your ex-boyfriend, Rob Tyler? Sure, what about him?" Before Jordan could answer, Laura put it all together. "You don't mean that you've run into Rob and he's been spending time with you and the boys, do you?"

"Yes."

"Why would you do that to yourself, Jordan?"

"Do what? We ran into him in town one day and he's come over a couple of times. It's no big deal. Really."

"Uh-huh." Laura stayed silent for a while and waited to see if Jordan would offer up any more information. When she didn't, Laura continued. "So? Is he still as cute as he was back in high school?" Her tone was playful and Jordan couldn't help but smile.

"Oh, yes. If anything, he's gotten better with age." Images of Rob running on the beach with the boys sprang to her mind, and she felt that familiar flutter in her tummy.

"Is he married?"

"Nope. Never got married. He's an architect now with his own firm here in town and he also owns a restaurant he inherited from his grandfather."

"Sounds like he's doing well for himself." She paused again. "You're not thinking of doing anything with him again, are you?" Before even giving Jordan a chance to respond, Laura rushed on, "Because I remember how devastated you were when you broke up back in high school. I mean, I know you're not kids anymore, but I just don't want to see you get hurt again."

Jordan sighed. "I was thinking along those lines at first, but it turns out he has a girlfriend. One he's with right now."

"You sound disappointed."

"I guess I am, a little. But I'll get over it."

Laura wanted to press Jordan for more details but held her tongue. It was a good thing Jordan was at least tempted to go out and have an interest in the opposite sex once again. After all that Eric had put her through, Jordan's whole family had begun to fear she would just give up on that part of her life and try to be content being a single mother for the rest of her life.

Not that there was anything wrong with not wanting to date, but Jordan was made to be in love and to be married. It broke Laura's heart that Jordan's marriage had ended the way it had. Having a successful marriage herself, Laura knew she'd be devastated if it ended.

She was proud of Jordan for being so strong and for overcoming so much. Someday she'd have to tell her how much she admired her strength. Tonight was not that time.

The conversation went on for a few minutes after that, and Jordan felt herself getting depressed, so she feigned exhaustion and pleaded off the phone. Besides, she knew Mark would be arriving early, and she needed to get some sleep so she'd be up and ready for him when he showed up. The boys were going to be so surprised!

Monday morning dawned bright and early. Jordan had made sure to set her alarm so she would be ready for Mark's arrival. The boys were already up when she came out of her bedroom. "You haven't eaten yet, have you?" she called out on her way to the bathroom.

"No. Why?" they asked.

"I just want us to eat together this morning, okay? Give me a few minutes." Jordan entered the bathroom and washed up quickly. A glance at her watch as she walked back to her bedroom told her it was almost eight o'clock. Mark would be here soon.

No sooner had that thought hit her than there was a knock at the door. She stepped out of her room, still dressed in her flannel pajama pants and a T-shirt. "Who could that be?" she said dramatically as she let the boys run to answer the door.

"Uncle Mark!" they squealed as they jumped into his arms. Mark swung them around in turn and then took them out to his car to get the things he had brought with him at Jordan's request. She had followed them outside to Mark's car, heedless of the fact that she wasn't properly dressed.

"Nice of you to dress for the occasion," Mark commented sarcastically with a smile. His blue eyes sparkled with mischief and an early morning breeze blew his blond hair around.

Jordan stepped forward and hugged him tightly to her, thankful for a friendly face from home. Neither she nor the boys noticed the black SUV parked several houses away, observing the scene on the front lawn of the bungalow.

"You sure Laura sent enough?" Jordan asked as Mark released her and she looked into the interior of his car at all the bags and boxes.

"God, I hope so," Mark laughed. "I'll get better gas mileage now that all this weight is out of the car." Mark carried a large suitcase and a couple of grocery bags. Joseph and Jake carried the remainder of the bags and Jordan carried a box. Back in the house, the boys began to tell their uncle about all they had been doing since their arrival while Jordan went to the kitchen to make breakfast for all of them.

"You brought all our favorite foods, Mark," Jordan commented as she unloaded the food. In a matter of minutes, everything was in its place and she had begun preparing their breakfast. Off in the distance she heard the boys telling Mark about their room, the town, and how their days were going and all the fun they were having. It warmed her heart to hear their voices filled with excitement and happiness. This trip had been the right choice.

She called them all to the table a few minutes later

and placed their food in front of them—western omelets with toast and home fries.

"I sure wish you'd teach your sister to make omelets like this, Jordan. No matter how hard she tries, they always just come out scrambled and a little burned. Don't tell her I said that," he joked as he pointed a fork at his nephews. They poked fun at Jordan's sister's cooking skills while they ate.

"You must have been on the road while it was still dark out to get here so early," Jordan said.

"I didn't mind. Laura's been out of her mind with worry since you left, so it was kind of a relief to get on the road so I could find out for myself that you were fine—like I assured her you'd be—and report back to her.

"Laura drove over to your house after you got off the phone last night to get the stuff you needed, and luckily all the food things you wanted, we had in the house. I did stop at one open-all-night supermarket for the pasta you requested."

"Well, I really appreciate all that you've done, Mark, and I'm sorry Laura's still worrying so much."

"She's a perpetual nurturer, Jordan. She can't help herself. I know she wants you to feel better, but there's always going to be a part of your sister that's going to want to take care of you, and she's going to worry about you when she can't. Believe me, it's best just to accept it. It makes our kids crazy but it's one of the reasons I love her." His words nearly brought tears to Jordan's eyes, and when she looked at her brother-in-law, she could easily see the love he had for his wife. Jordan envied their connection and had to stop herself from being out-and-out jealous of the fact that she did not have that connection with anyone.

At the serious turn in the conversation, the boys chimed in, eager to have Mark's full attention back on them. Jordan picked up her mug and took a sip of the steaming coffee, enjoying listening to Mark converse with her sons.

The black truck drove slowly past the house. Rob could see inside and it looked like a real family scene in there. His gut twisted. It wasn't Eric, of that much he was sure. He realized he never had asked Jordan if she was involved with anyone, but wouldn't the boys have mentioned that fact to him? They'd told him everything else about their lives; a boyfriend would be a hard detail to skip. Slamming his fists on the steering wheel, he quickly drove off before anyone noticed him.

After breakfast, Jordan excused the boys and relieved them of cleanup detail so they could spend some more time with Mark. She didn't mind doing the task and was sure her sons felt even more gratitude toward their uncle for getting them out of the chore.

Jordan had just finished loading the dishes into the dishwasher when Mark came into the kitchen and poured himself another cup of coffee.

"Boys are making their beds. So," he said as he casually leaned on the counter. "Who's this *Rob* I've been hearing about all morning?"

He was watching her with raised eyebrows and pure amusement.

Jordan closed the door to the dishwasher and started the cycle as she motioned for him to sit down at the kitchen table. Mark had been dating Laura while Jordan was still in school, and Jordan knew it wouldn't be hard for him to remember that time in her life. Honestly, Jordan couldn't remember a time when Mark and Laura weren't together and he wasn't part of their family. "I dated Rob before I started going with Eric."

Recognition dawned in Mark's eyes.

"I had no idea he lived here. We ran into him in town our second day here and he's come around a couple of times to hang out with the boys, that's all."

"Uh-huh," he said with a smirk.

"You sound just like your wife," Jordan said dryly. "Anyway, think what you want, Mark, but that's all there is to it." She took a sip of her coffee. "Besides, I'm not looking for a relationship and Rob already has a girlfriend. End of story." If only it didn't hurt so much to say it.

"If you say so."

"Well, I do," she said a little too quickly, and Mark put his coffee down and stared at Jordan. "What?" she asked.

"Okay, I may be completely out of line here so I'll apologize in advance."

"It's okay," she said hesitantly.

"You've had a rough time of it, Jordan, and believe me, I wish that there was more Laura and I could've done to help."

"Oh, Mark, you guys have been…"

He held up a hand and stopped what she was going to say. "I don't want you to think it's a bad thing to go back out there into the dating world. You deserve to be happy. Laura and I? We both want you to be happy. If this Rob guy can make you happy, then maybe you shouldn't shrug the whole thing off so quickly."

Jordan sighed. "I'm not shrugging anything off, Mark, I'm telling you, he has a girlfriend."

"Are you sure?"

"He was away with her this weekend."

Mark studied her for a moment and then leaned on the table, his expression serious. "Unless he said those words to you, that this girl is his girlfriend, I wouldn't be so sure. No man hangs around with a woman and her kids unless he's interested."

Jordan loved it when Mark went all "big brother" on her. "You're hanging out with a woman and her kids right now and I know for darn sure you're not interested," she teased.

He laughed out loud and reached for his coffee, shaking his head the whole time. "You always were a brat, Jordan. You know that, right?"

"It's why I'm the favorite." She rose to finish cleaning the kitchen and heard Mark leave the table and head down the hall toward the boys' room.

He hung around until after lunch, playing with the boys down on the beach while Jordan showered and cleaned up around the house. She appreciated some time alone to get things done without the constant interruptions that came with being with her children 24-7.

When Mark pulled away, Jordan kept her sons close as they all waved good-bye, feeling good about having seen someone they loved so dearly from home.

Both boys were a little sad Mark hadn't been able to stay longer, but were in good spirits as they headed back into the house. The phone was ringing as Jordan stepped inside and closed the door.

"Hello?" she said cheerily into the phone.

"Hi," Rob said stiffly.

"Oh, hi," she said breathlessly. "How was your weekend?" Jordan really didn't want to know, but secretly hoped that it was miserable. She was obviously some kind of masochist. And her stomach was so *not* fluttering just from the sound of Rob's voice. She would not allow it to.

"Fine," he said. "I was wondering if I could take the boys fishing sometime this week." Not *her* and the boys, she noticed, just the boys. He sounded tense and as uncomfortable as Jordan felt at the moment.

Trying to keep her tone light in opposition to his dark one, she said, "That would be nice. They've never really gone fishing but I'm sure they'd enjoy it. When did you have in mind?"

"Tomorrow," he said flatly.

Okay, no more Mrs. Smiley Face. "Fine," she responded with equal enthusiasm. After several strained and silent moments, arrangements were made and they hung up. If Rob had really wanted to ease out of this situation with her and the boys, why bother calling at all? Damned if she knew.

"Hey, guys! Guess what you're doing tomorrow?"

—⁓—

Early the next morning, Jordan woke her sons up and got them ready to leave. She packed up a cooler with snacks, drinks, and sandwiches for them and waited for Rob to pull up. Her plan was to send them directly out to him and to avoid having to talk with him at all. After his attitude toward her yesterday on the phone, she seriously began to second-guess her decision to let the boys go out with him and the heck with the consequences.

Why on earth would he have such an attitude with her? Was he mad she fell asleep while they watched a movie? If he was, it was a damn lame excuse and she'd be happy to tell him so if she wasn't so hell-bent on not seeing him at the moment.

She knew by avoiding him she was being a coward, but she didn't have the strength to care. For far too long, Jordan Manning had spent the bulk of her time caring about everyone else's feelings. Well, no more! It had become painfully obvious that all her caring had only caused her more disappointment. She had given her heart to him at sixteen and he had stomped all over it. She had done the same thing with her ex-husband, and he had not only stomped on her heart, but gone for an all-out removal of it.

Let Rob think her a coward. She thought no more highly of him right now.

Rob showed up while she was dressing. He was early. *Dammit!* He was waiting for her in the living room, dressed in what Jordan could only assume to be clothes that Goodwill had refused: ripped jeans, an old sweatshirt with paint stains on it, and a ridiculous-looking fishing hat. A quick glance out the front windows showed her the boys were loading their cooler into the truck and getting settled.

She walked toward him but stopped several feet away and tried to act completely unaffected by his presence by folding her arms across her chest. "What time should I expect them back?" she asked coolly as she reached up to comb a stray strand of hair behind her ear.

Rob's expression was equally cool, but his eyes were dark and seemed to bore into hers. "We'll be back sometime after two."

"Fine." Jordan strode passed him out to the truck to say good-bye to the boys and remind them how they were expected to behave. She leaned into the truck to kiss them, and when she backed out and stood, she very nearly collided with Rob.

"Oh!" she cried out as she turned around.

"Sorry," he said through clenched teeth. Jordan stepped around him and watched as he leaned into the vehicle himself.

"Hey, boys, just give me one minute and then we'll be on our way." The boys both nodded and started conversing with each other about all the fish they were going to catch.

Rob closed the door and walked over to where Jordan stood. "So?"

"So, what?"

"Will this give you enough time today?" he asked snidely.

"Rob, what on earth are you talking about? Enough time for what?" She was clueless as to why he had an attitude with her and it was royally ticking her off. If anyone deserved to be bitter toward anyone in this scenario, it was her.

"I saw you had company yesterday. I thought you might like some time alone with your male *friend* without the kids around." He crossed his arms solidly over his chest.

Oh, this was unbelievable. "So you thought you would take it upon yourself to protect my children, is that it?"

He made no reply.

"Do you think I am so depraved that I cannot go

without male companionship for more than a week?"
Her voice was beginning to rise and she caught herself
before giving in to a full-blown scream. Rob cocked
an eyebrow at her. "I see. Well, if memory serves me
correct, and I believe it does, *I* was never the one to
have that problem—you know, being unable to control
myself with the opposite sex." She crossed her arms
over her chest smugly, mimicking his pose and seeing
that at least he had the decency to look ashamed at what
she was implying.

"And for your information, that was my brother-in-
law you saw here yesterday morning. You might remember Laura's husband, Mark? And just for the record,
what were you doing? Spying on us?" Jordan noticed
his jaw clench a little. "Mark was driving through town
on his way to a conference and was bringing me some
supplies from home that I had forgotten!"

Rob shifted his feet a little, holding a firm stance with
his own arms still folded, his hands clenched tightly.

She was fuming but good now and steamrolled on.
"And just so we're on the same page here, these are *my*
children and they've done just fine without you being
around to protect and entertain them. We were fine
before you came along and we'll continue to be fine
after we leave. Do you have a problem with that?" Her
breathing was hard at this point and she was so angry
she was shaking a little. He had a nerve!

Jordan stood there and waited for Rob to make some
sort of reply, but he just turned and walked away. The
only thing he said to her as he climbed into his truck
was, "We'll see you sometime after two." And then they
were gone.

—∾—

"Hey, Rob? Check me out! I'm about to reel in my third fish," Joseph bragged, his face a little red from the sun but completely full of pride.

"Great job, Joe. At this rate, we'll have more fish than we'll know what to do with! We'll have to invite the neighbors over for dinner or something," Rob teased.

"That would be fun!" Jake chimed in.

Rob sat out there on the boat and watched the two boys he was coming to love. If he hadn't been such a fool at eighteen, these would be his own children he was out fishing with. His and Jordan's.

She was never out of his thoughts for long lately. Learning that the man at her home yesterday was her brother-in-law was like winning the lottery. He couldn't remember the last time he had felt such relief. But how could he be sure there really wasn't someone else waiting for her back in Raleigh?

"Hey, I hear you had a visit from your Uncle Mark yesterday."

"Yeah, Uncle Mark is great. He used to coach my little league team when I used to play," Jake said, and he shook his fishing pole in hopes of making a fish take note of his bait.

"You don't say?" Rob commented. "So, I was just wondering, does your mom plan on having anyone else from home come to visit? You know, any friends or boyfriends or anything?" *Smooth, Rob. Real smooth.*

"A boyfriend? Yuck," Joseph said. "Mom's never had a boyfriend. I mean, I guess she's pretty and all, but... She's a mom! Moms don't have boyfriends!" At that point, the boy shuddered as if the very thought of his mom having a boyfriend was repulsive.

"Well, some moms do," Rob suggested. "Would you hate it if your mom had a boyfriend?"

"Not me," Jake said.

"It would depend on the guy," Joseph said diplomatically, but not wanting to have that picture in his head. "Like, there's this guy at the bank who always acts all goofy whenever Mom goes in there. I wouldn't like it if he was her boyfriend."

"Well, is there anyone you would like?" *Easy there, Casanova. Your desperation is starting to show.*

"You'd be a cool boyfriend for Mom," Jake said with a smile.

"Oh, yeah. You'd definitely be cool," Joseph agreed.

"Do you want to be her boyfriend?" Jake asked.

"Shut up, stupid," Joseph said as he rolled his eyes. "You don't ask somebody that!"

"I am not stupid! You are!"

"Am not."

"*Rob…*" Jake whined, clearly hoping Rob would jump in and break up the fight.

Rob smiled at them both. In the short time he'd known them, he had learned it didn't take much to make them argue. He also learned they didn't hold grudges and they'd work out this particular fight soon enough. It was slightly amusing. Besides, he was too busy being fully satisfied with what he had learned.

Now the only problem he saw was convincing the lovely Ms. Manning that he wasn't some creepy jerk who had been spying on them and hope that she'd be in a better mood when they got home.

Home.

Maybe if luck was on his side, it wouldn't be long before he had a real home to go to at the end of the day where Jordan and the boys would be waiting for him. It wasn't such a far-off fantasy. They had been on the path to this once, and Rob had no doubt in his mind they could get back on that path again. He was still in love with Jordan—had probably never stopped loving her—and he was crazy about her kids. He now knew they liked him too. Maybe it wouldn't be too long at all.

He sighed with contentment and cast his line out to fish for more dinner.

Chapter 6

THE DAY SEEMED TO DRAG ON ENDLESSLY. JORDAN definitely enjoyed the peace and quiet, but had to admit she missed the boys. Not only did she miss her boys, she missed Rob. He was jealous. That thought caused her to smile, but at the same time made her heart ache. He was involved with someone—someone with whom he'd spent the weekend. She couldn't get past that. She couldn't reconcile his jealousy about her being with another man while he was with another woman.

Maybe they were just never meant to be. Surely if two people were right for each other, there wouldn't be so many darn obstacles and misunderstandings. If Rob was going to continue coming around and spending time with her sons, they were going to need to clear the air. Parameters needed to be set, and it couldn't be put off any longer.

She was fine with the thought of being just friends with Rob; what she couldn't handle anymore was wondering if it was possible, and if he would be receptive to the idea. It was time to put into practice her commitment to letting go of the past and dealing with the present.

The sound of his truck pulling up in front of the house at two thirty interrupted her inner pep talk and had Jordan's heart skipping a beat. Was she prepared for this? Unfortunately, she had no choice; she had to be. Hearing her sons' laughter had her nearly ripping the front door off its hinges to get to them. She had missed them; for those few short hours, she had missed them all.

The boys were smelly, wet, and a little sunburned, but were bursting with excitement to tell their mother about their day.

"I promise I will listen to every detail about your day and hear all your fishing stories if you just go inside and wash up and put on clean clothes," she said playfully. "You guys stink!"

"Aw, Mom," they whined but did, indeed, go right into the house to do as they were told.

Rob climbed out of the truck and fetched her cooler. He walked casually past Jordan and placed it inside the front door, then went back to the truck to retrieve a larger cooler.

"We had a lot of success today," he said as he shut the tailgate to the truck. "The boys are natural fishermen." He stopped in front of her and smiled. "I hope you are in the mood for fish for dinner." At her blank expression, he walked past her again and went directly into the house.

She wasn't prepared for him to come back and be in such a pleasant mood, nor was she prepared to have dinner with him. Jordan had just assumed he'd leave the boys with what they caught and be on his way. When she stepped inside and saw him setting up to clean the fish in her kitchen, she knew she had to express her feelings and clear the air.

"What's going on here?" she asked, hands planted firmly on her hips. She stood on the side of the breakfast nook opposite from where Rob was setting up a butcher block cutting board and sharpening a filleting knife.

"Well, Jordan, we've got to clean the fish before we can cook them," he said as he waved the large knife around. He looked adorable. He, too, had gotten some sun and his skin was bronzed and glowing. He was still wearing that goofy fishing hat and he smelled just as bad as the boys had, possibly worse.

"That's not what I meant," she said irritably. "What's going on here with us?"

Pretending to stay focused on setting up his butchering station, he asked without looking at her, "Why?"

"What was that all about this morning? You come here making all kinds of crazy accusations...and... What difference does it make to you if a man came to visit us?" She hated to sound desperate, as if she were trying to force him into admitting that he had feelings for her, but her heart couldn't help it.

Without a word, Rob placed the knife on top of the cutting board and went over to the sink to wash his hands. Jordan watched and became increasingly agitated. He turned slowly toward Jordan as he dried them with a paper towel. "Because I'm concerned about the boys, that's why," he said in a deep voice that sent chills throughout Jordan's body.

"Oh," she whispered. "I see." She felt the rejection pierce her heart as she stared at the floor.

He stopped in front of her and reached down to cup her face in his hands. "I'm concerned about their mom, too," he said as he bent forward and placed a gentle, featherlight kiss on her cheek.

Jordan sighed and leaned in to him. She was no longer concerned with the smell of fish or what she was supposed to do. She just wanted to be near him, to touch him, and to feel him touch her. As his mouth moved toward hers, she remembered why they couldn't do this.

Friends, dammit, they were just going to be friends, she chanted in her head. She awkwardly cleared her throat. "What about Kelly?" she asked as she stepped back and nervously smoothed her hair.

"What about her?" he asked, confusion written all over his face as his brows furrowed together.

"You spent the weekend with her and now you're here like this with me. Correct me if I'm wrong, but isn't that the exact same reason we broke up all those years ago, Rob? You were spreading yourself around a little too much?" Sure, it was a childish statement and totally went against her whole commitment to letting the past go, but she had to protect herself.

There were many responses she had expected.

Laughter was not one of them. His hearty amusement made her that much angrier.

"That's priceless, Jordan! Kelly is my cousin's fiancée. Why would you think she's my girlfriend?"

She wished a giant hole would open up in the floor and just swallow her. Her face must have been twenty-seven shades of red. "Well, like I, um…said, you…you went away with her for the weekend, so I just assumed…"

He chuckled again. "She and my cousin are getting married next month and I designed their new home. He's a builder, so we spent the weekend working on the house to get it done in time. Honest." He reached out and pulled her into his arms, planting a kiss firmly on her lips. There was nothing romantic about it at all and as soon as it started, it was over. He released her and went back to working on the fish.

"So, should I wait to cut off the heads until the boys are here to watch?" he asked with a wicked grin.

Dinner was an early and boisterous affair. After Rob had cleaned and filleted all the fish, he set about frying them while Jordan prepared rice pilaf, salad, and biscuits. Jake and Joseph had watched, full of pride, as their day's work was being prepared. It was a real family effort.

Tall fishing tales were thrown at Jordan from every angle. Her boys, who had never fished before in their young lives, were suddenly little Hemingways. They talked and laughed throughout the meal. Rob sat back and realized this was what he wanted: to be part of a family. *This* family.

They were all so much at ease with each other, and the sounds of childish laughter and the look of pure joy on Jordan's face as she listened to her sons' stories caused his gut to clench. It filled him with happiness that he had contributed to the fun they were having tonight.

Jordan's comments from earlier in the day came back to haunt him. *"We were fine before you came along, and we'll continue to be fine after we leave."* He frowned. He didn't want them to be fine when they left. Well, that wasn't completely true; he didn't wish them any ill will, but he didn't want them to leave.

Period. Time was going by too quickly as it was and he knew he hadn't had his fill of being with them yet. He doubted that he ever would.

As the boys rose to begin cleaning up, Joseph's voice brought Rob back into the present. "Hey, Mom? Do you think we can go to Kings Dominion this weekend?" The brown eyes that mirrored his mother's looked at her expectantly. "It's not that far from here and they're only open on the weekends. Maybe it won't be so crowded since the season is over."

"Joe, we talked about this before we came here, remember? I'm just not up to it this year, baby. I'm sorry." Rob noticed both pairs of brown eyes were brimming with tears.

"Yeah, I know." Joseph sighed. "I'm sorry. I just thought now that we've been here a little while, maybe you were feeling better and might change your mind." He slowly walked over to the sofa and quietly sat down.

Jordan sat at the kitchen table and placed her face in her hands and sighed wearily. She hated this. She hated how her boys had to suffer because of her. Before the accident, she could run around at an amusement park, or anyplace else for that matter, all day long. Now, even the task of walking around a supermarket could cause her extreme fatigue and muscle aches.

Though she was beginning to feel better, Jordan didn't want to take the risk of overdoing it and hampering her recovery.

Without looking up, she heard Rob murmur something to the boys and then heard the sound of footsteps heading down the hallway to their bedroom and the door closing. He came and sat next to Jordan and took both of her hands in his.

"I'm sorry, Jordan. I'm afraid that was my fault," he confessed as he ran his thumbs over her knuckles. "We were talking while out on the boat today and they mentioned wanting to go to the park. I told them how great it was and I got them all wound up about it. I really had no idea this was a topic you and the boys had already discussed. I wasn't thinking. I'm sorry."

"It's not your fault, Rob. You'd think by staying close to the park that we'd go, but there never seems to be the time." She smiled weakly at him, reveling in the feel of his strong hands wrapped around hers. She wanted to draw on that strength, have it fill her and take all her pain away.

That thought nearly stopped her breath; if just having him touch her hands gave her such a strong reaction, how was she ever going to come to grips with just being friends? Who was she kidding—now that she knew Kelly wasn't a threat, the thought of being just friends with Rob was completely unappealing.

She looked at his face and saw he was waiting for her to continue. "The thing is, I get tired so easily still and I just can't do all the things they want me to. Believe it or not, up until about six weeks ago, I was still using a cane to get around."

Rob dropped her hands and kicked the chair out from under him. He paced the length of the kitchen with a scowl on his face. Jordan eyed him hesitantly. She had never in all her life seen Rob when he was angry. She remembered Eric's anger well. He had directed it at her often enough during their marriage and even well into their divorce. She silently prayed what she was about to witness wouldn't be anything like what she'd experienced in the past.

"Jordan," he snapped but then caught himself. He took a moment to breathe and calm himself down before beginning again. "Jordan, I am just sick inside when I think about what you and the boys have gone through.

I know I can't erase any of it, but dammit, it breaks my heart to see them look at you that way!"

Jordan finally let the tears she was fighting back fall. She knew exactly what he meant. "It's not easy for me either, Rob," she sobbed. "I have to live with the bad decisions I've made every day, and unfortunately, my children have to pay the price for them. A normal woman would have taken her children someplace fun for a vacation, but because of what I am now, we have to take quiet vacations where they have to look after me!" As her tears freely flowed, Rob stopped his pacing and came to kneel down beside her.

"Look," he said as he reached up and wiped the tears from her face with his thumbs. "Let me do this for them. Please."

"Do what?" She sniffled.

"I want to take us all away for the weekend." He stopped and waited for her refusal. When she stared at him with wide eyes and a watery grin, he went on. "We'll leave on Friday night and drive up. We'll get a hotel room or a suite someplace, and we'll spend all day Saturday at Kings Dominion and then spend part of the day Sunday relaxing around the hotel before coming home."

Home. Oh, how he would love to have a home with Jordan and the boys that they all could come back to and live in together.

Calm down there, Romeo. You're going all soft and emotional and getting way ahead of yourself. Get a grip!

"Rob," she began, "I can't. I—"

"Shh. You can go at your own pace. I'll do all the running around. You can take as many breaks as you like—sit down in the shade and enjoy the view, have a snack, whatever you want. The boys will get to enjoy the rides, and you can sit back knowing they are having a good time." Rob let that scenario play through Jordan's mind for a moment before asking, "What do you think?"

"That's far too much, Rob," she said and reached up to touch his face. The fact that this man wanted to do something nice for her and the boys touched her more than anything else in the world could have. It had been so long since she'd known this type of kindness—no, tenderness from someone, and she wasn't sure how to respond.

"It's not too much, Jordan. I *want* to do this for you and the boys. Trust me. It'll be fun. Come on. What do you say?" His eyes were sweet and pleading, and Jordan would have given him anything in that moment. Staring deeply into his eyes, she knew she was lost.

"I say you are the sweetest man I've ever known." She leaned in and kissed him briefly on the lips, only meaning to express gratitude, but at the initial contact, she realized it wasn't enough.

Rob still held her face in his hands and Jordan reached up to do the same to his as they tasted and teased each other's lips with shy remembrance. They nipped at each other, both painfully holding back.

Jordan sighed and leaned in to him, and all Rob's restraint left.

He slanted his mouth over hers again and again, and when he gently probed at her soft lips with his tongue, she willingly opened for him and let out a soft cry of pleasure.

And then found herself alone. Rob stood and released her while he caught his breath. She feared she had disappointed him in some way. Maybe she had misread the signals, but she thought he wanted her as much as she wanted him. Placing her face in her hands, she cringed with embarrassment. And then he was back at her side.

"Jordan? I'm so sorry. I didn't mean to get so carried away. I…I promise I won't let that happen again. I'm not expecting anything from you in return for this weekend. That's not why I asked, so please relax. I promise to keep my hands to myself." There was a trace of desperation in his voice that caused Jordan's head to snap up. Her eyes were full of questions.

"I don't think I understand."

Looking down at the ground because he couldn't bring himself to look her in the eye, he spoke. "I know you've just been through a hellish few months and you're here to recover, and I go and practically attack you. I'm so sorry. I don't want you to worry about me pouncing. I promise to control myself and…" He stopped speaking at the sound of her soft laughter. "What's so funny?"

"Pouncing?" she laughed. "I think we'd have to admit that we both pounced. You have nothing to be sorry for. I just thought you were regretting kissing me because…well…"

"What, Jordan?"

"Because you didn't enjoy it," she admitted in a quiet voice.

She couldn't bring herself to look at him, either, but he left her no choice. Using his index finger, Rob lifted her chin so she was forced to meet his gaze.

"Oh, I enjoyed it," he said softly as he inched closer to her. "I enjoyed it very much." His lips touched hers briefly. "In fact, I'll probably dream about it for a very long time."

Unfortunately, they couldn't let it go any further than that. Noises were drifting down the hallway from the boys' room, and they both knew this would lead them nowhere for right now.

Resting her forehead on his, she asked, "Are you sure you really want to do this? An entire weekend with my children has been known to take down many brave adults."

Rob stood and took her in his arms and held her close. She felt so good, and he just absorbed the sensations before speaking. "I'll make all the arrangements," he stated. "Besides," he added playfully, "it isn't fair for them to get stuck going to a theme park with a *girl* who doesn't fully appreciate all the scary rides." He winked at her and stepped away.

"Oh, I see. So this isn't really about helping me out. This is to spare Joseph and Jake the embarrassment of having a chicken for a mom, is that it? The fact that you are just a big kid who enjoys thrill rides is just a bonus, right?"

"Absolutely," he said as he headed down the hall to talk to the boys, leaving Jordan standing in the kitchen, smiling at his retreating form.

Chapter 7

IT WAS A PRODUCTIVE WEEK FOR THE MANNING trio. Jordan was truly feeling stronger, and the boys were so thrilled about their upcoming weekend that they were on their best behavior at all times. Jordan figured if she'd made them a meal like liver and onions, they would have eaten it, complimented her on it, and asked for seconds, just to keep her happy and not rock the boat.

In preparation for the weekend, Jordan had begun taking short walks around the neighborhood several times a day. She didn't explain to the boys what they were doing or, rather, why they were doing it; she used the excuse of them needing to be outside, enjoying the fresh air, for their daily jaunts.

In truth, Jordan knew these little walks weren't going to suddenly make her able to keep up with Rob and the boys while touring the theme park, but by exercising her body like this, she'd speed up her recovery. She didn't want anyone worrying about her at the end of the day, when their focus should be on how much fun they'd had.

When Friday finally rolled around, they were all about ready to burst. The boys woke Jordan up at the crack of dawn to help them pack, even though they weren't leaving until after dinner. She indulged them mainly because she knew going back to sleep was impossible and it was something to do to pass the time.

While they were sat around the breakfast table, she stared sleepily at her two sons. Slouched to the side with her head resting in the palm of her hand, she asked, "Why exactly are we up so darn early?"

"We're too excited to sleep!" Jake said, his smile wide, his eyes twinkling.

"I can't believe we are *finally* getting to go to Kings Dominion. Rob is the best!"

"Yes, he is." Jordan nodded around a yawn as she reached for her coffee and realized she was going to have to do everything within her power today to keep them all occupied until it was time to go.

After breakfast, she made them clean around the house while she packed, and even talked them into a walk on the beach for a picnic lunch. The distraction was as much for her benefit as theirs. Jordan was finding it hard to keep her own anticipation in check. The only difference was that she didn't want to let on to the boys how excited she was. What would they think if she were to tell them she was excited about going? Would they think about it on their level—that she was excited about seeing the park? Jake probably would. Joseph, who was so intuitive, would probably realize she was excited because of Rob.

They had never discussed Jordan dating, and in truth, she was afraid of how they'd react to having a man back in their lives full-time. She knew they loved having Rob around, but they knew it was temporary. Had Eric damaged their view on having a father figure in their lives? It was a topic Jordan knew would have to be discussed eventually, but she was unsure if she wanted to face that right now. Now, as they were about to embark on a fun weekend away, was not the time. First she'd like to have time with Rob to explore a little more of what was going on with the two of them.

But what if they didn't want her to get involved with anyone? She had made a life for them, just the three of them. Perhaps they would resent someone joining their family. It was too much to deal with on top of this weekend, so Jordan decided to push all thoughts of it aside until it simply *had* to be dealt with.

It was nearing two in the afternoon when they arrived back home covered in sand. Jordan had just sent them to get cleaned up and had collapsed on the sofa when Rob called.

"Hi," he said smoothly when Jordan answered the phone.

"Hi, yourself," she said softly. Since their dinner on Tuesday, they hadn't seen each other but had spoken on the phone several times a day. Rob was catching up on work so he could be away for the weekend, and she found herself missing him while enjoying hearing his voice on the phone. Jordan longed to see him and was almost as excited as the boys at the prospect of spending the entire weekend with him.

"Listen, don't worry about cooking dinner tonight. I thought we could grab some pizza on the way out of town. Is that all right with you?"

"Are you kidding? Not having to cook is what I live for on days like this!" she joked. "Although getting them involved in a complicated recipe would make a nice distraction at this point."

"Eager to leave, are they?" he chuckled.

"We all are," she said huskily, barely recognizing her

own voice. She sighed into the phone and smiled again at the thought of being with Rob all weekend.

His response told her he was thinking the same thing. "Mmm… You're killing me, you realize that, don't you?" he asked in a dark tone that held many promises.

"Am I?" she teased.

"Absolutely. It's been torture not seeing you these last days. I've been dreaming of that kiss nonstop, Jordan."

She smiled. "I know exactly how you feel." Now there was a double entendre if she'd ever heard one.

"I'll see you around five." He hung up before she could reply.

Jordan wasn't sure what had gotten into her, but it felt really good to be so much at ease that they could flirt with one another. Though the thought of spending time with Rob was thrilling, it was also a little unnerving. The fact that the kids were going to be with them the entire time put to rest any notions of being *alone* with Rob. She wasn't even sure Rob wanted to be alone with her. Was he getting as desperate as she at the thought of what it would be like to be alone together, to make love to one another again after all these years?

That thought sent a shiver down Jordan's spine.

Rob had been her first lover, and she had been his. It was always amazing to her that when all her friends spoke of losing their virginity, they all said how awkward it was, but with Rob, it had been beautiful. They had been so in love at seventeen and so confident of their future together that making love had been as natural to them as the simple act of breathing.

Just the thought of how they used to meet after school and go to the beach or to his father's boat to be alone and make love had Jordan smiling. If she closed her eyes, she could almost still feel his hands on her body.

It had never been that good with anybody else. Well, she had only been with Eric after Rob, and between the two, there had been no contest. Rob was, by far, a more caring, *thorough* lover.

She longed to find out if the sparks would still be there, if her body would still quiver at his touch.

When Rob arrived at five o'clock sharp, Jordan had her answer.

He climbed out of the truck. Seeing her standing in the doorway, he walked very slowly toward her, like a predator stalking its prey. He was a man on a mission, and Jordan stood frozen to the spot. Rob stopped short in front of her and, without any notice, cupped her face and brought his mouth down on hers.

Jordan willingly opened underneath his command. His tongue darted inside and she leaned heavily into him, clinging to the front of his shirt for dear life. Oh, how the man could kiss!

As his arms wound tightly around her tiny waist, Jordan released the shirt and threaded her fingers through his silky brown hair at the nape of his neck and sighed. Blood swept through her veins on a wave of heat, warming her. His tongue found hers and gently persuaded hers to join in mating with his.

When his large hands started to travel up Jordan's rib cage and touched the sides of her breasts, she let out a whimper of need and did, indeed, quiver.

She lifted her mouth briefly from his to regain her breath. "Rob…" she sighed.

He wasn't ready to release her yet. He had been away

from her for too long. He had ached for days with the thought of touching her, and he was greedy in his need at the moment. He pulled her so close he could feel her nipples poking through the fabrics of both their shirts and she could feel the proof of his desire gently pulsing against her belly. At the sound of approaching footsteps, he reluctantly released her.

"Who's killing who?" she whispered. He smiled and shifted uncomfortably before going inside the house to start collecting luggage and loading the truck. Once they had everything secured in the back of the vehicle and everyone was buckled in, they headed into town and to his restaurant for dinner.

Jordan did not allow the boys to indulge in video games this time because she was eager to get on the road. Remarkably, they didn't argue.

"So what's this hotel like, Rob?" Joseph asked. Bless his heart; her son loved going away from home and staying in hotels, any hotel.

Jordan had only recently learned from her sister that Joseph had confided in her that he loved going to hotels because his home life was so miserable. While Eric was still living with them, there was constant fighting going on, and once Eric left, times were tough. To Joseph, a night at a hotel meant a reprieve from the dismal life they had been living.

"Well," Rob began, " I couldn't get us into the resort I had wanted to tonight, so we'll just get a room at one of the smaller ones and then check into the Virginia Crossings Resort sometime tomorrow."

"What's the Virginia Crossings Resort like?" the boy asked, intrigued.

"Well, from what I can tell, because I've never been there, it's kind of a formal, colonial-style place. It's got swimming pools and a golf course, plenty of stuff to do to keep everyone entertained including an Xbox 360 system in the room. I booked us a two-bedroom suite." He looked at Jordan to gauge her reaction.

"Is that all right with you, Jordan? One of the bedrooms has two full-size beds so you and the boys can use that one, and the other bedroom has a king-size bed—for me." His eyes were dark with desire and Jordan wished the sleeping arrangements could be different, that the second bedroom with one bed could be for the two of them. Being a responsible parent was one of the most difficult things she had to do that day.

Just once, she wished she could kick her conscience to the curb and do what she wanted. Everyone else these days did and to hell with the consequences— but that wasn't her and she knew it. Jordan knew she would do the right thing and lie in her bed and dream of being wrapped in his arms in the aftermath of mind-blowing lovemaking.

Rob watched as Jordan swallowed and licked nervously at her lips, and he seemed to read her mind. The action of her tongue fascinated him.

"That sounds fine," she croaked as she tried to clear her throat, hoping he couldn't see right through her, but knowing full well that was exactly what he was doing. He always could. "What about the place for tonight?"

He took his last bite of pizza before answering. "Well, it's a smaller hotel, a Best Western. Now that the park is only open on the weekends, due to the off-season, places fill up fast. I had to take what I could find. Besides, it's only for one night." He shrugged and stood to leave, praying she wouldn't freak out when they arrived at tonight's destination.

"Everybody ready?"

———∾∾∾———

An hour later, Jordan's worst fears were confirmed—she knew this hadn't been a good idea. Standing in the lobby of a Best Western, she nearly let out a cry when the clerk handed them one room key.

"Yes, sir, that's one room reserved for Tyler," the man behind the check-in desk said.

"*One room*?" Jordan hissed as she leaned over the desk, careful not to alert her sons to her dismay.

Rob stood there silently signing the necessary paperwork. "Sorry, ma'am. It's one of the last rooms in town. I can try to check around elsewhere, but I don't think we'll have much luck for you." In all fairness, the man did seem sincerely sorry for their inconvenience and tried to be optimistic for them. "It's a nice size, non-smoking room with two queen-size beds, a refrigerator, and a microwave. I'm sure you'll all be very comfortable. Will you be needing any extra pillows?"

Jordan nodded numbly and wanted to say "only if they come with extra beds—in an extra room!" Still, she couldn't suppress a look of anxiety in Rob's direction as he turned to collect their luggage.

"Now what?" she said.

"Thank you," Rob said over his shoulder as he guided Jordan by the elbow away from the desk. "Now, we go up to our room and try to convince these children of yours to get some sleep."

"*Where*?" she cried again. He kept her moving up to the room without answering any of her questions.

Luckily the boys were too wound up to notice their mother's dismay. Rob kept an eye on them and smiled.

Joseph was daring his brother to ride one of the monster coasters and Jake, trying not to look terrified at the prospect, puffed up his chest and accepted his brother's challenge. Rob had never had a brother, but he certainly remembered similar dares with his sister. He wished Jordan would relax enough to enjoy the exchange going on between her sons.

Once inside the room, he turned on the TV for the boys to find something on cable that interested them, while he pulled Jordan over by the vanity alcove to speak with her in hushed tones.

"Look, I knew if I told you they only had the one room, you would have backed out of the entire weekend and that would have devastated the boys." When she started to correct him, he placed two fingers over her mouth to silence her.

"I've thought it all through, Jordan. We have two beds here." He pointed toward them for dramatic effect. "You and Jake take one; Joseph and I will take the other. It's not ideal but it's only for one night. Nothing inappropriate is going to happen. No one will be scarred for life over it, right?" Rob gently placed his hands on Jordan's shoulders and then began to slowly caress her arms.

"Please, *please* make this fun for the boys and try to relax and enjoy yourself. Don't let them see you all freaked out." His tone was soothing, silky, and, worse, he was making complete sense. She would have agreed to anything at that point just to continue to hear the deep baritone of his voice and feel his hands on her bare arms.

"Okay," she said and reluctantly stepped away from him. She walked fully into the room to check it out. Begrudgingly, Jordan admitted to herself it would be fine for the one night. The room was plenty big for all of them, and by the time she had the boys settled and sleeping, there'd be hardly any time for her to worry about anything before they were packing up and heading to the larger resort.

She announced to the boys that they needed to take their turns in the bathroom, showering and getting ready for bed. Once they were clean and pajama clad, they all agreed on a movie to watch before going to sleep. Personally, Jordan had no interest in watching a movie, but it kept her mind off the fact that Rob was lying on the bed not three feet away from her, sprawled out and looking far too attractive for his own good. Forcing herself to at least pretend she was interested, Jordan turned to make a comment to Jake about the movie but found him already asleep. Joseph, apparently, was going to be a night owl.

Jordan excused herself to take her turn in the bathroom to get ready for bed. She spent as long as she could in the small space, trying to get over the wave of nerves crashing over her at the prospect of Rob seeing her in her nightie. It seemed so personal, so intimate, so childish. So exactly what her body was screaming for! They'd never spent a complete night together before. As young lovers, it had all been about stolen moments and curfews.

Even with the kids in the room, there was a part of her that told her it felt right. Not that she would share a

bed with Rob in front of her children—certainly not—
but it felt right being there and sharing a room, the four
of them, together. It felt nice to be away from the pain
and drudgery of the last year and to feel like part of a
family again.

Jordan did not regret for one moment the end of her
marriage, but she did regret the feeling of loss over the
full family unit. Her boys desperately needed a father
in their lives and it obviously wasn't going to be Eric.
Would Rob even want to be the father her sons needed?
Would it be hard for him to raise another man's children
as his own, particularly Eric's?

If she hadn't been so spiteful and so unwilling to
work things out with Rob at eighteen, she wouldn't even
need to be thinking these things because the children in
that room *would* be his. No amount of worrying or regret
was going to change that, but it still caused an ache deep
in her heart at all they could have had. Still she was
thankful for her marriage to Eric because he had given
her the two wonderful sons she now had. For that reason
alone, she would never regret marrying him.

Pushing all negative thoughts aside, Jordan checked
her reflection in the mirror.

*You're not eighteen anymore, Jordan. You're a
thirty-two-year-old divorced mother of two. Did you
honestly expect to see anything different in the mirror?*
Would Rob still find her attractive after all these years?

Gathering up her courage, Jordan flipped off the light
and emerged from the solitude of the bathroom.

She heard Rob's sharp intake of breath at the sight of
her. She was wearing a simple white cotton nightie that
came to a little above the knee. It had thin straps and a

scooped neckline with tiny buttons down the front. It was in no way sexy, in Jordan's mind, but from the look in Rob's eyes, she felt as if she were standing before him wearing nothing at all.

Averting her eyes, she climbed into her bed next to Jake and tried to focus on the movie. Joseph was beginning to look like he was losing the battle with keeping his eyes open and Jordan encouraged him to shut them and get some sleep. With Jordan's permission, Rob turned off the television and all but one small light, and moments later, the only sounds in the room were those of the two sleeping boys and the pounding hearts of the two adults.

"I guess it's my turn in the bathroom," Rob said as he stood and stretched. His jeans hung low on his hips, and the top button was undone. Jordan had to force her eyes away. "You could join me in there," he suggested softly, and for a split second she considered it.

"I don't think that would be wise." Somewhere in the back of her mind, she was sure there was a reason for her to feel that way, but sitting there and looking at him, she couldn't remember what the reason was.

Rob turned and looked at her before closing the bathroom door. His eyes were dark with desire and Jordan would have given anything to go in that tiny bathroom with him, but it was the little snoring body next to her that reminded her of why she could not.

Jordan tried to force herself to relax, but couldn't. She heard the shower turn on and when she closed her eyes, all that was visible was the image of Rob naked under the steamy spray, water coursing all over his skin, soap suds clinging to him, his muscles gleaming with beads of water… She groaned and placed a pillow briefly over her face.

At the sound of the water shutting off, Jordan decided it would be best for all involved if she feigned sleep. The bathroom door opened and she could smell the clean scent of his soap and shampoo and heard the faint rustle of sheets as he climbed into the bed opposite her.

Waiting until the last light was turned off, she opened her eyes, needing one last look at him. She was surprised to find him lying on his side, watching her, longing written all over his chiseled face. Slivers of moonlight spilled into the room through the curtains, and it was just enough to see what they each needed to.

They lay like that for some time, each on their side, facing one another from opposing beds, just looking. Her body longed to reach out and touch him, but the space between the two beds made that impossible.

It was torture to be this close, close enough to smell one another's scents and hear each other's breathing, and not be able to do something about it. Not to be able to touch Rob was almost more than she could bear. She couldn't remember the last time she had felt such longing, such frustration.

Eventually, her body began to calm itself and she accepted the inevitable. There would be no meeting in the bathroom, no stolen kisses. Not tonight anyway. Tomorrow night in the bigger suite, however, all bets were off. If her body was still as on fire as it was right now, she might be willing to risk being alone with him in his bedroom depending on how far away it was from the boys.

Jordan smiled at him weakly and whispered good night before closing her eyes, feeling light and happy.

Sometime later, Rob had looked his fill and closed his own eyes, happy to have Jordan there and be the last thing he saw before going to sleep. It wouldn't be the first time. Only this time, she was really and truly there and not just an image burned into his mind.

A day at a theme park under normal circumstances was hard work. A day at a theme park with two overexcited boys was pure exhaustion. Jordan was extremely thankful for Rob because there was no way even in good health that she could have kept up with her sons. He went on every thrill ride with them.

Twice!

The closest she came to a thrill ride was the log flume. Not that the ride in and of itself was thrilling; quite the contrary, it was pretty tame. The thrill came from sitting between Rob's hard, muscled legs with her back pressed against the solid wall of his chest while he took advantage of the fact that the boys were in front of them and nuzzled her neck. Jordan wiggled against him and could easily feel his growing arousal pressed firmly against her bottom.

It was a little comical to watch him gingerly climb out of the log at the end of the ride. At her look of barely contained laughter, he walked up behind her and smacked her on the bottom.

"Witch," he whispered. Jordan let out a shriek of delight and walked away, her head still swimming from the sensations his touch had surfaced in her.

Throughout the remainder of the day, they carried on like a family. Jordan took Jake on some of the less-than-thrilling rides while Rob took Joseph on more of the coasters. Meeting up at dinnertime, Jordan cringed at the fast food fare but seeing as this was supposed to be a total day of fun for the kids, she put her adult tastes aside and indulged in a chili dog, fries, and an extra-thick chocolate milk shake. Completely sinful but totally worth it.

Later that night as they settled in at the resort, Jordan collapsed on the oversized sofa, her body screaming with fatigue. She forced one eye open to look at her surroundings. The suite was beautifully decorated with Thomasville furniture in jewel tones. It had been newly renovated, and Jordan couldn't remember ever staying someplace so nice, not even on her honeymoon.

The boys remained unfazed by their surroundings, even Joseph, who normally carried on and on about how nice a hotel room was. No, tonight both he and his brother were so worn out from the events of the day that Jordan knew it would be a breeze to get them to go to sleep.

Without a word of complaint, the boys stuck to their nightly ritual of showering before bed. As each headed in the direction of the bedroom, Jordan reminded them they had to share a bed because the second one was for her. They each mumbled in return but did obey. They were too tired to put up much of a fight anyway. She still felt a wave of disappointment at the thought that she couldn't share a room with Rob.

Rob felt comfortable that they were on their way to winding down and finally took a seat on the sofa next to Jordan. She sat up briefly and he took advantage of her position to ease in beside her so she could recline against him.

They stayed in that position long after the boys were in bed; Rob reveled in the feel of Jordan's body next to his. He had been longing for it ever since the flume ride. Enjoying the closeness while they attempted to watch a little TV, they channel surfed for a while before Rob clicked the set off and pulled Jordan more snugly against him.

"So tell me," he said as he smoothed her hair away from her face, "what was the real reason for your beach retreat?"

She loved the feeling of his hands raking through her hair and felt so much at ease and relaxed, like it was the most natural thing in the world for them to be in this place together. She sighed softly before replying.

"After my accident, my family convinced me to file a civil suit against Eric since the accident was his fault. Rather than go to court, we ended up settling out and it was all very ugly." She took a deep breath before continuing. "You see, Eric is a financial big shot on Wall Street right now and is starting a new life. We were baggage." Jordan could feel tension coursing through Rob's body at her words but forced herself to go on.

"I had stayed in the house where we had lived for the boys' sake, and because that was what Eric had dictated in our original divorce agreement. It was his way of keeping me under his control, you know?

"At first I thought it would be okay and that it would be best for Jake and Joseph, but the longer we lived there, the more miserable I was." She shifted her position a little. "Anyway, Eric had cut his visits down to once or twice a year and once we received a settlement from him... Well, now I can afford to move us to wherever we want and start over." Jordan felt Rob's hand still for the briefest of moments.

"My lawyer drew up papers that stated Eric gave up his parental rights to my children. Can you believe that? How could someone just walk away from their own kids? I mean, I always knew Eric resented being a father but I never thought he'd walk away and ignore his own flesh and blood." Jordan sat up and faced him, wanting no secrets between them. Rob deserved to know exactly what he was getting involved with.

"You have to understand how traumatic all of this has been for the boys. Jake doesn't remember too much about Eric living with us, but Joseph does."

Rob took both of Jordan's hands in his and waited for her to continue.

"On the day Eric signed the papers that terminated his parental rights, he came to the house to gloat. Joseph heard everything." She sighed. "He was so cruel. I was still pretty banged up and had bruises and casts, and he laughed at my appearance. And as if that weren't enough, he went on to belittle the boys too, saying how disappointed he was in them." Her voice quavered with remembrance.

"I had no idea Joseph was home; I had thought they were still out with my mom. They had come back early. I'll never forget the look in his eyes when we turned and saw him standing there. Eric just shrugged and walked out, muttering, 'Oh well. Not my problem anymore.'" Her eyes brimmed with tears and Rob wrapped his arms around her and pulled her close.

"He had said he was glad to be rid of me and my kids because we didn't *fit* his image. It didn't bother me so much because I had always hated his image, but his little

speech really hurt Joe. He's been in a funk ever since."
Sadness filled her voice.

Rob felt a pang of regret for the boy. It must have
been horrible to hear that your own father didn't want
you. No wonder Joseph had become so attached to him
so fast—he was starved for a father figure in his life.
Rob would love to fill that void.

He placed a feather-soft kiss on her temple. "So
you just needed to get away." It was a statement, not
a question.

"Yes and no," she replied as she mindlessly began
to stroke the strong muscles of his chest while her head
rested on his shoulder. "I pulled the boys out of school
and I'm homeschooling them now." He pulled back and
looked at her with surprise written all over his handsome face.

"They didn't want to start the new school year in a
school they were possibly going to leave. Plus, I felt we
needed some time together to decide, as a family, where
we go from here. I wanted us to be free of distractions
and anything that might sway our decisions." When her
eyes met his, she saw his were full of so many emotions:
pride, tenderness, and possibly, love.

"You're an amazing woman, Jordan," he murmured
as he carefully twisted her around in his arms so she was
now lying across his lap.

"No, I'm not."

"You're more than amazing. You're wonderful,
smart, and sexy as hell," he growled as he leaned
forward to kiss her. Jordan had met him halfway and
looped her arms around his neck to bring him closer.
"I don't think I've ever met another woman who is as

courageous as you. You've had an awful time and while some people might just admit defeat, you've come back swinging. You're taking care of your boys and doing all you can to ensure them a good life." He kissed her gently on the nose. "Your boys are lucky to have you." Then he was done talking.

His mouth was hot and sweet on hers, but it wasn't enough. She had wanted this closeness with him all day, all week, heck, probably her whole life, and just lying in his lap wasn't enough. She shifted her body and helped him maneuver until they were lying down on the sofa together, facing one another.

Their kisses were very gentle, teasing. It made Jordan think of their first kisses when they were sixteen. It was a time to get reacquainted, and it was thrilling.

Rob had his hand pressed firmly against her bottom, holding her to him. They were lost in the sensation of the kiss, tongues gently teasing, lips clinging, breath mingling. When Rob traced Jordan's full lower lip with his tongue, she moaned her approval.

Rob stopped suddenly and looked down at her through heavy lids. "I want you, Jordan." He swallowed hard. "I want you so badly I ache, but I know this isn't the time or the place." She had wanted to protest, but she knew, deep down, he was right. They couldn't continue on this path with her children in the next room.

"When we make love"—he kissed her lightly on her neck, just below her ear—"and we will, I want to have you all to myself, with no worries, no distractions. Just you, me, and this incredible need we have for each other."

Jordan groaned with frustration at his words. He was

right, of course, but she did not want to move out of his embrace just yet, so she decided to be a little wicked.

"You're right," she murmured against his throat. "We need to wait." She sucked lightly on his neck and then pressed her breasts a bit more firmly against him. "We can't take the chance of being interrupted." She flicked her tongue against his earlobe and he shook.

"When we are finally alone, we'll make up for all the years we've been apart. I think we'll need at least an entire day to get our bodies reacquainted." Jordan deliberately pressed her hips forward and blatantly cradled his erection in the juncture of her thighs. She placed featherlight kisses along his strong jaw and then licked her way softly up to his ear and whispered, "Don't you agree?"

Suddenly, she was pinned beneath him. His dark-brown eyes sparked with desire and a bit of anger. "It's not nice to tease," he growled, and pressed his erection firmly into her most sensitive spot. Jordan arched her back off the couch and ground herself against him.

Rob took her mouth fiercely and she loved it. There was no forcing; he took and she gave equally. He reached between them and palmed one aching breast and she cried out at his touch. "It's been too long," he panted. "Too damn long."

"I know, I know," she replied between heated kisses. Jordan raked her fingers through his glorious silken hair and held him near to her, not willing to let him go. "I need you," she whispered roughly as she slid a hand between them and stroked his hardened length through the denim.

He shot upright and sprang off the couch. He looked

down at her as he tried to catch his breath. Her own breathing was just as ragged and he almost dove back down on top of her at the sight of her kiss-swollen lips and the desire in her eyes.

"I can't do this with you now, Jordan. I want to—God, do I want to—but I want it to be right." Slowly he sat back down beside her as she forced herself to sit upright. Rob cupped her face in his hands and rained tiny kisses along her cheek, jaw, and throat.

"But we're not kids anymore. I used to dream of making love to you in a bed, not in the backseat of my car or off in the woods like we used to." Jordan blushed at the memory. "I wanted the thrill of taking you to bed and loving you all night long. I've fantasized about it." He bowed his head so only their foreheads touched. "I want you too much to take you here on the couch like a boy." Then he looked directly at her. "I'm going to make love to you like a man." With that, he stood, turned, walked to his bedroom, and closed the door without looking back.

Well, how was she ever supposed to sleep again after a declaration like that?

—⁓—

Jordan tossed and turned all night long, and before she knew it, the blasted alarm clock was going off to remind them there was more fun to be had. Great.

She shared the bathroom with her boys while Rob had one to himself and they all came together eventually in the living room of the suite to go for breakfast. Jordan noticed Rob looked as unrested as she did, which consoled her a little.

On the elevator ride down to the dining room, Rob discreetly reached for her hand and held on to it. She smiled weakly at him and was tickled to see the same expression on his face. How much longer were they supposed to last before the sexual tension and frustration got the better of them?

They ate a leisurely breakfast in the dining room and decided to spend some time touring the grounds. It was unseasonably warm out and Jordan decided it would be okay for them to use the pool.

When they all met up again in the living room after changing into their swimsuits, Jordan thought she'd faint. Seeing Rob in nothing more than a pair of swimming trunks made her mind go blank and her throat go dry. Her body was still on high alert after their encounter on the couch last night, and seeing him walking around half-naked did nothing to squelch that desire. Would he feel the same way once she took off her cover-up down by the pool?

Absolutely.

Jordan placed their towels on a lounge chair as the boys instantly jumped into the pool. Rob was about to dive in after them but the motion of her lifting the blue cotton number over her head stopped him. A quick glance over his shoulder told him the boys were thoroughly distracted by a game of pool volleyball; the coast was clear.

Slowly he walked up behind her and placed his hands on her hips, gently pulling her back against him.

The red one-piece suit she had on was cut high on her hips and low down her back and had him feeling weak. "What are our chances of getting a little time alone in the hot tub?" he whispered against her ear.

Jordan shivered. "I think it's too far away from the pool and Jake isn't a great swimmer." She cursed the fact that he had missed out on swimming lessons this summer, because the thought of time with Rob in the steamy hot tub was exactly what she had in mind.

He took Jordan by the hand and headed over to the pool. "In that case…" he began before scooping her up in his arms and jumping into the cool water.

Jordan let out a scream when they broke through the surface of the water. "Rob!"

He laughed and released her. The boys swam over and soon had their own game of volleyball going. Rob was mesmerized by the sight of Jordan jumping up out of the water. Her skin glistened and he could clearly see the shape of her hardened nipples beneath the clingy Lycra. Her sons soon tired of the game and went off to swim on their own. Rob swam over to join her, pulling her toward a more reclusive spot shielded by potted plants and tropical shrubs.

Sometimes, his hands would linger as he swam around her, or he'd be bold and press his body full against hers while he stole kisses. Jordan thought surely her body would burst into flames even in the cold water.

At three that afternoon, Rob herded them all back up to the room to pack and get ready to check out. No one was happy at the thought of leaving. Jordan wished they could stay longer, but realized she'd be torturing herself even more. At least back at the beach they weren't sharing a residence—he had his own place to go home to and wasn't sleeping in the next room. If they spent one more night under the same roof, Jordan would surely let all her insecurities go and seek him out in the night.

They were on the road by five. The ride home took less than three hours, including a stop at a fast food restaurant for burgers for dinner. Once back at the bungalow, Jordan immediately got the boys settled and ready for bed. They fought her on it, wanting to continue talking about how much fun they'd had over the weekend, but Jordan was barely hanging on by a thread.

Selfishly, she wanted time alone with Rob, and after having spent the entire weekend entertaining her children's every whim, she felt entitled to a little time of peace and quiet without them.

Each boy took a turn thanking Rob for a great weekend and replayed their favorite parts just to linger before calling it a day. Just as Jordan was about to herd them down the hall to bed, Jake rushed over and threw himself into Rob's arms. "Thank you," he whispered.

Jordan almost had to wipe tears from her eyes. She was so touched that this one weekend meant so much to her children. She hugged them both a little longer than usual as they climbed into bed. This was a memory they would cherish always.

"Get some sleep, guys," she said softly as she backed out of their bedroom. "We'll talk more in the morning."

"G'night, Mom," they said together as Jordan closed their door.

Walking down the hallway to the living room, Jordan's tummy was full of butterflies. They would finally be alone for the first time today. She found him sitting on the sofa flipping through the TV channels in an obvious attempt to kill some time.

"Can I get you something to drink?" she offered as she opened the refrigerator to get herself some water.

"Sure. Whatever you're having."

Drinks in hand, she headed over to the sofa, sat herself next to him, and placed the drinks on the coffee table. Rob held an arm out for her and pulled her close beside him while he caught the tail end of a police drama.

"Well, I think the weekend was a complete success, don't you?" she asked.

"Absolutely."

Once the token conversation about the weekend was done, Jordan found herself in Rob's arms, kissing him. She wanted to giggle because here they were "making out" on her sofa like they used to when they were teens. Then they had feared getting caught by Jordan's parents; now they feared being caught by her kids.

Jordan broke the kiss first. "I can't do this with you again and then watch you go," she admitted, her breathing ragged. Her skin tingled all over where their bodies touched and it felt as if it were over a thousand degrees in the house. She stood and greedily drank her glass of water. She slowly walked into the kitchen to place her glass in the sink, trying to put distance between them.

This was so much harder than she'd ever expected it to be. Never once in all her planning for this monthlong trip had she imagined the possibility of meeting someone and wanting to become involved. The prospect of dating again had never entered her mind. Eric had done such a number on her and his desertion was such a blow to her ego that she'd never thought she'd feel attractive to the opposite sex again.

Yet here stood Rob Tyler. There was so much mutual attraction between them that the air nearly bristled with it. Jordan was not an aggressive woman, but right now she wanted to take control of this situation and have her way with this man who had haunted her dreams for the last two weeks. She was tired of her body aching with need and going unfulfilled.

She was tired of stealing kisses and barely touching him and then watching him leave. It wasn't fair. Something had to give and soon, or Jordan would surely lose her mind. Right now, the space between the kitchen and living room felt like a football field and she needed all of it to clear her mind.

Unfortunately, Rob followed. "I know, baby. I know," he said as he pulled her into his embrace. "I want to take you out, just the two of us. I want to be alone with you."

"I want that too, but it's not possible," she said with a shaky breath. "I can't leave the boys here alone and I don't know anyone here I would feel comfortable leaving them with."

Unable to resist, Jordan stood on tiptoes and kissed him. She needed to feel his mouth on hers again. Rob instantly responded, and within seconds, they were right back where they'd started. He scooped her up in his arms and carried her back to the sofa, where he lay down on top of her. Jordan shifted beneath him so she could feel him in all the places that were crying out for attention.

"Do you trust me, Jordan?" he asked as he lifted his mouth from hers.

A few weeks ago she would have had doubts. "Yes."

"Leave it to me then. Okay?"

"Leave what to you?"

"We're going to have the time alone that we both desperately want. Just leave it to me."

Jordan wrapped her arms around his shoulders and pulled him close while she enjoyed the weight of his body on hers until it was time for him to go.

Chapter 8

TWO DAYS LATER, JORDAN WAS SITTING IN THE KITCHEN having breakfast with the boys when the phone rang.

"What are you doing for lunch today?" Rob asked casually.

"The usual," she yawned.

"How about I pick you guys up around eleven?"

That perked her up a little. "Where are we going?" Jordan asked curiously.

"We're going to Claudia's for lunch."

Jordan was a little disappointed they weren't going someplace a little more romantic than that. "Oh."

"She said she'd love to watch the kids for a little while so you and I could go out for a bit." His tone was seductive and Jordan fully grasped his meaning.

"Oh," she said with understanding. "We'll be waiting," she said huskily as she hung up the phone.

The boys were staring at her as she walked back to the table where they were devouring the last of the cereal. They'd need to go shopping again soon.

"Who was that?" Jake asked, milk dribbling down his chin.

She smiled at the sight of him. "That was Rob. He's going to pick us up and take us to lunch at his sister's house."

"Why?" Joseph asked.

"Because Aunt Laura and I used to be friends with

his sister back when we were in school, and he thought it would be fun for us to get together."

"Great," he mumbled.

"She has kids…" Jordan began.

"Boys?"

"Um, well, one boy, three girls."

Joseph shrugged and he went back to his cereal, clearly unimpressed with the afternoon's prospects.

"I'm sure they have video games…" she said, hoping that was true and smiling when both boys perked up in their chairs and started chattering at her all at once.

"Is it an Xbox or Playstation?"

"Do you know what games they have?"

"I knew I should have brought my extra controller!"

"When are we leaving?"

She held up her hands in surrender as she walked toward the coffeemaker and poured herself another mug. "I have no idea what system they have or what games, but whatever they have, I'm sure you'll play it and you'll have fun. Rob's not coming over until eleven, so I would appreciate it if you two got this breakfast mess straightened up and tried to contain yourselves until it's time to go."

They readily agreed and as Jordan left the kitchen to go to her bedroom, she couldn't help but smile as she listened to the boys continue to debate, plot, and plan all the possible scenarios of a video-game-infused afternoon.

Closing the door to her bedroom, Jordan was a bundle of nerves. Would she and Rob come back here to the bungalow? Would they go to his place? A hotel? Her mind raced. Maybe she should call him and ask for some details. Should she dress casual or dress up a little? Should she bring something slinky she could slip into in her purse?

Slinky? Who was she kidding? She didn't even own anything slinky anymore. What was the use? No one had seen her in any form of undress in a long time.

Rummaging through her drawers and closet, she sought something to wear that would look enticing, but not as if she was trying to look that way. Feeling depressed at the items that lay before her, Jordan chose a deep-violet lace bra with matching panties. Lacy underwear had always been her weakness and she hoped Rob wouldn't be disappointed.

Going about her normal routine wasn't easy. She knew the boys had no idea what was going to go on this afternoon, but Jordan was acutely aware of everything she was doing. She took a little longer in the shower so she could shave her legs.

She took a little extra time putting on her makeup and wondered if the boys noticed. She walked around straightening up the house just in case she and Rob came back here, wondering if the boys noticed her slightly nervous flitting around the house.

They never said a word, and Jordan breathed a sigh of relief when at last she felt everything was in place— including herself. She checked her image in the full-length bedroom mirror at least a dozen times, and with each look, her anticipation of seeing Rob increased.

When he knocked on the door at eleven o'clock sharp, Jordan could see her own anticipation mirrored in his eyes. He mentally devoured her right there in the doorway and Jordan shivered with thoughts of what was to come.

Her sons came running down the hall to greet him and began questioning him as they had their mother earlier on what kind of games his nieces and nephew had.

Rob patiently answered as many questions as he could as he herded them toward the truck and got them settled inside. When at last he had Jordan settled in next to him, he felt himself relax.

All morning he had had his doubts; in the back of his mind, he feared something was going to go wrong and Jordan would back out. Did she want him as badly as he wanted her? Did she realize he was slowly going insane for wanting her?

"How is all this going to work?" she asked quietly once they were in the car and on the way.

"We'll go. We'll eat. Then…" He turned and smiled at her. "I remember I wanted to show you some real estate since you're considering a move, and we make our exit." His words held so much promise and he said them quietly enough so Jake and Joseph couldn't hear.

Jordan started to giggle. "Very clever. Does your sister know all this?"

"Who do you think suggested it?"

Jordan blushed fiercely. It was bad enough they had to sneak off to do this, but to know his sister had helped plan their intended lovemaking embarrassed her immensely.

"Rob…" she began hesitantly. She was beginning to have second thoughts about pulling this afternoon off. She was no good at this sort of thing; sneaking around was definitely not her style.

"Don't think about it, Jordan. Let's just go and have some lunch. Claude's eager to see you again."

The house Rob pulled up to had Jordan catching her breath. The property was large with tons of trees. She could see a swing set in the backyard and a basketball hoop set up in the driveway. The actual dwelling was so lovely, so welcoming, it almost pulled Jordan from the car. A porch ran along the entire front of the home with a swing and tons of hanging plants. If Jordan could have picked a home for herself and the boys, it would have been one just like this.

Rob noticed her intense stare and was curious to know what was going on inside her head. Was she having second thoughts about the day? Was she feeling self-conscious about being here with his family? Unable to hold the question in, he turned to her and asked, "Everything okay?"

"It's just so lovely," Jordan sighed. "We live in a subdivision in Raleigh where all the houses look the same, all the yards are landscaped the same. But this…" She sighed dreamily. "This is a home. This is a place that says family."

She turned to look at him and smiled. *He must think I'm a nut.* She suddenly felt self-conscious. "Sorry, I'm babbling," she finally said to break the silence.

In that moment, Rob wanted to lean forward and wrap his arms around her, but held back because of the boys. He looked into Jordan's eyes and his gaze said it all; he understood exactly what she was feeling and didn't think her foolish in the least.

"Who's ready for some food and video games?" Rob asked as he climbed out of the truck, feeling confident in the way the day was going so far.

—〜〜—

Lunch was a lot of fun and Claudia made Jordan and the boys feel as if they were part of the family. Joseph and Jake were in their glory with Claudia's kids; there were video games galore to be played, and once they had finished eating, all the kids had taken off for the play room without a second glance at their parents.

Rob had excused himself to make sure the boys had gotten settled in, and that left Jordan and Claudia alone. Suddenly remembering why exactly they were there and who had helped plan the midday rendezvous, Jordan had a hard time meeting Claudia's gaze.

"I couldn't believe it when Rob told me about running into you in town," Claudia said to break the tense silence. "It was like, wow, blast from the past!"

"Yeah, it was a bit of a shock seeing him, too." Jordan sat, stiff backed, at the kitchen table, expecting Claudia to say something about this awkward situation or about the past Jordan and Rob shared. She wasn't disappointed.

"You know, Jordan, I was a little bit hesitant when Rob first mentioned his spending time with you. I mean, he's a grown man who can make his own decisions, but I remember what he went through when the two of you broke up back in high school."

"We're not teenagers anymore, Claudia," Jordan reminded. "I don't think either of us is going into this, whatever *this* is, blindly. Besides, high school was a long time ago and—"

"Relax, Jordan. I'm not trying to accuse you of anything or make you feel uncomfortable. I just worry about my brother, that's all." Her tone held no condemnation, just love for her brother.

"He's lucky to have you. I know I depend on my sisters' love and support. I don't know how I would've gotten through these last few years without them."

"Do me a favor, and remind him of that!" Claudia said with a laugh and then her expression turned serious again. "Rob has a tendency to jump in with both feet; he doesn't know how to ease into anything. He leads with his heart, Jordan, and I know he's happy with his life and tries to make it seem like it's no big deal that he's not married with kids of his own, but deep down, I know it does bother him. Oh, he'll never admit that out loud but…I just want you both to be careful."

Jordan let Claudia's words sink in before responding. "I don't know how much Rob shared with you about my marriage and everything I went through with Eric, but believe me when I tell you I am beyond cautious these days. I don't know what's going to happen when Rob and I leave here today, but I think we owe it to ourselves to at least explore it a little bit. Does that make sense?"

Claudia smiled. "Absolutely."

Fearing Rob would return to the kitchen and find the two of them talking about him, they switched gears and the conversation centered on what had been going on in Jordan's life while the two worked to clean up the kitchen. Then they discussed motherhood and even shared a laugh at how different it was from what they dreamed it would be. When Rob returned to the kitchen some twenty minutes later—he had gotten sucked into a level of dragon fighting—both women turned to him and smiled.

Jordan would fit in well with his family, he thought. So many years ago, she had been welcomed into his life, his home, his family, and he was sure this time around it would be no different. He was more than ready to find out for sure.

"Ready?" he asked lightly, and Jordan ducked her head and blushed at the thought of gracefully making an exit when Claudia knew what they were going to do. In that moment, she looked exactly like the girl of sixteen he had first fallen in love with.

She slowly nodded and stood. Rob walked over and kissed his sister and then led Jordan up to the playroom, where she could say good-bye to the boys. She informed them that she was leaving with Rob for a little while, but they barely acknowledged her. She was glad for that because she was sure the word *guilty* was written all over her face.

"We'll see you later, Claude," Rob said as they walked out the front door, and his sister waved to them both, smiling like the proverbial cat that swallowed the canary.

"Well, that was awkward," Jordan whispered as they walked down the front steps.

Rob chuckled and reached for her hand. "We're grown-ups, Jordan. We're just going out for a quiet afternoon alone. No one's thinking anything bad about us." He placed an arm around her waist as they walked over to his truck. He helped her inside, closed the door, and walked around to the driver's side and hoped Jordan didn't notice the way his hands shook as he put the key into the ignition.

Back in the truck, Jordan hoped Rob couldn't see her

trembling. This was it. It was really going to happen. They were going to be alone and they were going to make love. Her whole body was tingling with anticipation.

Jordan kept her eyes focused on the view out the passenger side window. Not sure of where they were going—she'd never asked—she was surprised when they pulled up in front of his architecture office. She looked at him quizzically.

"I have a studio loft above my office," he supplied. "Keeps things simple." Jordan nodded and stayed in her seat as he got out of the car. She was suddenly too nervous to move. Rob walked around to her side of the vehicle and opened the door.

"We don't have to do this if you don't want to, Jordan," he said softly, placing one large, tanned hand on her thigh. She noted the look of quiet desperation in his eyes and knew this was exactly where she wanted to be. "We could go someplace else if you'd prefer."

"No," she said quietly. "This is perfect." Rob took her hand and led her from the truck up the stairs to his loft.

His home made her want to cry. It was a place to live— functional, but by no means a home. The walls were bare and it was only one large room. It was immaculate—all white walls and hardwood floors, not a thing out of place. She couldn't find one personal item in the room. She felt as if she were in an office space, except for the bed.

At the sound of the door closing behind her, she turned around to face him, knowing this man needed her and she desperately needed him. They were like two lost souls who had been fortunate enough to find each other. Again.

Jordan walked slowly toward his embrace and

kissed him gently on the cheek. Words were not necessary as Rob took Jordan by the hand again and led her toward his king-size bed, which seemed to dominate the entire space.

Standing beside it, Jordan leaned into him. This was what she wanted: to be with him, holding him, kissing him. Rob slipped his arms around her waist to pull her closer. He trailed kisses down her throat, loving the feel of her bare skin against his lips as he worked his way back up to hers. He let his hands begin to roam—up and down her back, over her bottom, around to her hips, and up her sides to cup her breasts.

"Jordan." His voice rumbled with barely contained passion.

The sound of her name was her undoing.

Jordan became the aggressor as she captured his mouth. It had been too long since she'd been with him, felt this with him, although somewhere in the back of her mind, she knew as teenagers they had never felt this kind of mindless need for one another. They were mere kids back then, and the emotions involved right now were more mature. They had been formed through years of knowledge and longing, and they threatened to carry her away.

Every inch of her burned for him; the need to touch him overwhelmed her. As she let her hands skim the broad planes of his chest, he captured her wrists and lifted his head.

"Are you sure?" he asked, his breath ragged. "I don't want to rush you. I don't want there to be any regrets at the end of the day." He held her gaze steady. "I need to know that you want this."

"Absolutely." She nodded. "More than anything." She tilted her head back as he kissed her neck. The feel of his mouth on her body was exquisite torture. Rob released her wrists and then let his hands wrap around her middle again as he cupped her bottom and pulled her tightly against him. The hard evidence of his arousal pressed firmly against her belly.

Jordan shivered at the contact and before she knew it, Rob was gently guiding her to lie down on the bed.

He stood and looked down at her as he removed his shirt. He saw Jordan swallow hard, licking her lips, and desire pumped through him with such ferocity that he needed to take a minute to compose himself or he'd take her too roughly.

Their eyes never left each other's as Rob's shirt hit the floor, followed by her shoes. When he reached for his belt buckle, she sat up to help him, needing to put an end to this ache throbbing deep inside of her. She was impatient and it turned him on.

She kissed the taut muscles of his stomach as she pulled his belt off and trailed her tongue around his navel. She smiled at the sound of his breath hissing through his teeth. It made her bold; she reached for the button on his jeans and felt him tremble as she lowered his fly.

Rob cupped her face in his hands and gazed down into her desire-filled eyes. "I don't believe this is happening," he rasped.

Jordan stood and removed her own shirt. "Believe it," she whispered into his ear as she nipped at his earlobe, her breath hot.

He shifted his position so he could look at her. She

stood before him in her jeans and a lacy purple bra, and he knew that this image would be burned into his brain forever. He had never wanted a woman more than he wanted, no, *needed* Jordan right now.

Tucking his head down, he kissed her luscious breast through the lace as she arched her back. He brought her rosy center to a tight peak and made her cry out for more. His tongue worked her while he reached up and unclasped the flimsy garment, roughly pushing it aside so they could be skin to skin.

Jordan wrapped her arms around Rob's neck and pulled him down to the mattress with her. The feel of his weight on top of her was like a bolt of lightning. She writhed beneath him, craving a more intimate contact. She couldn't remember the last time she had felt such an intense buildup of passion. Eric had never been one for foreplay. And as for her past relationship with Rob, there was never the time or opportunity for them to take it slow. Their time together was always heated and rushed. What Rob was doing to her now was an entirely new and wondrous experience.

She held on tightly to him as he lavished attention on her breasts, gently licking, sucking, and kissing her with his hot, wet mouth. Her world was spinning out of control, and when she was sure she'd die from his erotic machinations, he came up and scorched her again with a kiss.

She ran her greedy hands down his hot skin, around his waist, and finally into the waistband of his jeans. As she began to lower them from his hips, Rob broke their kiss. "Let me," he growled as, in one swift motion, he kicked off both jeans and briefs. He lay beside her, fully naked and fully aroused, as the heat built in Jordan's eyes.

Leaning forward, she kissed his chest, licking at his flat nipples, and he shivered. Rob nudged her gently onto her back. He kissed her lips, then her chin, working his way down her body. He stopped and lavished attention on both of her breasts again before moving lower. He undid her jeans and worked them over her hips and down her legs.

Jordan felt a moment of panic. She knew she no longer had the body of the eighteen-year-old girl he remembered. Her body now bore the faint markings of having had two children. Would it turn him off? As turned on as she was, she had the sudden urge to cover herself and wished it wasn't broad daylight outside.

When she lay there in nothing but the skimpy lace panties she had chosen, Rob seemed to stop breathing.

"You're even more beautiful than I remembered," he said as he lowered his head to kiss her hip bone. In that moment, all shyness slipped away and Jordan let herself relax once again and enjoy what he was doing to her.

He sighed her name as he ran his hands over her hips and thighs, then up again, hooking his fingers into her panties and dragging them down her silky smooth legs and then off.

Now he pressed his body fully against hers and Jordan let out a sigh of pleasure. His mouth swooped down onto hers. His tongue imitated what their bodies would soon be doing as Jordan wrapped her legs around him, silently begging for his attention.

The thick head of his arousal was poised at her entrance, and she let out a frustrated plea and closed her eyes.

"Look at me, Jordan," he said huskily. She obeyed.

"I want you to watch me as I love you." His words were like silk and soon he slid inside her. Hot, slow, and hard.

Jordan gave a groan of complete pleasure, loving the feel of him filling her in ways she hadn't imagined possible. He belonged to her. He felt so good and she tilted her hips up to take all of him as deeply as possible. He began to move above her, watching her face, taking in every detail of her response to him. Soon he heard her breath begin to quicken, and Jordan pulled his head down for a soul-robbing kiss.

Taking her hands and pinning them above her head, he rocked even deeper as Jordan cried out his name. Rob buried his face against her neck as his hot breath beat against her racing pulse. He growled out his release and called out her name again and again until all that he had was emptied into her. Only when his breathing returned to normal did he move to roll beside her.

Rob pulled her close, feeling the still-rapid beating of her heart against his ribs. She felt so good in his arms, and nothing in the world could have prepared him for the overwhelming need he felt to keep her there. He placed a kiss on the top of her head, and she snuggled closer to him, wrapping around him like a silken blanket.

She placed a soft kiss on his chest before her breathing slowed and evened out. Rob could tell Jordan had dozed and he didn't mind; he was just enjoying having her there with him. With infinite gentleness, he caressed her arm that was splayed across his chest. He knew it had never been that good between them when they were younger; there had been passion, but it was much better now that they had matured.

Jordan had been so responsive to his every touch, and

hearing her cry out his name could possibly count as the most erotic thing he had ever experienced in his life. She shifted a little next to him and sighed. In that instant, he realized in their intense haste to be together, he had not used any protection. He stiffened a little at the thought but relaxed almost immediately.

Normally, he never slipped like that. He was emphatic about birth control and left nothing to chance. Of course there was a chance Jordan was on the pill. Rob frowned for a moment. He didn't want to think of the possibility of her *needing* to be on the pill. Just the thought of her being with another man, responding to him as she just had with him, caused his gut to clench. He couldn't go there.

But the thought of being one with Jordan with no barriers, or better yet, the thought of his child growing in her belly, only made him smile. He had no regrets, and that thought kept him smiling as he closed his own eyes to doze.

Jordan woke him an hour later. The sun was shining brightly in the loft, but she still had the look and feel of a woman in a dream state. Her hands lazily trailed all over his body with no particular purpose. Featherlight kisses seemed to trail her fingers. She was slipping over him as he opened his eyes in wonder. It wasn't a dream; she was real and she was there with him. Straddling him, she kissed him gently on the lips as she felt his manhood stir to life.

She lazily reached between them and guided him inside her. Without more than a sigh at his entrance, she rode him, slowly, seductively, silently. As she climaxed, she arched her back sharply and reached behind her to hold on to Rob's muscular thighs. His own explosive release quickly followed.

Neither spoke; words weren't necessary.

Jordan draped herself over him and Rob hugged her to him; they both fell back to sleep with Rob still deeply buried inside her, two hearts beating together as one. As far as fantasies went, Rob knew this would top them all.

As the afternoon sun was starting to fade, Rob woke up. They were now lying spoon style and he had a hand cupping her breast, teasing her nipple to alertness. When Jordan stretched and purred like a contented kitten, he nuzzled her neck and pulled her beneath him.

"We need to go soon," he said as he claimed her mouth. She wiggled around until she found his hard length and guided it back into her. They cried out together in frantic need, knowing their time together was coming to an end. All too soon, they lay completely spent in each other's arms.

"Yes…soon," Jordan panted.

They dressed quietly; neither had wanted the afternoon to come to an end and now that it had, there weren't any words to describe how they were feeling.

Jordan knew she should be anxious to get back to the boys, but selfishly she wanted more time here with Rob. She watched him from across the room as he pulled his shirt back on and tucked it into his jeans, remembering the exact moment he had taken it off earlier, and felt herself ready to throw caution to the wind and ask if the boys could just stay at Claudia's for the night.

But the practical woman and devoted mother in her kicked in, and she finished getting dressed, wishing things could be different.

Chapter 9

IT WAS ALMOST DARK BY THE TIME THEY ARRIVED BACK at Claudia's. "Well, well, well…" she nearly purred as Jordan and Rob walked hand in hand into the house. She had a knowing smirk on her face but managed to converse about how well all the kids had gotten along and how she'd fed them dinner since it was getting so late. Jordan and Rob looked at each other guiltily and smiled.

"Oh, so you decided to come back?" From behind Claudia, a tall man appeared. He shook hands with Rob and gave him a wink and then turned to Jordan. "Hey, Jordan, I'm Dave, Claudia's husband. It's nice to meet you."

Jordan shook his hand, mortified that now someone else knew what they had been doing all afternoon. An afternoon of sex should not involve this many people! "It's nice to meet you, too, Dave," she answered shyly, and was relieved when both men turned and walked away.

"Thank you, Claudia," Jordan said as she noticed Rob going upstairs to claim the boys. She knew the second he had found them when she heard the telltale whine of, "Aw, do we have to?"

"I hope that we'll get to see you again, Jordan," Claudia said as the two women hugged and said good-bye.

"I would like that. And again, thank you for keeping the boys today. I'm sorry we were gone so long."

"It was no bother and I'm glad that you guys had the

chance to have some alone time. If you need to get away again, just let me know. I'm always here."

Jordan managed a smile but thought it would be a long time before she would be comfortable having a group discussion about her sex life again.

With that thought, she turned to the boys and reminded them to say thank you to Claudia and the kids for having them over today. They both did as they walked out the door, still talking excitedly to their new friends.

As Jordan watched Rob while he said good night to his family, she waited with hers in his truck. Her sons were talking nonstop about how much fun they had.

"Man, I wish we had a game room like that," Jake said excitedly. "Do you think we could make a room like that at home, Mom?"

"They had a really cool bike trail behind the house, too. I wish there was something like that where we lived," Joseph added. "Do you know of any biking trails back in Raleigh, Mom?"

"You don't even ride your bike, Joe," his brother said. "You spend all your time playing video games!"

"That's only because we've had to stay home so much while Mom got better."

Jordan's head snapped around and she looked at her boys, her expression stricken. This was her reality; while today with Rob had been wonderful, it was but a moment out of time. This trip was not supposed to be about her; it was supposed to be about reconnecting with her children. In her haste to please herself, she had pawned them off on someone who was a stranger to them and now she had a glimpse into what her children really thought.

It was in no way the kind of connecting she was hoping for and took a little of the glow off the day.

Joseph noticed the look on his mother's face and his mouth worked to say something, to take back what he had just said. "Mom…I…um, I didn't mean for it to come out like that. It's just that…"

She held up a hand to stop him. "It's okay, Joe. You're entitled to feel the way you do. I know these last couple of months have been hard on you, and I am really hoping to rectify all that and make a better life for us from now on."

Smiling at both of her sons, she continued. "I'm sorry you've had to sacrifice so much, but I promise you, when we get home, that's all going to change."

She looked at Jake. "We'll start making plans for a game room." Then she turned to Joseph. "And we'll look up biking trails on the parks and recreation website and invest in some real mountain bikes. Would you like that?" They both cheered and as Jordan turned forward in her seat, she heard their excited chatter start up again and plans being made. It warmed her heart.

With this latest crisis averted, she was able to put her focus back on the day she had just had. It had been magical. In Jordan's wildest dreams, she couldn't have imagined a more beautiful connection between two people. Rob was a thrilling yet tender lover and she sorely wished their time together could've lasted longer; her bed would feel far too big and lonely tonight after he was gone.

But what did it all mean? She had always known they were compatible physically. That was never a problem in their previous relationship. There was more at stake now, however. This wasn't some silly, adolescent crush. They were grown-ups with real responsibilities and commitments. Not only that, but Jordan had to face the reality that her time here on the Virginia coast wasn't going to last forever, and when it ended, where would that leave her and Rob?

Though she'd never had one personally, she was sure a long-distance relationship would not satisfy either one of them. Plus there was the fact that Jordan's life was in transition right now and she had no idea where she and the boys were going to end up. There was the possibility of moving here to Virginia, but was that the best move for her boys or was she letting her mind get clouded from the afterglow of a passionate afternoon? Worse yet, could her already-fragile heart deal with the answer?

They had been so focused on satisfying their physical needs, they had never addressed the emotional ones or where this relationship was going. At least, she hadn't. Funny how when they were younger they were so free with their words and how they felt, and now that they were older, it seemed so much harder to put their feelings into words. At least, it was for her.

Jordan sighed as she thought about where she wanted to see this relationship go. Her heart screamed out that she wanted to stay here with Rob; to marry him, have babies with him just as they had planned in their youth. But the divorced woman in her calmly reminded her of all that could happen when you rushed into a relationship and a marriage. Could she really consider this a *rush* when it had been where they were heading all those years ago? If anything, she could argue they had waited too long.

But what kind of a husband would Rob be? She knew him as a teen and now as a firmly established adult, but what would he be like to live with every day? How would he handle the responsibilities of a wife and two children? Had he even *had* a long-term, committed relationship in all these years? What if a situation arose like the one in the past and he reacted the same way?

Would he be faithful this time? Jordan knew she couldn't handle that kind of betrayal from him again.

Did he have a temper? Would he be kind to her boys? Jordan rubbed at her temples. He had been the epitome of kindness with Jacob and Joseph since he'd met them, but would that continue once they were his?

Eric hadn't been kind or gentle with them and they were his own flesh and blood. While Jordan didn't think Rob capable of the same kind of behavior Eric had exhibited, she was wary of making that leap of faith.

Smiling warmly to herself, she admitted that in all their years together, Eric had never been as attentive or loving to her *or* the boys as Rob had been these last two weeks. Could he be what her little family needed to finally heal? Was she willing to step out and take that risk, or was she getting too far ahead of herself? Rob hadn't mentioned anything about continuing this relationship, or love or marriage. Maybe she *was* getting too far ahead of herself.

"So, did you guys have fun today?" Rob asked as he climbed into the truck, beaming.

"Yeah," the boys responded eagerly and then went on to tell them all about every level of every video game they had played that day. Jordan couldn't help but smile at their enthusiasm.

"…and then I took my giant key-blade and slayed the dragon, Rob," Jake said excitedly. Rob looked into the rearview mirror and smiled at the boy, and was rewarded with a dimpled smile in return.

"Great job, son," he said with pride, and Jordan's heart lurched at the word. *Son.* Oh, how easy it would be for him to slip right into all their hearts and be a part of the family if she let him.

She held on to that image on the short drive back to the bungalow.

Once at home, it was too early for the boys to get prepared for bed, although they were slowly winding down from their exciting day. Knowing their senses were on overload from all the video games, Rob suggested a walk down to the beach and was met with a positive response.

Jordan and Rob walked together, wanting to hold hands, but Jordan was hesitant to show even that simple gesture of affection in front of her sons just yet. The sun was low on the horizon, and it seemed the perfect ending to a perfect day.

The boys headed down toward the surf in their never-ending search for shells, while Jordan and Rob lagged behind, enjoying the sunset and listening to the laughter of her children. Unable to control himself, Rob took one of Jordan's hands in his, brought it to his lips, and gently kissed her.

"They certainly seemed to have fun today," he said with a chuckle, watching as Jake carefully inspected a shell he'd found.

"Well, your sister had all the necessary ingredients to guarantee a fun-filled day: food, video games, kids…"

They stood close together and, heedless of whether the boys saw, Rob drew Jordan even closer and put his arms around her.

"How about you?" he asked tentatively. "Did you enjoy yourself today?"

"Fishing for compliments?"

He chuckled and with Jordan's head resting on his chest, she felt the vibration. "Would I do something like that?"

"In a heartbeat," she teased. Easing back a little, she looked at his face. "I had a wonderful day. I don't think I can remember anything quite like it." Her words ended on a sigh and she wished they could stay like this forever.

It wasn't long before it was too dark to see much of anything, particularly tiny shells in the sand, so Jordan called to the boys and they headed back to the house. Once inside, she laughed at the fact that they'd all walked along the same stretch of sand and yet only her sons managed to be covered in it from head to toe! At this rate, they'd have their own beach to take back to Raleigh with them.

"Okay, guys, showers, pj's, and then it'll be time for bed."

"Aw…already? It's not like it's a real school night or anything, Mom," Joseph whined. "Why can't we stay up late? We're supposed to be on vacation."

Although he had a point, Jordan was a stickler for routine. She liked having order around her and knew if she let the rules slip or change, restoring things would become increasingly difficult and soon she wouldn't be the one calling the shots; her boys would.

Maybe it was foolish, maybe she was overreacting, but after being under Eric's thumb for so long, she needed to be in control. She didn't think she was being too restrictive with her sons.

"I know we're on vacation, Joe," she said diplomatically, "but that doesn't mean we don't have to have any rules. You had a busy day and got to do all the things you love to do. Let's not ruin a perfectly good day by arguing, okay?"

Although she could tell he wanted to argue some more, the boy nodded and headed down the hall to take his shower. Jake was sitting in the living room with Rob, laughing and watching the TV. The sight of the two of them together made her smile.

Within the hour, both boys were showered and ready for bed. They both thanked Rob again for bringing them to Claudia's house and asked if they'd be able to go there again. Without looking at Jordan for her approval, he told them he would definitely arrange it so they could and wished them a good night. The boys each hugged him and then kissed Jordan before heading to their room.

Rob reclined on the sofa with a smile as Jordan rummaged through the refrigerator in search of something to eat.

"I am starving," she commented over her growling tummy.

Rob slowly rose from the couch and came up behind her, wrapping his arms around her middle and reminding her of why she had missed dinner.

He kissed her throat and Jordan could feel his growing arousal pressing against her.

"Oh yeah," she said.

"Maybe I wasn't thorough enough," he growled against her ear, sending chills of delight coursing through Jordan's body.

"If you were any more thorough, I wouldn't be able to stand," she teased. He let out a low chuckle. "Now, what about some dinner?" She continued to rummage around in the refrigerator, calling out ingredients and meal ideas. She really did need to get to the supermarket again because the most appetizing item she could come up with was grilled cheese sandwiches, and even that felt like too much work.

"Why don't I run out and get us something? I could swing by the restaurant or maybe get some Chinese?" he suggested, and Jordan readily accepted.

"Surprise me," she said and laughed as he scooped her into his arms and dipped her dramatically. "My hero." She beamed as he planted a quick kiss on her lips before setting her back on her feet and heading out the door.

—◊◊◊—

On the short drive back and forth, Rob couldn't help but smile. This was where his life was meant to be: here, with Jordan and her sons. Suddenly, it was as if there was clarity in his life, like the missing pieces of a puzzle had finally been found and everything now fit. This was always where he had wanted to be, and after the incredible afternoon they'd shared, he had no doubt Jordan felt the same way. He'd talk to her about moving them here after dinner. The anticipation he felt was so great that he could hardly wait and had to keep himself from speeding back to her house.

Thoughts and ideas were already racing through his mind. He wouldn't dream of moving them into his loft, so they'd have to act quickly and find a house. They'd probably have to rent first and then he and Jordan could design their dream home. He sighed with contentment. He knew the schools here were good, and he was sure with Claudia's help, they'd be able to get the boys settled in and involved in some sports and clubs in no time.

Of course there was the issue of having to sell her house in Raleigh and moving all their things here. Hell, he had no problem with moving them here before their house sold; if it were up to him, he'd hire someone to pack up the house so Jordan and the boys wouldn't have to leave here at all. Deep down, Rob knew it wasn't practical, but he was eager to start their life together, and the thought of being apart for even a little while caused an ache in his chest.

As the owner of the firm, he could delegate some of his responsibilities to others in his office and take time to go back to Raleigh with Jordan and help her wrap things up there. Maybe with his help, they could get it done quickly and be back here on the beach within a week.

Jordan wasn't working right now, but would she want to go back to work once they were settled in, or would she be as anxious as he was to start a family? Well, they already had a family but he would love to add to it and have babies that were his—his and Jordan's. That thought had him grinning like a lovesick fool. Hell, he'd always known he wanted to have kids but had finally accepted that it probably wasn't going to happen. But now, now with Jordan back in his life, he knew it was a very real possibility—especially after today.

Swiping a hand across his jaw, Rob allowed himself the luxury of thinking that Jordan was already pregnant. If there were any possibility of Jordan being unsure of their relationship, a baby would cement it. She would see they were meant to be together, just as they had planned so many years ago. The thought of watching Jordan's belly grow with his child was just too much to even think about. He didn't think any man deserved to be this happy, but he was.

By the time he pulled back up in front of the bungalow, everything was worked out in his head.

There wasn't a single doubt in his mind that Jordan wouldn't want all that he did. Climbing out of the truck, he grabbed their food, locked the doors, and tried not to look quite so smug and confident as he walked through the door.

The boys were in bed, so they had some time alone. Jordan had set up a place for them to eat in the living room in front of the TV. He had brought back Chinese food and they fed one another, taking pleasure in licking fingers and heated kisses. It was the perfect ending to a perfect day.

Jordan was feeling deliriously happy; it had been far too long since anyone had made her feel this alive.

The conversation had been light; they were enjoying being in each other's presence. Jordan shared how much the boys had enjoyed themselves and how they'd still been talking about it up until a few minutes ago when she'd gone into their room to remind them they were supposed to be going to sleep.

"I'm telling you, Rob, you'd think they'd never gone to anyone's house before! I know I didn't get a very good look at the bonus room, but it must be like Disney World up there the way they're talking about it."

Rob chuckled. "I think between Dave and me, we sort of started out using that room as a 'man cave' and then as the kids came along, we used them as an excuse to buy more toys. There's a big-screen HD TV, video game systems, a Foosball table, Ping-Pong, darts… I have to admit, it's darn close to perfect."

Jordan rolled her eyes. "Typical man," she mumbled.

"I don't hear the kids complaining. They have benefited greatly from all our hard work and I completely understand how the boys feel; it's a place I hate to leave at the end of the day." He looked a little like the boy she'd first met as he admitted, "Most times, Claude has to throw me out because I've overstayed my welcome."

"Aw, poor baby," she cooed. "Well, then I'm sorry I took you away from your man cave today."

Rob reached out like he was going to caress her face, and she caught a glimpse of mischief in his eyes as he lunged lightly and tickled her. "I prefer the kind of playing we did back at my place," he said. "That was way better than any game we've got set up at Claudia's." They laughed like naughty children.

The mood was light, they were laughing and just enjoying their time together, and Jordan was feeling a sense of peace and ease that had been missing from her life for far too long. She nearly choked on her last bite of dinner, however, at Rob's serious statement.

"So, I was thinking," he began, "we'll want to go out tomorrow and find you a house here." Taking a sip of wine, he continued. "I figure we could rent someplace nearby, because the loft is way too small for the four of us, and then we can find some property and build a house of our own." At her silence, Rob tried for a little humor. "I know a really good architect and I think we can afford him."

Jordan had been too stunned to answer him, but the look in her eyes apparently said it all, and Rob's face was a mask of devastation.

"Maybe I spoke too soon," he said as he stood and ran a hand through his hair. Unable to find her voice, Jordan could only sit and stare.

He was offering her all that she thought she wanted, but somehow, having it stated so bluntly caught her off guard. She had hoped they would ease into this discussion after confessing their feelings and then make the decision for her to move here *together*, not have it tossed out like she had no say in it. She was terrified to make that commitment because there were so many other hurdles for them to get over. One was that Rob hadn't once spoken of love or commitment.

"You're amazing, Jordan. You know that?" It wasn't a compliment. "Your face just turned into a wall."

Still she couldn't force herself to speak; tension was working its way up her spine and beginning to choke her.

"I mean, you're sitting here, but I feel like that one sentence put me here all by myself. Are you going to say anything to me? Do my words mean anything to you?" He wasn't shouting but Jordan could tell it wouldn't take much to make that happen.

She cleared her throat and forced herself to speak. "You took me by surprise," she said, her voice sounding cold and very unlike her usual tone.

"That much was obvious," he spat, and bent to clear their dinner dishes. "So? What do you have to say?"

"Rob," she began calmly, following him into the kitchen and farther away from the hallway so the boys couldn't hear them if they were still awake. "I'm just not sure what to say to you. We had a wonderful day today, but is that enough to make me move my life here?" It was an awkward attempt to get him to tell her how he felt toward her, but pride kept her from asking outright.

"Make you? *Make you?*" he said incredulously. "No one makes you do anything, Jordan. That is one thing I clearly remember about you."

"What is that supposed to mean?" she whispered angrily, now trying to keep her voice down so as not to wake her sons.

"When we were dating, I made one mistake and you just took off, refusing to listen or work it out. I couldn't *make you* listen to me!"

"That was completely different, Rob, and you know it! We're not dealing with you screwing around with the easiest girl in school; we're talking about a life-altering decision. *My* life-altering decision!"

"You don't think this is going to alter my life in any way? Jeez, Jordan, I've lived alone for years. I think living with you and the boys qualifies as life-altering!"

Living with you and the boys...not "marrying you," Jordan noted quickly in her mind, and that one statement seemed to stick in her craw, irritating her all the more.

"Rob, please," she began, as if talking to a child, and pinching the bridge of her nose. "Unlike you, I have to think not only about myself, but about what is best for my children."

"And you don't think that being with me is what's best for your kids, is that it?"

"That's not the point and you know it! And don't try to change the subject!" she snapped. "Do you have any idea what it's like to be responsible for anyone but yourself? Do you have any idea how one tiny choice can alter more than your own life?"

"Maybe I would've if you had given us a chance all those years ago."

"Are we back to that?" she said sarcastically. She was frustrated with the direction of this conversation and found herself pacing the room like a caged animal. Rob remained, arms crossed, feet firmly planted.

"Look, Jordan, I'm not saying there was nothing else wrong with our relationship back then. It wasn't perfect, but I never thought you'd walk away from me like that."

"It was for the best at the time," she said, rubbing her temples.

"Oh, yeah. You picked yourself a real winner to run off with. Eric wasn't what was best for anyone, and I still cannot even *believe* that you would not only date him, but marry him!" Rob stalked across the room and grabbed his keys and headed for the front door.

"I didn't run off with Eric and you know it. We had broken up. I just moved on because I didn't know what else to do."

"You could have talked to me, Jordan; you could have tried to work things out, but you were so hell-bent on being pissed that you never gave us a chance!" He stared at her for a long moment and then grabbed the doorknob and yanked the door open.

"So that's it? You're leaving?" she hissed. "Just say something stupid like that and then run off? It was probably the same way when we were eighteen. You had no excuse for yourself then and so you put the blame on me for not talking to you, and you're going to try to put all the blame on me right now.

"I'll admit marrying Eric was not the smartest choice, but I was young and I was hurt. At the time, he was kind. It wasn't until after we were married that another side of him emerged." She sighed wearily. "If nothing else, he gave me my sons. For that fact alone, I will never regret marrying him. I just can't."

Rob had a death grip on the doorknob, ready to take his leave. His shoulders slumped with resignation; his words were spoken softly, sadly.

"They could've been our kids. I loved you then, Jordan, and I would have moved heaven and earth to get you back."

"Oh, really? Well, I think I would definitely have remembered the planets moving, Rob. As I recall, I moved on because I never received so much as a phone call from you after I caught you with that girl. If you had tried, even once, maybe…" She let that thought hang. It was too late for what-ifs.

Rob bowed his head, knowing she was right. In his mind, he always went back after her and made her listen to him. But he'd never done it. He had stood on the sidelines and watched her move on, ashamed of his own foolish behavior. He'd felt he knew Jordan so well that he could predict exactly what she would say to him, how she would look when she said it, and his heart had just never been able to bear it. He hated the reality of her thinking so badly of him, of letting her down for no good reason. So he'd stayed away.

"All this is a moot point right now," Jordan stated blandly. "We aren't talking about the past; we're talking about the here and now. Why do I have to make this decision tonight? I need time to sort things out and figure out what it is that I want to do with my life. I don't think I'm asking for something unreasonable here, Rob."

Why are you making this so difficult for yourself, Jordan? she screamed internally. *He is offering exactly what you want! The hearts-and-flowers nonsense can come later! Stop him before it's too late. Most people don't get a second chance. Grab it and don't let go!*

Rob turned around and leaned heavily against the door, his eyes boring into hers. "What do you need to sort out?"

"How could you even ask that? I'm recovering from a bitter divorce, a near-fatal car accident; I'm a single parent to two growing boys… I mean, isn't that enough? I'm contemplating moving from the home I've lived in for the last thirteen years, uprooting my children from the only home they've ever known! They'll be leaving their school, their friends… Everything they know, that we know and are comfortable with, will be gone. I cannot make that kind of decision on a whim, Rob. That's not fair to the boys. I need to discuss it with them, see how they feel about the whole thing. Did you honestly think one afternoon of making love would make all of that go away?"

Rob winced as if she'd slapped him. "No, I didn't think it would make it all go away, but I thought it meant we were both heading in the same direction, that we wanted the same things."

"What direction is that?" God, how she needed to hear the words from him! She needed reassurance that he loved her and that everything was going to be all right, but she also needed to know he would be patient with her. Eric had never been patient. Every decision had to be made quickly and on Eric's timetable. For once in her life, Jordan needed someone to wait for her, to let her come to her own conclusions, no matter how long it took her to reach them. Was that so unreasonable? Was she really asking for too much?

Apparently so.

Ignoring her question, he let her know where he was coming from. "Do you know not a day has gone by where I haven't kicked myself for what I did to you? Even when I was involved with other women, you were always there." His voice was deadly quiet.

"For years, you have haunted me. I didn't want to admit it to myself, but there was never anyone who compared to you. From the first day we met, you and I had a connection. I tried harder than a man should have to to get you out of my mind. But I guess my guilt just wouldn't let me let you go. I may not have said it then, but I'm saying it now. I'm sorry, Jordan. I am just so damn sorry for what I did to you. There are no excuses, not then, not now. If I could, I would take it all back. God, when I think about the look on your face when…" His voice cracked with emotion; he couldn't go on, and tears welled in Jordan's eyes as she listened. "I never wanted to hurt you. Ever. I have no excuse for what I did and I won't insult you by trying to come up with one."

Jordan could only stand and stare. She had hoped they would share what they were feeling right now for one another, but apparently the past had to be dealt with first if they were ever going to try to have a future together.

He was looking down at the floor and whispered to no one in particular, "I was there on your wedding day."

"What?"

"I was parked in the lot across the street from the church. I sat there and watched you and Eric come out of that church. You looked so happy and so beautiful." He sighed. "It almost killed me. Up until that moment, I thought you'd come back. I kept convincing myself that you would come back and forgive me and we'd have the life together that we had planned." He swallowed hard and looked Jordan in the eyes. "I never wanted to believe we were over."

He straightened his posture and looked at her sadly. "I can't go there again." Turning, he opened the door and walked out. Jordan went after him.

"Why do we have to go there again?" Her words stopped him in his tracks. "You're not being fair, Rob! You spring some idea on me and because I don't jump up and instantly agree to it, we're done? Is that what you're saying? Am I not allowed to have time to think things over for myself?"

He walked toward her and Jordan felt a glimmer of hope. Her heart beat madly in her chest and she was certain they were going to be all right. The night air surrounding her was cool, and she longed to have Rob's body curved around her, warming her and telling her it was okay. But he stopped before fully reaching her, robbing her of his warmth.

"These last two weeks with you and the boys have been the best of my life. I never thought I'd get another chance with you," he said softly. "Making love with you today was more than I ever could have hoped for. But I've waited almost fourteen years for you, Jordan. I can't sit around and wait any longer. It's too much for you to ask."

Well, there was her answer to the whole *rushing into it* dialogue from earlier that evening.

"I didn't come here expecting to find you." Her words were filled with panic and she clutched the front of his shirt. "Please, don't leave like this. Let's go back inside and talk about this." The muscles bunching beneath the fabric told her he wasn't as immune to her as he was trying to be.

Rob traced the line of her jaw with his index finger.

"Baby, if you don't know for certain what you want from me after all these years, then we're not on the same page."

Jordan honestly *heard* her heart break. The pain of it was almost unbearable. Even after suffering so terribly both physically and emotionally at Eric's hands, this feeling was so much worse. As she watched Rob climb into his truck, she knew she should tell him she loved him and that she desperately wanted to live here with him, but fear paralyzed her. She had been so wrong about so many things in her life that she couldn't make herself say the words aloud.

Dumbfounded, she just stood and watched him drive away. When his taillights were out of sight, she crumpled onto the front lawn and cried. Her whole body ached, and she cried for all the things she'd had and lost. Of all the hopes and dreams Jordan had brought with her to the Virginia coast, none had included her finding love and losing her heart to a man who she knew without a doubt was the one and only man for her. The only man she would ever love.

As she knelt on the cool ground, she mourned for the heart that now lay broken. And she hadn't even realized it could happen.

―⁓―

Rob drove as calmly as he could until he was off Jordan's street, then he howled like a wounded animal and pounded on the steering wheel in frustration.

What had just happened? For the last few weeks, things had been progressing beautifully. They were happy with one another, relaxed, in love. Yes, he had no doubt in his mind it was love he and Jordan shared. In the wake of all that had just transpired, Rob realized he'd never *told* her he loved her. But couldn't she tell? He slammed on the brakes in the middle of a deserted street. Maybe that wasn't the real issue. Maybe Jordan didn't love him. That one thought caused a tightening in his chest that brought a tear to his eyes.

There was no way after the way they had made love this afternoon that she couldn't feel the same way about him. He saw it in her eyes, felt it in her every touch.

Then what was the real problem?

Removing himself from the middle of the issue, he conceded that yes, Jordan had been put through hell in her marriage and divorce. Of course, she would be hesitant to get involved again, but not with him! If he were any other man, he could imagine her needing more time and space, but they'd had a previous relationship, one where they had made plans for the future. How could she not believe in them?

Why would she need to think about things? Why would she have doubts? He was crazy about her and her children and the thought of it all being over and not having them in his life was surely going to be the death of him. A part of him wanted to go back to the bungalow and beg and grovel until Jordan agreed to stay with him, but he knew that, after all this time, begging and groveling shouldn't be necessary.

He wanted Jordan more than anything else, but he had his pride. He'd laid his heart out on the table, laid himself bare for her, and she'd rejected him. The squeezing pain in his chest nearly choked him as he drove aimlessly around town.

Not wanting to face the silence of his loft, Rob pulled up to a local pub and went inside to get a drink. He wasn't much of a drinker, but tonight, tonight he needed something to numb the pain causing his heart to seize.

The place was a local landmark and in the summertime, you couldn't get a seat, but on a weeknight after the season ended, there were only a handful of people scattered about. There was a band playing in the corner, crooning about love—great, just what he needed. Pulling up a stool at the bar, he ordered a shot of Jack Daniels. He drank it down in one gulp and accepted the burn. Rob sat, staring off into space for a long while, not paying attention to his surroundings or to the looks he was getting from people around him. People who knew him. People who had never seen him come into the bar, let alone have a drink before. He ordered one more shot, paid his tab, and walked out.

Climbing back into the SUV, he was no closer to wanting to go home but knew he could no longer put it off. He had no place else to go. Not at this hour. Getting behind the wheel after having two shots was probably not the smartest move, but clearly he wasn't the smartest of men right now. If he were, he wouldn't be drinking alone and sitting outside a roadside bar; he'd be holding Jordan in his arms and happily planning their future together.

He gave himself a few minutes to make sure he was okay and then pulled out his phone and called the one person he knew would understand. At the sound of his sister's voice, he almost let himself cry.

"Hey," he said gruffly.

"Rob? Are you all right?" Claudia knew her brother well enough to know that something was definitely wrong.

"No, I'm not all right…definitely not all right."

It was near eleven o'clock and Claudia was beginning to panic. "Rob, honey, what's going on? What's happened?"

He sighed wearily, his head rolling on the headrest. "I lost her, Claude. I lost her."

She muttered a curse. "I don't understand. Everything seemed fine when you guys left here."

"I thought so too. We went back to her place and the boys got ready for bed and I went to pick up dinner. Everything was fine. I get back and tell her that we'll go and find her a house here tomorrow so we can move her here, and she tells me she has to think! What the hell does that mean?"

"So you wait a little while. She's got a lot on her plate

right now. I know you're eager to have her here, but what's a couple of months waiting time?"

Rob couldn't believe his ears. He pulled the phone away and looked at it, offended. "A couple of months?" he snapped. "Dammit, Claude, I've been waiting for Jordan my whole damn life and now you think I need to wait more, too? What is it with everyone? Why do we need to wait? I love her and I want her and the boys here with me! Why is that such a crime?"

"What did she say when you told her you love her?" Silence. "Rob? You did tell her you love her, right?"

"No…but she should know that by now! After all we've been through, after all we shared this afternoon, she should know I love her! And the boys," he added.

"Rob, you may not want to hear this, but women like to be told they are loved. We like to have choices when planning our future. It seems to me you didn't give her any reason to want to be with you."

"You're out of your damn mind, you know that? You're supposed to be on my side. Mine! You're my sister and I called you because I knew you'd understand, but no, you go and take her side!"

She chuckled. "I'll tell you what, call me tomorrow when you get your head cleared a little and we'll talk, okay? I think you're a little too upset right now to see reason. Are you going to be all right?" .

"Like you even care…"

"I love having my baby brother back," she said sarcastically. "Seriously, Rob, are you going to be okay? Do I need to send Dave over to the loft?"

"I'm not at the loft." He pouted.

"Where are you?"

"At a bar."

"Oh, for crying out loud! Are you kidding me? Did you drink? Do not go driving around, Rob. Do you hear me?"

He cringed at her loud voice. The effects of the alcohol were starting to set in. "I'm fine, Claude, really. I need to go. I'll call you tomorrow." He didn't wait for her response and hung up. Sighing wearily, he knew he had to get home. He probably should have taken her up on her offer to have Dave come out, but there was no sense in making everyone's night miserable.

Shaking his head as if to clear it, he started the vehicle, opened the windows, and drove as slowly as possible back to his place. There wasn't a lot of traffic, and he'd lived in this town long enough that he could have driven through the streets with his eyes closed. Still not a smart move to be driving at all in his condition and frame of mind, but what was done was done.

Pulling up to his lonely loft, he paused on the threshold, wary of going inside because he knew that all he would see was Jordan. Their afternoon had been heavenly and he could still feel her against his body, taste her on his lips. The image of her sprawled out on his bed, naked and glowing from their lovemaking, would haunt him forever. The fantasy he had harbored as a teen about making love to Jordan in a bed in no way compared to the erotic reality.

With a sigh of resignation, Rob unlocked the door, went inside and up the stairs. His eyes instantly went to the bed. It was still rumpled and unmade from the afternoon. His first impulse was to angrily rip the bedding off and put it in the laundry to erase the sights and smells of Jordan. But the lonely, brokenhearted man in him could only allow himself to be drawn to the place where he had finally found peace. Pausing beside the bed, he stripped and crawled beneath the sheets, inhaling deeply.

Images flashed through his mind that momentarily had nothing to do with sex, but purely about how much Jordan, Jake, and Joseph had come to mean to him.

Before running into them on the street that fateful morning, Rob had thought his life was complete; now he realized he had been living a hollow existence.

Sure, he had his architecture firm and the restaurant kept him more than busy, but that was just it—he was busy doing things that didn't offer him any fulfillment. He had friends, clients, customers, and each of them had families of their own to go home to. At the end of the day, Rob was still alone.

He'd chosen a career he loved, and he helped build dreams for other people, but not for himself. He took over his grandfather's business, not because it was his dream, but that of his grandfather. He intended to honor that dream, but what about his own? What about his dreams? His wants? His needs?

Spending time with Jake and Joseph, teaching them how to fish or just tossing a ball around with them in the yard, *that* satisfied him more than he ever thought possible. Sure, he spent time with Claudia's kids and he loved them dearly, but they had a father who loved them; Jordan's kids did not. Foolishly, in the short time he had known them, he had come to think of himself as a father figure to the boys. Rob knew he needed them just as much as they needed him.

Tossing his arm over his head, he forced his eyes to close. The smell of Jordan's perfume surrounded him. He smiled sadly. It was the closest he was going to get to spending the night with Jordan ever again.

Chapter 10

FOUR DAYS AFTER ROB DROVE OFF, JORDAN STILL hadn't heard from him. *Typical.* He hadn't made any real effort to work things out when they were eighteen; why should now be any different? He didn't get his way, so that was that. Well, she'd survive now just as she had then. But deep down, she wanted him to call or come by and talk some sense into her.

The thought of just *surviving* left her feeling empty. Jordan didn't want to survive—she wanted to scream and yell and demand that he listen to her as she cried out her love for him. She could only hope his response would be that he loved her too. But after all this time without any contact, Jordan felt pretty sure she had her answer. If Rob loved her, really and truly loved her, wouldn't he have called by now? They had specifically talked about how they should have done that all those years ago, so it seemed this was going to be their pattern of behavior—one mistake and then never speaking again. She sighed with frustration.

Jake and Joseph had asked nonstop questions those first few days regarding Rob's whereabouts. Not feeling up to a lengthy discussion, she told them Rob was out of town, and because she did not want to get caught in her lie, they stayed close to the bungalow and avoided going into town at all costs. It was just easier that way. There was no reason for her boys, who had lost so much in their young lives, to deal with the reality that their mother had caused them to lose again.

Though neither boy had said the words out loud, Jordan knew Rob had come to mean a lot to them. It had been so long since they'd had a father figure in their lives, and Rob had shown them what it was like to be important to someone other than their mom.

Although she prided herself on her parenting skills, she'd never be one to go fishing or to run around a football or soccer field. It just wasn't who she was, and all boys deserved to have that opportunity at least once in their lifetimes. Her boys deserved to have every chance to have fun and follow their dreams with someone who completely understood them, someone who understood how little boys think. It was a role that only a father could fill.

To fill the void Rob left, Jordan and the boys did some of the schoolwork they had been avoiding and started to settle into a homeschool routine. Their mornings were spent on schoolwork, and she managed to incorporate marine life into their lesson plans, so it gave her the perfect excuse to keep them at home and make daily trips to the beach. The schoolwork was a necessity, but finding a way to stretch it out into a full day with only two students was a bit of a struggle. They walked the beach and studied shells and plant life, and Jordan breathed a great sigh of relief that the boys were interested in what she was teaching and seemed to enjoy the work she planned for them each day.

With one week left in their rental agreement, Jordan was seriously considering leaving sooner. Rob wasn't the only one who could just walk away. Just the thought of leaving her sunny little bungalow and Rob to return to her cold house full of bad memories in Raleigh made her ill. In truth, she hadn't felt well since Rob had left. Getting out of bed every morning was a struggle because she knew he would not be there. She got up for the kids' sake. It was important to her that they not know how upset she was; she was just finally starting to feel normal again after the accident, and now this.

Unfortunately, she was no closer to having her life in order than she had been when they'd first arrived. If anything, she was more confused. There hadn't been a time in their vacation when she'd sat down with the boys to discuss what they wanted to do with their lives from this point on. It was only fair to get their feedback, since any decision that was made was going to affect them as well. And, though she hated to admit it, Jordan had to own up to the fact that she was a major basket case who didn't want to make the wrong decision again.

By the time they were done with dinner on Sunday evening and there still had been no call from Rob, Jordan knew it was time to sit down and talk to the boys and discuss their future as a family.

As they worked together cleaning the kitchen, Jordan introduced the subject by recapping all the fun they'd had on their trip so far, choosing to omit any mention of all the things they had done that included Rob. Not an easy task considering most of the exciting things they'd done had included him.

Dammit.

"We've had a lot of fun together, right?" she asked

encouragingly. "This wasn't such a bad idea after all, agreed?"

"Absolutely." They nodded in unison.

"You know," she began cautiously, "one of the reasons we came here was to get away from it all for a while and to think about our future together." The boys stared at her expectantly as they came to sit around the kitchen table. "The thing is, guys, we no longer have to stay in our old house in Raleigh." The words were said cautiously as she tried to gauge their reactions.

"Where would we go?" Jake asked, his brows furrowed in confusion.

"We can move wherever we want to. Have you ever thought of someplace you'd like to move to?" Now both boys were staring at her with wide eyes.

"We can live *anywhere*?" Jake asked, his curiosity piqued.

"Anywhere." She nodded.

"How about Disney World? Can we live in Disney World?" Jake asked with a huge grin on his face, flashing a dimple.

"You don't *live* in Disney World, stupid," Joseph replied with clear disgust. "You visit Disney, right, Mom? I mean, how stupid can you be?"

"I'm not stupid! Mom…"

"Okay, we're getting off topic here. But for the record, no, we cannot live in Disney World. I promise we'll try to visit there on a vacation, though," Jordan said with a smile. "So, any other suggestions? Anyplace that you're thinking about, Joe?" she asked hopefully.

"Can we move here?" Joseph asked, and Jordan's heart stopped. She had feared one of them would ask, but certainly not Joseph, who had hated the thought of coming here just a few weeks ago.

"Why would you want to live here? You hated it here when we arrived." Jordan knew she was getting defensive and her voice quavered a bit. She hoped the gentle reminder of how he had originally felt about the place would work to her advantage.

"Well, it's not as bad as I first thought. I mean, there's Rob, Miss Claudia and her kids, and the beach…" His list of reasons seemed to go on forever.

Soon Jake chimed in with reasons of his own.

"The movie theater…"

"Rob's restaurant is so cool…"

"Miss Claudia said the schools here were great…"

"I like the ice cream down by the beach…"

Jordan felt a headache coming on; she had lost control of the entire discussion and needed to reel it back in immediately.

"Okay, okay, I hear you. You like it here and I'm glad. We can make this an annual vacation spot, perhaps. But Virginia is only one state; we can go anywhere. Wouldn't you like to explore someplace new?" *Please, please, please,* she silently begged, *please have someplace else in mind that you want to move to. Anyplace else but here.*

"Don't you like it here, Mom?" Jake asked, his big blue eyes full of hope.

"I do, sweetheart, really. It's just that I was thinking of trying someplace new, that's all. When I brought us here for vacation, I never thought of it as a potential permanent move for us." Jordan tried to keep her voice even and calm, praying they didn't notice the slight tremor in it.

"We've always lived on the East Coast," she

reminded them. "We could try the West Coast! Maybe go to California? Disneyland is there. We could move close to it and be able to go all the time! Wouldn't that be fun?" Desperation was starting to set in. "Or maybe we could go to Texas and you could be cowboys! How cool would that be?"

"But what about Rob?" Joseph asked. "Why do we have to move away from him? He's been really cool to us and I just thought that…that…" He looked away. He quickly stood and tried to walk away.

"You thought what, baby?" she prompted, reaching a hand out to stop him before he could move. He looked at her with tears in his big, brown eyes.

"I just thought you guys were getting along great and that we could stay here with Rob and maybe he could be our new dad."

Nothing could have braced Jordan for that statement. *Dammit!* This was exactly what she had feared when she'd first invited Rob to join them for dinner, and here it was becoming a reality. How did she explain to a child the complexity of a relationship she didn't even understand? How could she make a twelve-year-old understand his mother was too afraid of messing up again to take a chance on a relationship when she couldn't clearly rationalize it herself?

"We were getting along, Joe, but we can't just assume he'd want to marry me and become a dad. Things like that just don't happen overnight." *Oh, but they did.* "We can see Rob again without living here, you know."

"No we won't. We'll move away and then we'll get busy and so will he, and next thing you know, he'll forget all about us. Just like Dad did."

Her heart lodged in her throat at Joseph's words. There was so much truth and wisdom in them that Jordan wanted to cry out in frustration. *This isn't fair!*

"I am so sorry, guys. I've made a mess of everything," she admitted sadly. "I keep thinking I'm doing the right thing for us but it all keeps turning out wrong." She stood and walked to the sink to get herself a glass of water; her head felt ready to explode. Glass in hand, she turned to grab the bottle of ibuprofen and hoped it would magically work immediately when the room began to tilt and spin.

Jordan blindly reached out for the countertop to steady herself but missed her mark. The last thing she heard before everything went black was the terrified screams of her sons.

"Mom!"

The light is too bright.

That was the first thought that registered in Jordan's mind sometime later as her eyes began their attempt to flutter open. Her head was pounding and even the hushed voices around her sounded as loud as a marching band parading through her head.

With eyes tightly closed because the light had been too hard to handle, Jordan raised a hand to where her head hurt the most. There was a lump there and just touching it lightly made her wince.

"Easy now," came a soothing voice. "Don't touch that. We'll get you some ice."

Was that Rob's voice?

Forcing her eyes to open, Jordan looked over and saw Rob sitting beside her. Before she could say anything, a nurse appeared on her other side, hovering over her and asking her a bunch of questions, which Jordan answered to the best of her ability. Irritably, she wished the nurse would just shut up.

"What's going on?" Jordan finally asked. It even hurt her head to hear her own whispered words. Joseph stepped toward her, his face full of worry.

"You fainted, Mom," he said through teary eyes. "You hit your head real bad on the counter and you were bleeding. I called 9-1-1 and then Rob and…and…" He started to cry again. He looked terrified, and Rob walked over and placed a reassuring arm around him.

Jordan looked over at Rob and he nodded somberly in agreement at Joseph's words. Jordan drank in the sight of him but couldn't get him to quite meet her eyes. Before she could say anything, the nurse started bustling about again.

Just listening to Joseph recount the story had Rob's heart racing. When he had answered his cell phone earlier and had seen Jordan's number on the caller ID, he'd felt more alive than he had since driving away from her bungalow that fateful night. But once he'd answered and heard the boy's frantic voice… It was a feeling he never wanted to experience again. He was in his car and driving toward the bungalow before Joseph had a chance to finish telling him all that had happened. And when he had arrived and seen Jordan bleeding on the ground… He had never known such fear. He was afraid to move her and cursed every moment until the EMTs arrived.

"What is the last thing you remember, Mrs. Manning?" the nurse asked, interrupting Rob's thoughts.

"The boys and I were sitting around the table and

talking. I had a headache. I got up to get some water and ibuprofen and…that's the last thing I can remember," she said solemnly. Rob took her hand in his and held it firmly, his expression grim. Jordan felt a little hope in that one simple gesture.

Simply nodding at Jordan's words, the nurse turned toward Rob. "Do you have the number for your wife's doctor back home?" Before Rob could even register the question, she went on, "It would be helpful for us if we knew the extent of her injuries. Your son mentioned she's suffered from dizzy spells before but, as you can imagine, there are dozens of reasons why a person can get dizzy. Have you noticed an increase in these spells since the accident?"

He knew his jaw was moving, but no words came out. Looking at Jordan, he silently willed her to step in and fill in the blanks. The feeling of helplessness was beginning to grate on his nerves.

She waited to see if Rob would correct the nurse, but luckily that subject got glossed over. Knowing he had no idea of the extent of her medical issues, she knew she'd have to be the one to answer all the questions, even though just whispering caused her great pain.

"If I stand up too quickly or sometimes when I step out into the sunlight, I get a bit dizzy, but I haven't noticed it happening much until the last week or so," Jordan said quietly. "This is the first time it happened along with a headache."

Another simple nod. "The doctor will be in to see you shortly but we're going to keep you overnight for observation," the nurse stated as she made some notes on Jordan's chart.

"No. No, really, I'm fine. I can't stay here overnight. I have children and…" She tried to sit up but a firm hand on her shoulder eased her back down.

"It's all being taken care of, Jordan," Rob said softly. "I called Laura from the car earlier as we followed the ambulance and she's on her way. I'll stay with the boys until she gets here."

Jordan stared at him helplessly, her brown eyes huge. He looked and smelled wonderful and just the sight of him had made her feel better. She didn't want to be here in the hospital. The last time she had to stay in one was after her accident, and just the thought of being in one again filled her with anxiety. Couldn't they see that?

There was nothing she wanted more in this world than to go home with Rob. As much as she loved her sister, it wasn't Laura she wanted taking care of her. If she could just convince them to release her, maybe she could regain control of the situation to her benefit and Rob would be forced to talk to her and hear her out.

Unfortunately, it was not to be. Her eyes begged him not to leave her here, even if it was only overnight, but Rob's attention was now focused on talking with the nurse. She continued to drink in the sight of him and if she could get his attention for just a minute, Jordan was sure she could get him to see how pointless it was for her to stay.

Jake and Joseph came to stand beside her, their little faces tear-streaked and full of worry.

"I'm fine, guys. Really," she reassured them with more confidence than she actually felt. They would be okay as long as they knew she was fine. So no matter how much Jordan did not want to be there, no matter

how badly she wanted to kick, scream, cry, and demand
not to have to stay overnight, she would let her children believe she was okay with the whole thing. "I'll
be home tomorrow and you get to hang out with Aunt
Laura in the meantime. That should be fun, right?" It
was important that they see their mom was positive with
the situation. There was no need to make them feel any
more anxiety than they already were.

Both boys nodded their heads, their expressions serious. "I don't want you to worry. Everything is going
to be fine, okay?" Again they nodded and Rob walked
back over and placed a hand on each of their shoulders.
They leaned into him and Jordan had to close her eyes.
The sight of the three of them like that reminded her of
what she'd always wanted. The reality was he was here
because he'd been forced to be. Joseph had called him
and he didn't want to make a twelve-year-old handle this
mess all by himself.

If he had well and truly wanted to be with her,
with them, he wouldn't have needed an emergency
call to bring him back. The fact that he wouldn't even
make eye contact with her hurt more than the bump
on her head.

That thought caused Jordan to grimace. "Are you
okay? Should I get the nurse?" Rob asked, his own voice
shaking with anxiety.

"No, please. I'm fine," Jordan responded weakly.
There was no way she wanted that damn chatty nurse
hovering over her again. Experience had taught her
she'd have a night full of hovering nurses ahead of her,
so why invite one here now?

"Why don't you go ahead and take the boys home?

There's no point in hanging around here waiting for me to get moved to a room. Sometimes it can take hours." She looked down at her hands, unable to look at Rob's handsome face and see everything she wanted but could not have. "Sorry you had to get dragged into this mess. Hopefully, Laura will get here soon and you'll be able to get back to your own life. She's a pro at looking after us."

Rob looked at her, his expression closed. Taking a deep breath, he nodded his head. "Give your mom a kiss, guys, and let's get out of here so the nurses can get her to her room and she can rest."

The boys obeyed his command, and Jordan watched Rob usher them out of the room. They each waved to her as they walked through the door.

Rob didn't look back at her or say good-bye. She closed her eyes to hold back the tears.

—⁓—

Never before had Rob been in a situation like this one; part of him wanted to call Claudia and have the boys spend the night with her and her family because leaving Jordan alone in the hospital made his whole body tighten with anxiety. He'd seen the fear on her face when the nurse stated she'd have to stay overnight. Rob might not have been back in Jordan's life for long, but he knew enough about her recent past to know she was fighting her own demons by being forced to be in a hospital again.

Then there was the fact that he wanted to talk to Jordan and fix everything, but unfortunately, now was not the time. She had fainted and no one seemed to know why, so for him to stand there and demand that she listen to him so that he could feel better would be beyond selfish.

Looking over his shoulder at the two boys in the backseat of his car upset him the most. They looked utterly devastated and lost. How many times had they had to sit back and have someone else take care of them since Jordan's accident? They must be used to it by now, but that didn't make it right and it didn't mean it was a good thing.

A lone tear slowly made its way down Jake's cheek and Rob's grip tightened on the steering wheel. A quick glance at the dashboard clock showed it would be at least two hours before Jordan's sister would arrive. He had to do something to lighten their burden and take their minds off what they had witnessed that afternoon.

Making up his mind quickly, he started the engine and plastered a smile on his face before turning and facing the boys.

"Who's up for some ice cream?" At the sight of their slight smiles, Rob knew he'd walk through hell and back for these boys and nothing was going to stop him doing everything in his power to make sure they never felt alone again.

<hr />

Just as she had predicted, the night was unbearable. Nurses woke her every hour or so to check her vitals. How was anyone supposed to get any rest under these circumstances? The only positive point to all these disturbances was it forced Jordan to put her own personal misery aside for brief periods of time while she was poked and prodded by uncaring medical personnel. Right now she'd kill for a sleeping pill that would let her sleep through the next couple of days. Maybe she'd wake up and find out the last week had been a bad dream. That she and Rob hadn't fought; they were still together, in love, and making plans for the future.

Unfortunately, there were no drugs to dull her senses, and her mind was fully alert to all that was going on and all that had gone on before. None of it brought her any comfort. Thinking back on that night made her ache. She knew she had some lingering control issues. If only she had just responded differently. If she'd had the confidence to engage Rob in a logical conversation, things would be a lot different right now.

Eventually she was going to have to face the reality that Rob was nothing like Eric. She needed to stop letting her ex-husband have this kind of control over her, making her doubt her every move. Jordan knew she was an intelligent woman who was more than capable of taking care of herself and her children. There was going to come a time when she was going to have to learn to trust in herself above all and not let her past keep ruining her future.

As she lay there in the darkened room, her thoughts were of the accident. She remembered how she had been riddled with anxiety over whether she would recover enough to take care of her children on her own and how desperately she'd missed them.

This time around, she had similar concerns, but they were compounded by a broken heart. Jordan felt miserable and alone. Her sons, no doubt, had already gotten their hopes up at seeing Rob again tonight.

Maybe he could explain to them why he wasn't going to be around in a more diplomatic way than she could. Should she have mentioned that to him? No. The closed expression on his face before he left showed he had no feelings left for her. She had blown it. She had broken his heart for the last time.

She had broken his heart. That thought made her angry. He had no right to claim a broken heart over their initial breakup because it was completely his fault! All she could be guilty of was moving on with her life! Leave it to a man to turn the tables—and shift the focus of blame.

Her emotions and memories seesawed through the night. One moment she was locked in the past, and the next, she was banging her head on the brick wall of reality. By the time the sun was starting to streak through the flimsy window blinds, Jordan knew what she had to do.

As much as it pained her, she would have to return home to Raleigh with Laura; their vacation was over. No matter what diagnosis the doctor came to her with this morning, Jordan did not want to take the chance that something like this would happen again and force her boys to handle it on their own.

Sighing wearily, she closed her eyes and waited for the shift change that would bring a new nurse in to check on her. It was when her body finally accepted the hopeless truth with resignation that Jordan fell into a deep yet dreamless sleep.

Sometime later, she was awakened again, but this time by a doctor.

"Good morning, Mrs. Manning. It looks like I may have some wonderful news for you!" he beamed.

Great. A morning person, Jordan thought bitterly. Her head was pounding and she wanted nothing more than just to get out of here and go home. Forcing a smile, she waited for his news.

"I've consulted with your neurologist back in Raleigh as well as looking over your x-rays from last night, and they're all clear." When she gave him a puzzled look, he continued. "We feared you might have a blood clot, possibly from your accident, but that's not the case. You do, however, have a rather nasty inner ear infection. That essentially is what caused you to get dizzy when you stood, therefore causing you to faint."

Jordan heaved a sigh of relief. "And my head?"

He waved his hand dismissively. "Just a minor bump from the fall." He smiled and made some notes on Jordan's chart. "No signs of a concussion. Our main concern in keeping you overnight was your medical history. Luckily it's just an ear infection. We'll give you your first dose of antibiotics now and as soon as you're ready, you're free to go."

"Thank you so much," she said with relief and a grateful smile.

"Your husband is waiting outside for you in the waiting room. I'll tell him he can come in," he said as he exited the room. She heard the man converse with someone briefly and figured it was probably her brother-in-law Mark, who had most likely driven down with Laura. She was sure that after last night, Rob would not willingly come back into this situation.

Jordan was climbing out of the bed and nearly fell

over when Rob entered the room. He looked like hell. There were dark circles under his eyes, and it looked to Jordan as if he hadn't slept all night. Or was that just wishful thinking?

"What are you doing here?"

"I thought it would be too hectic for Laura to bring the boys in to pick you up, so I told her I'd come and get you." He moved only a foot into the room, afraid to get too close, gauging her reaction to his being there.

"Oh." They stood there for long moments, struggling for something to say. "What time did Laura arrive last night? Did she get settled in okay? Is Mark with her?"

"She got in around eight," he said flatly. "When I left, the boys were moving her luggage into your bedroom and trying to convince her to let them stay up and watch some TV."

"I'm sure they probably played the sympathy card and, knowing my sister, she caved. She normally lets them get away with just about anything for the first few days she's with them, and then goes back to being tough as nails."

Rob winced at the thought that the boys had been away from Jordan enough for a pattern to form. He almost spoke the words out loud but decided it would be best to hold his tongue.

When Jordan turned to grab her clothes, Rob let his eyes feast on her. Keeping his distance, he simply watched. He knew if he got any closer to her, he'd make a fool of himself and haul her into his arms, kissing her senseless and begging her to stay with him because he wanted so desperately to take care of her.

It bothered him that he had to sit back and let Laura

take over. Not that he had anything against Jordan's sister; it was just that if she weren't here, if her help weren't an option, Jordan would have no choice but to accept his. Now he not only had to deal with Jordan's objections, but probably Laura's as well.

When he had arrived back at the bungalow with the boys, he had felt in control. He kept himself busy trying to distract them. They'd stopped for ice cream on the way home and then watched some TV together. But once Laura had arrived and started asking questions, Rob found himself struggling for answers. There was so much about Jordan he didn't know. Aspects of her life since the accident that she hadn't shared with him but Laura had. He had greedily soaked up any tidbit of information he could get. The more he knew, the better his chances of convincing her to stay with him.

As much as he resented Laura's being there, he was grateful for the opportunity to learn more about Jordan's life. If he could understand her, not only her health, perhaps he could unveil the truth behind her reluctance to be with him.

The last twelve hours had been hell on him. Since he wasn't related to her, he couldn't get a doctor to talk to him. He'd let the nurse's assumption in the emergency room go without comment at the time, but when he'd come back after getting the boys and Laura settled back at the bungalow, he'd foolishly told the truth about who he was and at that point everyone seemed to clam up and just offer him a seat in the waiting room. All night, he had paced out in that damn room hoping for some scrap of information on how Jordan was doing.

At one point, he had even called Laura and asked

her to call the hospital to get information for him. Unfortunately, he hadn't bothered to look at a clock and it had been near two in the morning. She had been patient, even kind to him, as she reminded him that a doctor would be in to see Jordan in the morning. With every hour that passed, his anxiety had grown until finally the sun was up and there was activity around him once again. With no choice but to lie, he'd found the doctor who was heading into Jordan's room and gotten an update on her. Once he knew she was going to be all right, Rob was able to relax.

Her cool tone when she spoke snapped him out of his reverie. "I'll be ready shortly," she said as she walked to the private bathroom to get changed. Though she didn't slam the door, the soft click still had the sound of finality, like she wasn't just shutting the door so she could change but was shutting him out permanently.

Rob nodded. "I'll wait out in the hallway," was all he said as he exited the room.

Looking at her reflection in the dingy bathroom mirror, Jordan wished she had a way to fix her appearance. Other than the few toiletries that had somehow appeared in her room, she had nothing to make herself look less like someone who'd suffered a minor trauma and spent the night in the hospital.

Finger-combing her hair, she stared at herself and wondered what Rob would see when he looked at her now. Would he still see her as someone he wanted, or would he take one look at her horrid appearance and thank God he'd dodged this bullet? She could agonize over that one for days and all she would manage to prove was she was nothing more than a coward hiding out in a hospital bathroom. It was an all-time low for her and she knew it.

Jordan gave herself a pep talk about how immaterial her appearance was at this point. It shouldn't matter to Rob, and if it did, she didn't need him anyway. She squared her shoulders and left the safety of the bathroom.

True to his word, Rob was standing against the wall in the hallway right outside her room when she emerged. There was a wheelchair waiting for her beside him, hospital regulations, and he escorted Jordan down to his truck. His silence was a blessing because she still had a twinge of a headache. It was a relief not to have to talk.

Once in his truck, Jordan sat stiffly beside him.

There was so much she wanted to say, that she *had* to say, and yet she could not get her mouth to cooperate. Having no idea where the hospital was in relation to the bungalow, she was unsure how long this ride would even last.

Meanwhile, Rob kept sneaking glances at her and hoping she would talk to him. He didn't care if they only talked about the weather, just as long as she'd talk to him. Her eyes were closed and her head lolled to the side. He knew she had to be exhausted and probably couldn't wait to climb into her own bed and sleep. He really hated the distance between them. Just when he thought he'd lose his mind in the silence, she spoke.

"How were the boys when you got them home?"

"Better. We stopped for ice cream on the way and so it provided a bit of a distraction. Then we got back to the house and tuned in to a *SpongeBob* marathon." He smiled in remembrance of the way the boys had just laughed at the pure silliness of the show. It hadn't taken long for him to join in.

Jordan found herself chuckling a little as if reading his thoughts. "They do love that show." And there the conversation stopped. She wished she felt better, that she was up to having an actual conversation with him, but the headache and exhaustion were just a little more than she could bear at the moment. As if willing him to read her mind, Jordan hoped Rob didn't take her silence for still being angry with him. She knew eventually they were going to clear the air and talk things through, but right now it was all she could do to survive the bumps in the road that kept jarring the vehicle. The remainder of the trip was spent in silence.

Once they were back at the bungalow, they were greeted by three smiling faces. Jordan almost cried at the sight of them. She knew it was only a night, but it felt like an eternity since she'd seen her sons. Her sister stood back and let the boys greet Jordan first. When Jordan looked up at her, their smiles met. Laura came and wrapped her arms around her sister and Jordan sagged with relief at her presence.

"Thank you so much for coming, Laura. I don't know what the boys and I would do without you." Her words were a mere whisper, a choked sob.

Rob stood back and silently seethed. *I would be here taking care of you, proving I love you and you should give us another chance.*

"Are you kidding me?" Laura chuckled. "Joseph runs a pretty tight ship around here. He's got it all under control." Joseph stood a little taller at the praise his aunt heaped on him.

Rob followed them into the house and took note of just how alike Jordan and Laura looked. He didn't remember seeing that in them all those years ago while he and Jordan dated. But now, standing there and watching them, unobserved, he noted their similarities—the dark hair and eyes—but Jordan's features were a little softer and more delicate. Laura's eyes were filled with wisdom and experience, where Jordan's seemed constantly to be filled with wonder and longing. He could stare a lifetime into her eyes and it still wouldn't be enough.

Focusing his attention back to the present, he declined when Laura offered him something to drink. "I'm going to drop off this prescription at the pharmacy for you, Jordan," he said, not meeting her eyes. Then he turned to Laura. "You can pick it up later or I can bring it back, whichever is easier for you."

There was his opening to come back later and check on her without being too obvious. God, he was a desperate man!

"Laura can get it later," Jordan said a little too quickly and then wanted to kick herself. Why in the world was she sabotaging everything? Maybe later on in the day she'd feel better and they'd have an opportunity to talk. Maybe she could get Laura to take the boys out someplace for a little while so she and Rob could be alone. Maybe she could free herself from the paralyzing fear of making the wrong decisions. With a cold sense of dread creeping down her spine, she couldn't find the words to take it all back.

Both Laura and Rob turned to stare at her. Sensing the questions in both of their eyes, Jordan spoke, trying to redeem herself. "It's just that you've done so much already, Rob. Besides, it will give my sister a chance to get out and see the town a bit. I'm sure Laura would like to do more than just sit around the bungalow watching me. She does that enough at home." That sounded believable, didn't it?

"Fine," Rob said tightly. He looked at Jordan with a clenched jaw and seemed about to say something when Laura, reading the tension between the two of them, stepped in and spoke up.

"Just tell me where I need to go and I'm sure I'll find it," she said lightly. She smiled at Rob awkwardly and then shot her sister a look over her shoulder. "Jordan, why don't you lie down? I'll be in to check on you in a minute."

Wordlessly, Jordan chanced a quick look at Rob before turning to walk down the short hall to her room and shutting the door. Laura noted the longing in Rob's expression as he watched Jordan walk away from them. Maybe she had been wrong to discourage her sister from getting involved with this man again. After all, could you really judge a person from what they did at the age of eighteen? If that were the case, she'd personally be excluded from many of the church groups she was involved in now!

Turning to Rob, Laura got directions to the pharmacy and then turned and watched as he said his good-byes to the boys. It tore at her heart to see how much her nephews adored this man. It was obvious the feeling was mutual; they all seemed to cling to each other. Laura noticed the tears in Rob's eyes as he said good-bye on his way out the door. What on earth had gone on here over the last couple of weeks, and what was wrong with her sister?

"Will you come over tomorrow, Rob?" Jake asked. "We can go to the beach and build the sand castles like you told me about."

It took a moment for Rob to compose himself before he could answer. It would be so easy to give these kids what they wanted, what they needed. But he wouldn't do it by going against Jordan's wishes. Until they had the opportunity to sit and talk and he could finally tell Jordan he loved her, he had no choice but to play by her rules and not overstep his bounds.

"Let's see how your mom is feeling tomorrow before we go and make all kinds of plans, okay?" he said, his voice sounding overly optimistic.

"Okay," the boy responded weakly before turning and heading back to the living room.

"Thanks again," Laura said as he turned to leave. "For everything. It makes me crazy just thinking about what could have happened if you weren't here to help the boys out. I mean, I know Joseph is a very responsible boy but…" She hesitated for a moment. "But this is more than he should have to deal with. So really, thank you."

Rob could only nod. All night and into the morning he'd thought the same thing. The thought of Joseph having to take on all that responsibility and dealing with EMTs and doctors and watching over his little brother was way more than a twelve-year-old should have to handle. The boy needed to be a kid again, and Rob hoped he'd be able to make that happen again soon.

Laura saw the emotions written all over Rob's face and she hated to let him leave like this. She had to *do* something. "Hey, wait!" Rob turned, hand on the front doorknob, and looked at Laura inquisitively.

"The boys tell me you've got a restaurant here in town and I was thinking I'd bring them in tonight, you know…maybe give Jordan a little time alone, some peace and quiet, a chance to catch up on some sleep, that sort of thing. I'm already planning on taking them to a hotel with me for the night and maybe we'll even catch a movie. I'm sure Jordan won't mind the chance to be alone."

Laura hoped she wasn't being obvious in her attempt to let Rob know that the coast would be clear for them tonight. If she was reading both of them correctly, this would be the perfect opportunity for them to be together, maybe work things out.

"Why take them to a hotel? Are you sure Jordan should be alone? I mean, she just got out of the hospital. What if she passes out again and there's no one here with her?"

Okay, apparently it's not so obvious.

"That ear infection should be responding to the antibiotics she's taking rather quickly. I think what she needs most is to relax and get a good night's sleep." Laura glanced over her shoulder in the direction of Jordan's bedroom. "I really do appreciate everything you did last night to help Jordan and the boys, Rob."

Rob smiled sadly. "I'm just glad I was close by and could be here. The thought of Joe having to handle it all on his own…" The rest of what he was going to say was clogged in his throat.

Laura's heart went out to him and she shuddered at his words. Jordan had been lucky Rob had been nearby and able to help. They would all forever be in his debt. Hell, Laura knew she could stand here and thank him all day, but she knew she needed to tend to Jordan and figure out what in the world was going on. "So, I guess we'll see you a little bit later."

"Yeah, sure. That would be great. Mondays are normally quiet, so I'm sure there will be more than a few tables open for you. If I see that it's getting busy, I'll put a reserved sign on a table for you."

"Thanks, Rob. I'm sure the boys will enjoy it. I hear there's an arcade and everything." Rob smiled sadly at her, barely meeting her gaze as he left the house. Laura pivoted in her spot and turned toward Jordan's bedroom. "Okay, little sister, now let's hear your story."

Chapter 11

JORDAN WAS LYING STIFFLY ON HER BED AND PHYSICALLY cringed when she heard Rob leave. She'd had the perfect opportunity to see him again when he offered to bring her prescription back for her, and she had foolishly spoken up and shot that to hell, too. What was the matter with her?

The man had rescued her kids, made arrangements for their safety and well-being, picked her up from the hospital and brought her home, *and* he was dropping off her prescription for her! What more did she expect from him after breaking his heart? Shaking her head with disgust, Jordan realized she was being unreasonable. Curling up in the fetal position and squeezing her eyes shut, she cursed herself a thousand times over.

"You are unbelievable, Jordan Manning!" Those were Laura's first words as she walked into Jordan's room, brown eyes ablaze with fury.

Jordan was temporarily taken aback by her sister's outburst. "What are you talking about?"

"I'm talking about the fact that that sweet man is absolutely gaga over you and you fairly threw him out of here! What were you thinking?"

Sitting up on the bed and braced for battle, Jordan responded. "First of all, aren't you the one who advised me not to get involved with him?" Laura at least had the decency to look ashamed of her earlier comments. "And secondly, he isn't *gaga*, for crying out loud. Where would you even get that idea, Laura?"

"From the way he looks at you, for starters. Then there's the way he looks at your sons, who, by the way, look at him the same way." At Jordan's wide-eyed expression, Laura ranted on. "And let's not forget the way he came rushing over here to help you and the boys when Joseph called him or how he took care of them until I arrived."

Jordan sat up a little straighter in the bed and rolled her eyes at her sister's dramatic tirade. "And when he's not busy rescuing lonely women and protecting their children, he spends his spare time flying around in his red cape stopping all the evil in the world and getting stranded kittens out of trees!" Jordan said sarcastically. "Are you done or did you have more to say about 'Super Rob'?"

"No, Miss Smarty-Pants, as a matter of fact I'm not done. Did you know he spent the entire night at the hospital after he left here?" Laura asked.

Jordan opened her mouth to speak but the shock of Laura's words promptly shut her up.

"I didn't think so. He was so out of his mind with worry for you last night that I almost had *him* admitted to the darn hospital! When he got back there and they wouldn't tell him anything about your condition, he called me on my cell phone to ask me to call the doctors and get an update for him."

She took a deep breath to calm herself a little because she was severely frustrated with her sister. "He stayed there, even though they wouldn't let him stay with you and no one would even talk to him about you. Now, tell me what on earth is wrong with you that you would treat him the way that you just did!"

The floodgates opened and Jordan burst into tears—heart-wrenching, body-shattering tears that caused her already-throbbing head to feel as if it were ready to burst. Could life get any worse?

"I'm an idiot, that's what's wrong with me!" Jordan cried. "I was so afraid to believe that something good could possibly happen to me or that someone could actually *love* me that I forced Rob away. I'm too afraid to trust my own judgment anymore, Laura, and I hate that about myself!"

Laura instantly felt remorseful for her harsh words and her eyes softened as she watched her sister fall apart. She sat down beside Jordan on the bed and hugged her. "I find all of that hard to believe, Jordan. First of all, why don't you trust your judgment?"

Jordan's eyes widened with disbelief. "Do you really have to ask? I was completely oblivious to what a snake Eric was before I married him! I was clueless to everything he was planning while we were married and then, to top it off, I still trusted him a little after the divorce! Look where that's gotten me!"

"Okay, but if it makes you feel any better, we were all taken in by Eric's deceit. None of us knew what he was really like, not just you. Stop beating yourself up over it."

"It's not the same, Laura! I was *married* to the man! I shared his bed, lived with him every day! I should have been able to see what he was really like." Jordan stopped to wipe her eyes. "Maybe I didn't want to see what he was really like. I mean, he was there for me when Rob and I broke up and I guess it never occurred to me that he was anything but decent.

"Then again I thought that about Rob, too," she said with a mirthless laugh.

"Oh, sweetie, Rob is nothing like him."

"Rob wasn't honest with me either."

"You were kids back then, Jordan! He is nothing now like he was back then. Even I can tell that after spending some time with him. So what is it you think you've done to force him away?"

"The list is endless."

"Come on," Laura coaxed. "It can't be that bad. Tell me."

Jordan told of the time they had spent together, including the afternoon they'd left the boys with Claudia. "When we came home here that night, he asked me to move here and I just, I…I…clammed up. I told him I needed to think about it and he said that if I didn't know what I wanted with him by now, we weren't on the same page." Taking a tissue from the box Laura held out, Jordan attempted to clean up her face.

"I told him he was being unreasonable; I needed time to think about it because I wanted to be sure. He never once said he loved me. There was no mention of feelings; it was all just 'Move here, Jordan.' In the end, he drove off and I didn't hear from him until I woke up in the hospital." Taking a deep, cleansing breath, she looked at her sister. "Oh, Laura…I've made a mess of everything. Again!"

Big sisters were great for many reasons, Jordan realized. The main one being that they didn't judge too harshly and always seemed to know what to say.

Laura sat back down on the bed beside her sister and

hugged her while Jordan cried it out. Sometime later, Jordan just seemed to sag against her. "Why don't you rest for a little while? I'm going to see what's in the house for lunch. I'll come back in a few minutes and check on you, okay?"

Jordan nodded and reclined against her pillows. It felt so good to get it all out in the open. She was thankful to Laura for listening to her, and she found herself fighting to keep her eyes open. As soon as her head hit the cushioned softness, exhaustion claimed her.

Casually walking down the hall and into the kitchen, Laura suggested the boys go outside and play while she made lunch. Once the door was securely closed, Laura went in search of Jordan's laptop, booted it up, and began a people search. Only partially finding what she was looking for, she grabbed her cell phone and called information in search of her old friend Claudia.

—⁂—

Fifteen minutes later, Laura was wiping tears of laughter from her own eyes. She and Claudia had been close in high school, and this conversation had really reminded her of how much she had missed her old friend.

"You know, as much as I could sit here and reminisce with you all day, we have got to do something to help these two out," Laura began.

"The way I see it, you've got to orchestrate a way for them to be alone. How hard could that be?"

Laura described to Claudia how she'd tried to do that earlier and how Rob clearly had not taken the hint.

"Men," they said in unison.

"Do you think this is going to work?" Laura asked.

"It has to, Laura. I've been worried about Rob all week long. I told them both I wasn't sure if their getting involved again was a good idea, but I thought they deserved a second chance. Seeing them together that day? You'd have to be blind not to see how much they feel for each other."

"Same here. After seeing the two of them together this morning, well, it just about broke my heart watching him leave the boys. I wish Jordan wasn't so stubborn!"

"Please!" Claudia laughed. "My brother goes full throttle like a steamroller when he wants something. No doubt he just started making plans for them without even talking to Jordan about it first. Men can be such idiots."

"That I have to agree on."

"I tried explaining to him, from a woman's point of view, why he needed to give Jordan some time, but he just couldn't see my point." After a derisive snort, she added, "Well, maybe I should say he *wouldn't* see my point. He always was a stubborn one."

"I think Jordan's giving him a run for his money. She is so convinced she is incapable of making the right decision about anything that she's afraid to take a chance on this relationship. I never thought of her as being insecure, but after sitting and talking with her today, I am well and truly shocked."

"Her ex must have been some monster to turn her into such a mess."

"You have no idea." Laura sighed. "But to be honest with you, we've been dealing with her physical recovery for what seems like forever, and I guess Jordan didn't want any of us to know how much damage he'd done to her psychologically. I never saw this coming."

"And then there's my brother just plowing through and pushing her to do things his way and on his time-table. That poor woman hasn't had a chance to figure out which end is up in her life." Claudia got quiet for a moment. "I can only hope he'll learn something from this and figure out not everyone thinks and feels the same way he does."

"Amen to that," Laura said.

At the sound of the front door opening and the boys coming in, Laura cut the conversation short. "I'll call you later," Laura whispered into the phone as she quickly hung up.

"What's going on there, big man?" she asked as she put the finishing touches on the soup and sandwiches she had prepared while on the phone.

"Is lunch ready, Aunt Laura?" Joseph asked, poking his head through the doorway.

"Sure is, handsome! Tell your brother to come on in, too, and wash up while I go see if your mom is awake yet." Joseph agreed and ran around to the backyard to expedite the process of getting to lunch.

Gently knocking on Jordan's door before entering, Laura found her sister just beginning to stir. "Hey, are you hungry?"

"I don't deserve to eat," Jordan mumbled and pulled the blankets over her head.

Laura rolled her eyes, walked over to the bed, and yanked the blankets out of Jordan's hands. "Okay, drama queen, that's enough now." After a brief tug-of-war with the blankets, Jordan finally sat up.

"Look, you can sit and wallow in here all day if that's what you really want, but I'm telling you, it's not healthy, it's not going to help anything, and your children would really like to spend some time with you. I think it would go a long way toward making them feel better if they saw you up and about, trying to interact with them."

Laura simply stared down at Jordan and waited for her to make a move to get out of bed. Seeing she need a little more convincing, Laura sighed wearily, sat down on the bed, and offered up a lengthy list of reasons why it was important to get up and to be done with her pity party, for the boys' sakes.

After a long pep talk, Laura led Jordan out of the bedroom and helped her to the living room sofa. She stood in the kitchen and prepared Jordan a sandwich while Jake and Joseph chatted quietly with their mother about all they wanted to do that day with Aunt Laura. Jordan smiled at them and once again felt grateful for her sister's presence.

"Hey, guys, you know what I was thinking?" Laura said from the kitchen as she placed Jordan's lunch on a tray to carry out to her.

"What?" they asked excitedly.

"I was thinking that maybe we should give your mom a little peace and quiet tonight since I know she didn't get much of that at the hospital last night. I thought we'd grab some dinner, see a movie, and then maybe, just maybe, we could...oh, I don't know...maybe we could...get a room at that hotel I saw on my way into town. What do you think?"

"Yea!" they squealed with delight. Jordan cringed at the loud tone of their voices. "Can we, Mom? Can we? Can we go with Aunt Laura to the hotel?"

"Can we have dinner at Rob's restaurant?"

"Can we get the extra-large soda at the movie theater?"

"There's a really great ice cream guy down by the beach. Can we go there, too?" Laura's head moved back and forth as if she were watching a tennis match as she tried to keep track of her nephews' endless chatter.

"Laura," Jordan began in a hushed tone, hoping to prompt her boys into lowering their own voices. "You don't have to clear out the house for me, you know. I'll still sleep if you're all here."

"Well, maybe I'm not doing it for you," she said with a smirk. "Maybe the thought of sharing the bed with you or sleeping on the couch is unappealing to me." Her eyes twinkled with amusement. The sisters looked at one another and laughed.

"I don't kick anymore, Laura," Jordan said teasingly.

"Sure, and I don't snore anymore, either." They burst into another fit of giggles while Jake and Joseph watched them in confusion.

"Grown-ups are weird," Jake whispered to his brother.

"Look, if that's what you want to do, then far be it from me to stop you. All I ask is that I have my prescription here so I can sleep."

"Great. We'll hang out here until around four o'clock and then we'll be out of your hair. Besides, that hotel I want to stay at is right on the beach! It's not every day that I get the chance to sleep in oceanfront property." Waggling her eyebrows, she added, "I'm considering this a minivacation. Just don't tell Mark I said that! He'll think we cooked up the whole thing as an excuse for me to get away!"

Jordan tried not to take it personally that her sons

were packed up and bouncing up and down at the front door by three thirty that afternoon. After all, how could she possibly compete with dinner, a movie, ice cream, and a night away at a hotel? She knew her children loved her; it was just that at this particular point in time, she was pitifully boring.

Again.

"I'll hit the pharmacy and get your prescription back to you as soon as possible, okay?" Laura said as she grabbed her purse.

"Thanks, Sis. I took some ibuprofen earlier so I don't want you to rush back here. As long as I have something before I get into bed, I'll be fine."

"What are you going to do with yourself tonight?" Laura asked before handing her overnight bag to Joseph to place in the car.

"Oh, big night," Jordan teased. "I plan on sitting here on the sofa for an extended period of time channel surfing. Then I think I'll make myself a peanut butter and jelly sandwich for dinner, followed by a nice hot shower to wash the hospital smell off me."

"Sounds exciting," Laura enthused. "I know we'll all appreciate coming home to a cleaner you."

"Ha, ha, very funny," Jordan deadpanned.

"Do you want me to pick up some dinner and bring it back to you when I bring your prescription back? It won't be a big deal, plus it would save you having to do anything."

"Thanks for the offer, but I'll be fine. I don't have much of an appetite, and a sandwich sounds like the perfect thing. Just as long as I eat something with that pill, I'll be okay."

She stayed in her position on the sofa as she kissed them all good-bye and watched as her sister and sons left the bungalow, talking excitedly about all the fun they were going to have.

She wanted to pout; she wanted to resent the fact that she was missing out—again—on having fun with her boys, but realized it was pointless. She pushed the petty thoughts from her mind and reminded herself she was fortunate her boys had their aunt to have fun with and make them smile.

The sun was beginning its glorious descent in the sky and the bungalow was cast in sun-streaked shadows. Silence followed, which was almost deafening, and for a brief moment, Jordan panicked. It was almost as if she was, yet again, back in the solitude of the hospital room—alone with all her fears and worries.

Tossing all negative thoughts aside, she shifted herself into a more comfortable position and scanned the television channels until she decided on a home-make-over show to pass the time. The show reminded her of her own situation. It would be so much easier if all it took was a bulldozer and a pretty home put together by a team of designers to put her life back on track.

In a perfect world…

—⁓—

"See, Aunt Laura? Isn't this place great?" Jake exclaimed as he dragged his weary aunt through the doors of Rob's restaurant.

Since leaving Jordan, Laura had taken the boys to play on a local playground, had ice cream on the beach, and checked into the hotel, where her nephews promptly demanded to swim in the indoor pool before heading out for dinner. Walking through the door and looking around, Laura prayed for at least a few brief moments of silence while they ate.

Rob spotted them through the wide front windows before they came through the door. His chest ached when he realized they would be leaving Virginia Beach soon and this could possibly be the last time he'd see them. If he didn't do something soon, they wouldn't be coming to see him anymore. Forcing a smile to his face, Rob walked over to greet a weary-looking Laura.

"Are we having fun yet?" he asked with a chuckle as he led them to a table.

"If I were Jordan, I'd pass out more often just to get a night away from this! Even if it would be in a hospital, it would be worth it!" They both laughed, and Laura reached into her purse and handed the boys some quarters to spend in the game room. "I wouldn't doubt it if somehow that ear infection was related to all the nonstop talking Jordan has to listen to! The home version of these two is a lot less demanding than the vacation version! They never ran me this ragged during Jordan's recovery. And believe me, we spent a *lot* of time together. Must be the beach air or something." Laura laughed as she sagged a little in her seat. Rob smiled and was just about to hand Laura a menu and tell her what the specials were when suddenly Laura gasped.

"What's the matter?" Rob asked, his voice laced with concern. "Are you okay?"

"In all the hoopla that's gone on this afternoon, I forgot to run Jordan's prescription back over to her." Laura looked nervously over her shoulder in the direction of Jake and Joseph. "I hate to interrupt their fun, and I also hate the thought of them disrupting Jordan's rest if we wait until later, and then there's the movie we're trying to make…" She stood, still lost in contemplation for a long moment.

"I could take it over to her," Rob suggested.

"Really? You sure you wouldn't mind?"

Oh, Laura. You evil genius.

"Sure. You sit, relax and eat with the boys, and go on with your plans. I'm not really needed here; I just hang around for lack of something better to do," he said with an easy laugh.

"Oh, Rob, that would be great. I can't believe I forgot to run that stuff over to her! Where is my head at?" she said jokingly as she collapsed back into her chair.

"Those boys certainly can do that to you," Rob mused, remembering all the times in the last three weeks they had left him feeling a bit scattered, overwhelmed, and exhausted. He had loved every minute of it.

Laura fished in her purse and pulled out the bag from the pharmacy. "All the instructions are on the bottles." She showed Rob. "She seemed to be doing fine with just the ibuprofen earlier, but it might be nice to have something a little stronger before going to bed."

Rob took that comment in his own way. *I'd like to be that something stronger that she took to bed tonight.* Shaking his head clear, he took the bag from Laura.

"I'll call Jordan and tell her you're on your way," Laura said as she rummaged around in her purse for her cell phone. "You have no idea how much I appreciate your help." She smiled brightly at him as Rob nodded and waved good-bye.

"Hey, Laura?" Rob called from the doorway.

"Yes?"

"Dinner's on the house."

Laura watched Rob walk out of the quaint little Italian restaurant with a look of amused satisfaction on her face. Certain she had just orchestrated a promising evening between two of the most clueless people she had ever known, she mentally patted herself on the back. Closing her eyes with a feeling of peace, she awaited the insanity that would surely return when the boys ran out of quarters.

Snapping out of her inner praise for her evil-genius behavior, she went back to searching through her purse for her elusive cell phone, pulling it out triumphantly and putting a call in to Jordan.

When she received no answer, her first instinct was to panic, but then she realized Jordan was probably in the shower. Besides, after witnessing her sister's fragile state regarding Rob, maybe it was best if she didn't know he was coming over. After leaving a brief message on voice mail, Laura hung up and immediately dialed Claudia's number.

At the sound of Laura's voice, Claudia grew anxious. "Well?"

"I just sent him on his way. He looked a little like I was sending him off to the executioner."

"Oh, I think he'll be just fine. Now we can sit back and bask in the pure genius of it all!"

Laura was laughing like a loon when the boys came back to the table. She didn't dare explain why.

Chapter 12

HE CURSED HIMSELF AS EVERY KIND OF FOOL. HE questioned his own sanity. He seriously reconsidered his offer as he drove past Jordan's house for the third time. In the end, however, Rob finally pulled up in front, cut off the engine, and took a deep, fortifying breath before walking up to her front door and ringing the bell.

He waited. And waited. And waited some more. He rang the bell a second time and glanced through the front windows for signs of her.

Maybe she was sleeping.

Surely Laura would have called by now and told Jordan he was on his way. Just to be sure, he took out his cell phone and called Jordan himself. He heard the phone inside ring several times and then began to panic. Why wasn't she answering the phone? What if she was lying somewhere in the house bleeding again?

Oh God!

He began to pray as he searched for a way into the house. Taking a chance, he tried the front door and found it locked. *Good girl,* he thought, thankful she was safe from intruders. Remembering that there was a spare key above the door, nestled on top of the trim, he reached up and pulled the silver key down and opened the door.

"Jordan?" he called out hesitantly. No reply. Closing the door behind him, he walked softly into the bungalow and looked around before calling out to her again. "Jordan?"

"Rob?" Jordan's voice was weak and it took a moment for him to locate where she was calling him from. He found her sitting on the floor outside the bathroom door.

White-hot fear gripped him. "Oh God! Jordan? What happened? Are you okay?" He knelt before her and scanned her body, looking for any obvious signs of injury and yet afraid to touch her.

"I'm fine, really," she lied. "I was coming down the hall to take a shower when everything began to tilt and spin again. I eased myself down to the floor in hopes of it passing."

"How long have you been sitting here?"

"I have no idea," she said quietly, her head in her hands. Rob lowered himself to the floor to sit beside her. He cautiously put an arm around her and pulled her close. She was tiny and fragile, and he could feel her body tremble with both fear and relief that someone was there now with her. She let him hold her close as she steadied herself.

"You're fine now," he murmured into her hair. "I'm here. You don't have to worry."

"What are you doing here?" she asked finally, finding some strength to put into her voice but unwilling to raise her head from the comfort and warmth of his shoulder.

"Didn't Laura call you?"

"I heard the phone ring, but I couldn't get to it. Is everything all right? Are the boys okay?" Panic laced her voice and he hugged her tight for comfort.

"The boys are fine. They're just running your poor

sister ragged," he teased. "When they showed up for dinner, she looked like she'd run a marathon, and when she mentioned she had forgotten to bring your prescription to you, I offered to bring it instead. I hope that's okay." Sure, he was fishing for some comfort of his own, but pride had long since been tossed out the window. While he wanted to know she was glad he was there, he also knew he wasn't going to leave anytime soon, no matter what she said. His dark eyes fixed on her face, willing her to look at him.

"Yes, that's fine. Thank you." Slowly, Jordan lifted her head from its resting place on Rob's shoulder, looked at him, and smiled. His brown eyes were tender and comforting. Everything was going to be just fine, she assured herself.

"How's that head?" he asked softly, one hand gently caressing her nape.

"Better. Not so bad right now," she whispered back. Their lips were mere inches apart and Jordan wanted nothing more than for him to kiss her. His breath warmed her face and she inhaled its minty scent.

Would she be so bold as to lean forward and initiate a kiss?

Before she could, Rob removed his arms from around her and slowly rose to his feet, reaching a hand down to her.

"Come on. Let's get you up off the floor so you can take your shower and get some rest." It was a far cry from what he truly wanted to say and do, but he couldn't possibly take advantage of her in this condition, no matter how badly he wanted her.

Jordan reached for his hand and allowed him to

carefully pull her to her feet, where she landed flush against the solid wall of his chest with a soft thud. Feeling bold, she rested one hand over his heart and felt its erratic beat that matched her own.

Through thick lashes, she met his serious gaze and felt certain *he* would kiss her. Surely now he would put an end to one of the longest weeks of her life and tell her he still wanted her.

But he didn't.

He released her carefully and turned her toward the open doorway. "You go on in and do what you've got to do while I make you something to eat. Have you had dinner yet?"

Speechless, she shook her head. "I was planning on making a peanut butter and jelly sandwich. Nothing major."

"Not to worry. I'll whip something up. Now go." Rob gently shoved her into the bathroom, turned on his heel, and walked purposefully toward the kitchen, willing himself not to look back at her, because otherwise, he *would* take advantage of her condition and make love to her right there on the bathroom floor. The image caused him to smile as he opened the refrigerator. *Mmm... Jordan in the shower, all soft and soapy.* He shook his head and refocused on dinner.

He frowned, however, as he took in the contents before him. If he was smart, he'd just pick up dinner from the restaurant, but after finding Jordan on the floor when he'd gotten there, there was no way he was going to leave her alone again.

Rob thought of calling Laura and informing her of what he had found when he arrived, but then thought better of it. If he alarmed her, she would possibly come home with the boys and that would not only upset them, but it would also ruin his chance of being alone with Jordan and working things out.

In his more rational thinking, he also knew this could be the best, and maybe last, opportunity for him to prove to Jordan that he was here for her, that he would take care of her.

Laura might get mad at him for not being told of Jordan's condition, but in the end, Rob was sure she would understand. Was it just a coincidence that she had made herself scarce and needed him to come here and help Jordan? Could Laura be that devious?

God, he hoped so. And if she was, he would buy her the biggest drink, the largest bouquet of flowers, whatever she wanted, to thank her.

Resigning himself to a less-than-spectacular dinner, Rob decided on making western omelets and toast for them both. As he chopped up the ingredients, he was keenly aware of the sounds coming from the bathroom. He nicked his finger with a paring knife as the image of Jordan naked in the shower with hot, soapy water streaming down her body played through his mind.

Reaching for a bandage, Rob lectured himself on having some self-control and not pouncing on her. He shouldn't allow himself to picture her naked, or to remember how smooth her skin felt next to his. Cracking the eggs into a large metal bowl, he scolded himself for thinking about her silky heat when he was inside her or the sounds she made when she climaxed.

Wiping the cold sweat from his brow with a nearby dish towel, Rob heard the bathroom door open, Jordan's light footsteps, and then her bedroom door closing. Thank the Lord he hadn't seen her wrapped in a towel right now or all his recriminations would have been for nothing! He knew the last thing she needed was for him to be putting the moves on her, but he was holding on to his self-control by a thread; it was better if he didn't see her in anything but full covering from head to toe right now.

Popping the bread down into the toaster, he focused his attention on flipping his omelets and getting the table set for a casual dinner. He hoped Jordan didn't mind that he had invited himself to stay and eat with her. Too bad if she did. He'd kept his distance long enough. He'd kept his silence long enough, too—a fact he planned on changing after they ate.

As he'd driven around town tonight before coming here, Rob realized he wasn't willing to let Jordan or her sons go. The thought of never seeing them again wasn't an option. He'd stay here all night and talk some sense into her if he had to. He'd plead his case, tell her how much he loved her—hell, he'd beg if that's what it took for her to understand how much she meant to him.

Rob wanted a life with Jordan and was willing to talk through any concerns she had until their future was set.

With any luck, they would not spend the night merely talking.

Chapter 13

JORDAN WAS A BUNDLE OF NERVES AS SHE PACED IN her bedroom. Rob was here.

Again.

Rob was taking care of her.

Again.

In all her alone time in the hospital the previous night and during her few hours alone today, she'd realized she had to fight for him. The thought of moving forward without him was no longer an option. He may very well still be angry and hurt, but she'd do her best to apologize and make him see what a fool she'd been. She knew she was going to have to be strong so they could talk about all her fears. It was important that Rob realize it wasn't him she was struggling with but herself. With any luck, Rob would forgive her and they could have the future together that should have started so many years ago.

Her damp hair began to curl seductively around her face and Jordan opted to let it dry naturally. The thought of the noise from the blow-dryer was just too darn much to deal with now that the dull ache in her head had finally started to subside.

Opening her bureau drawer, she pulled out something to wear and slipped it on. She smiled at her own reflection and said a quick prayer that Rob would appreciate her pitiful attempt at being sexy. Seduction had not been in her initial plans to make Rob know how much he meant to her, but right now it seemed like a damn good idea. They were here alone, and desperate times called for desperate measures. Who knew when an opportunity like this would present itself again?

Jordan stopped for a moment. Could she possibly pull off being sexy after the last twenty-four hours? Would she end up making a complete fool out of herself? Silently she hoped she wouldn't and pushed all negative thoughts aside. She was a woman on a mission and finally going after the man she loved.

The last thing she did before leaving the room was to use a touch of lip gloss; it was the only makeup she'd use tonight. Taking a final look around her room, Jordan felt at peace. For the first time in years, she trusted herself to make everything all right.

Walking into the kitchen, she smiled as Rob placed two steaming plates on the table. She saw him swallow hard when he spotted her and he quickly turned away and busied himself with buttering their toast.

"Something smells wonderful," she said as she inhaled the wonderful aroma of the meal and slowly walked over to the table, where she sat herself in a chair.

"You didn't have much to work with, so I hope you like omelets."

"I was letting the food run out since we're leaving." The words came out without conscious thought and she noticed the stunned look on Rob's face before he looked away and went about getting them drinks. Cursing herself for not thinking before she spoke, Jordan tried to think up a change of subject to get Rob to relax.

Soon he was sitting beside her and there was a fine sheen of perspiration on his brow. They ate in silence for a long time before Jordan could think of a neutral topic, something that was safe, and spoke.

"So," she began, "the boys were running Laura ragged, huh?"

Rob laughed and repeated the story of how her sister looked when she had walked into the restaurant. "She sent the boys to play video games, but I think it was just a ploy to get some quiet time for herself." They both laughed, knowing full well how energetic Jordan's sons were. "She seems to think the beach air has given them more energy than they had before."

"I can't believe she came all the way down here and then took them away for the night to help me out," Jordan said, searching desperately for something to say and then found herself rambling. "I think secretly she's trying for a weekend getaway; unfortunately, my sons are along for the ride."

"She was clearly concerned for you and loves you and the boys a lot. You're lucky to have her," Rob agreed.

"Oh, believe me, I know I'm lucky. Not many people have someone who'd be willing to drop everything on a moment's notice to come and help out in a crisis." She let the words hang there, hoping Rob would realize it wasn't just Laura she was talking about. Though there was silence again while they finished their meals, it wasn't the awkward kind they'd been sharing of late.

When he stood to clear the table, Rob remembered Jordan's prescriptions. "Oh, I almost forgot." He handed the bottles to her. "One of those is for the pain and the other is the antibiotic for the ear infection. You really need to take them with food so maybe you should take them now."

Jordan looked at the bottles and frowned. She'd take the antibiotic now, but she didn't want to take the pain pill in case it put her to sleep. She needed to be fully awake to settle things with Rob. If she waited much longer, however, she'd run the risk of falling asleep on her own. The lack of sleep from the night before was catching up with her—that and the fact that she had taken a relaxing hot shower and filled her tummy.

Watching him work in her kitchen made Jordan realize her love for Rob all the more. He would always be like this, she thought. He would always take care of her and her sons. That thought brought a faint smile to her lips. She knew she could get used to the idea of having a man—*this man*—in her life again permanently. Why had she ever thought otherwise?

Rob seemed to be going out of his way to keep his distance, and she didn't like it. Taking a deep breath for courage, Jordan rose from her seat at the kitchen table, walked into the living room, and sat down on the sofa. Waiting a moment to see if he'd take her cue, Jordan finally asked him to stop cleaning and invited him to sit with her.

Reluctantly, he accepted and gave the kitchen one last look to make sure he hadn't forgotten anything. Once the kitchen light was turned off, he realized the only other light came from a small lamp next to Jordan. The room had a very soft, very romantic glow. Jordan had a very soft, romantic glow as well, and he swallowed hard at the sight of her.

Sitting on the sofa, Jordan observed Rob as he walked over. If she didn't know better, she would have sworn he was nervous. In all the years she'd known him, she would never have called him that. Rob was always confident and secure; seeing him now made her realize there was more to this man than she'd ever known, and she wanted to know all of him.

In a pair of well-worn jeans and yet another snug-fitting navy T-shirt, he was ruggedly sexy. She loved that he kept his wardrobe simple, casual, and very masculine. His dark hair was in disarray from raking his hands through it too many times, no doubt in frustration over her and this wild ride of a weekend. The stubble darkening his jaw only enhanced his ruggedly sexy look. He sat on the opposite side of the room and played with a loose thread on his shoelace, clearly uncomfortable.

Jordan felt a little disheartened. "Are you going to talk to me at all?" she asked softly with exasperation.

"What do you mean? We've been talking."

"Not really," she said quietly. "We've been talking without really *talking*. We've talked about the kids and Laura and anything safe and mundane; the only thing we've skipped is the weather."

"What do you mean?"

The man was completely obtuse, Jordan decided. Either that or he was going out of his way to make her squirm. He still wouldn't fully look at her, and Jordan felt all the wind go out of her sails.

Maybe she had misread the signals; maybe she had seen only what she wanted to see and things really were over. She wouldn't grovel, and if there was one thing Jordan was coming to realize about herself, it was that she was a survivor. She had been through hell and back and she was still here, finally willing to try to make her life better for her and her sons. Clearly that life just wasn't meant to include Rob.

"Oh, just forget it." She sighed. "Thank you for bring-ing my prescriptions over and for making dinner. You don't have to stay and babysit. I'm going to take my pills and go to sleep, so you can go now. There's nothing left for you to do here. You've done your good deed for the day." Her annoyance was beginning to show and it took Rob completely by surprise.

Jordan was always in control of her emotions. To see this side of her now was a completely new experience, and as much as he was annoyed that all her anger was seemingly directed at him, he enjoyed seeing this kind of fire in her.

When Rob made no comment after her little speech, she decided to move things along and get him out the door so she could put this whole stupid night behind her. Standing a little too quickly, Jordan had to catch herself and brace her hand on the arm of the sofa.

"What on earth is the matter with you, Jordan?" Rob snapped as he jumped up and snaked an arm around her waist to steady her.

"What do you mean?" she mimicked snidely.

"What the hell did that comment mean? *You've done your good deed for the day.* What's that about?"

"It's nothing. Really. I'm just tired and cranky. I didn't sleep much last night in the hospital with all their poking and prodding. My head is starting to hurt, and I would really like for this day just to end." *And for the floor to open up and just swallow me now.* "Just go. Please." She headed for the kitchen, deciding it would be a good idea to take that pain pill and pass out before she made mat-ters worse and embarrassed herself any further.

"Oh no, you don't," Rob said as he stalked over and

grabbed the medication from her hands. Jordan made to grab the bottles back but he held her off. In the blink of an eye, she found herself semi-wrestling with him before the bottles fell to the floor and Rob had her by the shoulders.

"You're not getting out of this that easily. You want us to talk, so talk. I want to know what you meant by that." He wasn't yelling, but his tone left no doubt he was equally annoyed.

"Look," she said wearily with a sigh, "I just meant… Oh, I don't know! I can't do this anymore, Rob. Please just go." Tears welled in her eyes as she turned out of his grasp. Rob took one step closer, placing his hands on her shoulders again and turning her toward him, his face full of tenderness.

"What can't you do anymore?" he asked softly.

Somewhere deep inside Jordan, courage grew. "I thought I could be here with you tonight and act as if everything were okay. I thought we'd be able to sit and talk like we used to and maybe try to work things out."

Rob stared down at Jordan, willing her to continue.

"And I wore this stupid nightie in hopes that you'd like it and I can't seem to do or say anything right." Her voice grew steady as her eyes met his. "I'm so sorry I hurt you and sent you away. I was just so damn scared and unsure of myself. I have a lousy track record with decision making and that night, that wonderful night after we first made love again, I got scared."

"Jordan…"

"You said you wanted us to move here and be together, but you never said you loved me! And maybe I was wrong to react the way I did, but I was just too scared to trust in how you made me feel." She paused for a moment. "I wanted to call you back as you walked out. I didn't want you to go. I wanted to tell you I love you, but I was paralyzed with fear. And after having you leave…" Jordan's voice broke then. "You left but you came back when we needed you. You took care of me and the boys even after I had treated you so horribly."

His only response was to reach up and skim his fingers across her cheek.

"I know I don't deserve you, but I need you." Her words were spoken softly and Jordan stood frozen to the spot, waiting for Rob to do something—to *say* something!

In that instant, Rob crushed her to him and hungrily claimed her mouth. Jordan's appetite matched his and her tongue darted out to tease his. Rob growled low in his throat as Jordan wrapped her arms around him. The kiss was urgent, frenzied, and neither was willing to let it end.

Jordan felt her knees weaken and as if Rob could sense it, he hauled her into his arms and walked over to the sofa where he laid them both down. He settled himself firmly beside her as Jordan raked her hands through his hair. Long moments later, they both surfaced for air. Rob gently stroked the side of Jordan's face before letting that finger travel down her slender throat and over the swell of her breast. He hardened at the sight of her nipples beading beneath the prim cotton fabric of the garment. He let his hand wander down to the curve of her hip, over firm thighs, smooth calves—all the way to her pink-tipped toes and then back again.

"Don't ever call this garment stupid," he said seriously. Jordan had chosen to wear the white cotton nightgown she had worn on their weekend away together.

"This thing is sexier than any damn item in Victoria's Secret, and I've had some major fantasies involving you wearing this since our weekend away."

"Really?" she asked, mesmerized by the too-soft caress of his fingers. She needed him badly and was growing frustrated that he seemed in no particular hurry. He was slowly torturing her, and she let out a low groan of frustration.

"Yeah, really." His gaze was fixed on where his fingers played with Jordan's breasts. Her breaths were ragged and shallow, and the sounds coming from her were driving him mad.

"So put all your fears out of your mind," he whispered as he placed his mouth a breath above where his fingers had been, "because I love what you're wearing."

His mouth took one hardened peak deep inside and Jordan groaned with pleasure. She arched her back and twisted until she was fully beneath him and his solid frame was firmly planted between her thighs.

"Rob," she sighed, lost in the ecstasy of having him with her again. Had it only been a week? "I need you."

He raised his head at her statement. "Do you?"

"Yes."

The only response he gave was to return his attention back to her breasts, nuzzling her slowly. Jordan thought she'd die from the heat flowing through her. He was in no hurry to move the fabric away to bare her skin, and she continued to squirm beneath him.

"Rob, please…"

"Tell me what you want," he softly demanded.

"I want you to take me into the bedroom and make love to me. All night."

No one sentence had ever sounded sweeter. In the blink of an eye, Rob lifted Jordan into his arms and did just that. Kicking the bedroom door closed behind him, he crossed the softly lit room and placed her down on the bed.

"Are you sure about this?" he asked. The slight tremble in his voice told Jordan he was waiting to unleash all the passion that had been building. "You spent last night in the hospital and you probably need to take it easy but…damn it, Jordan, I want you."

"Oh, yes." She anxiously awaited his next move. When he simply stood beside the bed and watched her, her concern grew. "I'm fine. I promise." She held out a hand to him. "Rob?"

His dark brows creased as he looked down at her sprawled out on the antique bed, her hair fanning out on the crisp, white pillows. She was every fantasy he had ever had.

"Before we take this any further, I think you need to know something, Jordan." His tone was darkly serious. She raised her eyebrows. "If I join you on this bed and we make love, I'm not leaving. Ever." He heard her gasp in surprise and noticed her eyes shining with unshed tears.

Rob waited to see if she had anything to say to his declaration. When she didn't, he continued—to make sure she understood his intentions completely.

"When your sister brings the boys back here tomorrow, we'll tell them you're all moving here with me. You and I are going to be married and I will be their father."

As a stray tear rolled its way down Jordan's cheek, Rob sat down beside her and brushed it softly away with the pad of his thumb. "I love you, Jordan, and I don't want you to walk out of my life ever again. I'm sorry I made you feel rushed and I was too pushy. I had waited so long for you…for this, that I couldn't help being greedy. I promise to never do that to you again. I want you to know it was never my intention to hurt you and I will have patience with you from now on.

"But I want you to know you mean more to me than anything else in this world, and if all I just said to you isn't what you want, then just say the word and I'll go." His heart hammered in his chest. He felt confident in her response, but then again, he had thought he was sure a week ago.

Jordan smiled weakly up at him. There were no words that could possibly convey what she thought, so instead of trying and having her poor way with words get her in trouble again, she cupped her hand behind his neck and pulled Rob down so she could kiss him.

What followed was erotic chaos. Jordan wasn't sure how their clothing fell into heaps on the floor; all she was aware of was the heat of Rob's body as he rolled her beneath him.

"Are you sure?" he said, afraid to make another move until he knew for sure.

"Yes," she groaned as she threw a leg over his hip, anchoring him to her.

"Good," he growled and kissed her with such ferocity that he scared himself.

Jordan linked her arms around his neck and pulled his weight back down on to her. Sinking deep into the kiss, she gave herself over to the earth-moving feeling of his mouth on hers.

Rob's hands raced up her sides to hungrily claim her breasts. They filled his hands so completely; their bodies fit together so perfectly, so naturally, that it seemed predestined. Under his skillful hands, Jordan felt treasured and loved as only Rob could ever make her feel.

She moved beneath him, urging him to take her completely before she lost her mind. "Please…"

Her words died off as he spread her thighs and entered her in one swift move. Her sigh of delight made him smile. Rob wanted to go slow, mindful of her recent injuries, but once she locked her legs around his hips, any sense of sanity was gone. Jordan was just as crazed for him, and when she began to chant his name, he knew he could no longer hold back. Thrusting wildly into her, he barely held on until she was done with her own cries of release.

Rob was exhausted; he could only imagine what Jordan was feeling. He cursed himself a hundred times for rushing her, but couldn't find the strength to truly feel bad about it. No, he could never feel bad about making love to Jordan, no matter what the circumstances.

Rolling to his side, he tucked Jordan in beside him as their breathing calmed. The light of the moon shone through the curtains, giving the room just enough light that they could make out each other's features. Though they were both sleepy, their hands never stilled as if afraid the other would disappear if they stopped touching.

Lying in each other's arms had Jordan feeling content and unafraid for the first time in what seemed like forever. Rob kissed the top of her head at the same time as she placed a light kiss on his chest. He'd thought she was asleep, but was glad that she wasn't. There was one more thing they needed to discuss.

"Jordan," he whispered.

"Hmm?"

"I know this is a weird time to ask this question, but…" He cleared his throat, uncomfortable with what he was about to say.

She raised her head and faced him with curiosity.

"That afternoon that we made love at my loft, we never… What I mean is, well, the subject of birth control never came up." He saw her blush a little, and instead of answering him, she returned to her original position: her head on his shoulder, her legs twining with his and seemingly unfazed by his statement. "Um, Jordan? Feel free to join the conversation at any time."

She chuckled and Rob loved feeling that vibration from head to toe. "I have to admit, I gave no thought to it that first time," she replied softly, her hands lightly trailing a path down the middle of his torso. "After that, though, it just didn't seem important."

"I don't think I'm following you," he said with some confusion. Did it not seem important because she had it covered or because she was as desperate to be one with him as he had been for her? Why didn't women just say what they meant?

With a heavy sigh, she sat up and looked at him again, talking to him as patiently as she would a child. "I'm not on the pill if that's what you're wondering. I know it was irresponsible of me not to say anything, but the idea of being with you, making love with you, making babies with you, well…it's all I ever really wanted."

"Really?"

"Absolutely." She bent over Rob and kissed him lightly on the mouth. Soon one thing led to another and she found herself wrapped in his embrace as he began to slowly seduce her again.

"I know we shouldn't be doing this," he said between placing kisses on her throat. "You need your rest."

"Oh, we so totally should," she argued breathlessly, turning the tables on him as she pushed him over onto his back so that she could straddle him. "Rest is highly overrated," she said as she rained tiny kisses all over his throat and chest.

Letting his head toss to the side at the sheer pleasure of Jordan's mouth on his body, Rob would have agreed to anything.

Rest was highly overrated, indeed.

In the wee hours of the morning, they lay tangled together among the now-cooling sheets. They had talked for a long time after making love the second time. She shared stories about the boys and about her life that she hadn't shared before, while Rob filled in some blanks about his own life from the last dozen or so years.

Instead of ruining the mood or cooling the passion, they found that the more they learned about one another, the more they loved. They made love one more time before finally giving in to the need for sleep. Jordan had been afraid to close her eyes in fear that this had all been a dream. She couldn't remember the last time she had felt so secure, so alive. It was a feeling she was looking forward to experiencing every day for the rest of her life.

"Rob?" she whispered, unsure if he would be easy to wake.

"Hmmm?" he answered sleepily, kissing her on top of her head as he pulled her naked body closer. "Were you expecting someone else?"

Jordan giggled and it felt good. "No, I wasn't looking for someone else. I was just making sure you were real and not just a dream."

Lazily, Rob let his hand wander up and down her back before playfully pinching her behind. "Real enough for you?"

"Very funny. I was lying here thinking that instead of finding me a house here today, maybe we could just extend the lease here on the bungalow."

Lifting his head to look down at her, his brows furrowed in confusion. "It's kind of small, isn't it?"

"Well, yes, but it holds so many wonderful memories and I really wouldn't mind staying here a little bit longer." She kissed him firmly. "Plus, I think it will motivate you."

"Motivate me? For what?"

"To quickly design a house for our soon-to-be expanding family."

Rob's eyes conveyed his confusion at her words and then twinkled with understanding. "Mighty confident of that fact, are you?" he teased, secretly hoping she was right.

"No doubt." She sighed as she snuggled closer to him before drifting back off to a peaceful sleep.

Rob went to sleep with a satisfied grin.

Epilogue

THE TINY LITTLE BEACH TOWN WAS HOPPING. JUNE WAS always a busy time on the coast, but it seemed to Jordan that half of the world's population was vacationing here. She had to circle the block several times before finding a spot close to the front door. They definitely could use some more parking. Peeved that so much time had been wasted driving around, she climbed out of her new truck, collected her things from the backseat, and headed for the restaurant. Today was a big day.

Opening the door, she was greeted by loud voices—all welcoming her. It was a Wednesday night, but the place was near capacity. Two of the loudest voices came from behind the counter. That's where she spotted Jacob and Joseph waving to her as they chatted about how they were making pizza dough. Even if they hadn't told her, the flour that covered multiple spots on their faces would have given it away. Rob was training them in the family business and the boys could not get enough. It did Jordan's heart good to see them so happy.

All traces of the sad little boys who had arrived with her almost a year ago were gone. Joseph finally was able to relax and just be a boy. He now played soccer on the school team and had come to make a lot of friends. He'd even let his hair grow a little and let it get messy. He still took on a lot more responsibility than most kids his age, but it was balanced out with the beginnings of some minor teenage angst.

Jacob had grown taller, and while not as cooperative as he was a year ago, he was constantly running on all cylinders. Baseball was his game of choice and he was the top hitter for the local rec team. Jordan stole a quick glance at the team picture that hung on the wall. The restaurant sponsored the team, and Jacob said he felt like a famous celebrity with his picture hanging up where everyone could see it.

With great clarity, Jordan could remember the exact date and time when things turned around for her sons: twelve hours after Rob had proposed to her. The afternoon that Laura had brought the boys home from their overnight trip for their hotel-movie-extravaganza, Rob and Jordan had been anxiously waiting for them.

Jordan didn't give Laura any hints as to what was going on, so when they asked the boys to sit down in the living room, Laura was invited to sit with them. While Jordan had figured she would do most of the talking, Rob had asked if it would be okay if he talked to the boys, man to man. Unsure of what to expect, she had gone along with it, and looking back, she wished she'd had a camera to capture the look of pure happiness on her sons' faces when Rob told them they were going to be a family.

Laura had jumped up and hugged them both before excusing herself somewhat awkwardly. It wasn't until later on that Jordan had found out exactly who had orchestrated their reunion and thanked both her sister and Claudia profusely. Now that they were one big family, the two women seemed happy to take all the credit for the happiness Rob and Jordan shared.

Breaking out of her reverie, Jordan brought herself back to the present and smiled at the scene around her. The sights and smells of the restaurant were always a treat, and tonight was no exception.

"We're making our special calzones tonight, Mom," Joseph told her. "Any requests?"

"Nothing spicy," she replied. The boys shared a sneaky glance at each other before Jordan added, "And no anchovies!"

"Oh, you're no fun." Out from behind them came her husband to sweep his newest son from Jordan's arms. She didn't think it was possible for a man to look any happier than Rob did at that moment. "It was going to get ugly in here if you hadn't brought him in soon," he teased as he took the baby carrier from her arms and placed a sweet kiss on her lips. Rob looked down at his sleeping infant son and Jordan swore she saw his chest swell with pride.

"Everyone," he bellowed. "I'd like you all to meet my son, Christopher." At the applause of the patrons, Rob accepted their warm wishes and congratulations as he pulled Jordan close to him. Christopher Robert Tyler was born nine months to the day after Rob informed Jordan that he wanted her as his wife. Now, at three weeks old, and with the blessing of their pediatrician, he was on his first official outing.

"I still can't believe it," he murmured against her ear with hot breath that still gave her chills.

"What?" she replied as she tried to stand on jelly legs.

"That you are my wife. That I have three amazing sons." He looked deeply into her eyes and saw she was on the verge of tears. "You've given me everything

I have ever wanted in this world." He leaned in and kissed her.

"I'm the one who is still in awe of it all." When he cocked an eyebrow at her, she turned and looked him squarely in the eye. "You came and healed me—body, heart, and soul. You made us a family again and have given me more love than I ever thought I deserved."

"You deserve even more, my love." He took her by the hand, and together they went around the restaurant greeting people, laughing, and smiling while showing off their newest family member.

Meet the Montgomerys

―⁓―

Wait for Me

The Montgomery Brothers

Book #1

―⁓―

Lucas

Former NFL superstar Lucas Montgomery is perfectly fine in his self-imposed solitude, until sweet, sexy, and completely off-limits Emma Taylor comes crashing into his carefully constructed world one snowy weekend and turns his life upside down.

―⁓―

From *Wait for Me*:

"It's going to be treacherous driving on your evening commute tonight. Snow is expected in the area early this evening and it's going to come down fast and furious."

"Damn weather," Lucas cursed under his breath as he pulled into his driveway. He was returning from his monthly trip into town to stock up on food and supplies. That was something new; he used to have everything delivered, but with a couple of days of stubble on his face and a ball cap pulled down low, no one bothered him.

Glad that he was fully stocked, it took a little time to

get it all from his truck and into the house. Once it was all inside and put away, he looked at his supply of wood. While he had a generator and knew that if the storm got bad enough to lose power, he'd be fine, he liked to be well prepared. Looking at the clock and seeing that there were several hours of daylight left, Lucas headed out into the backyard and toward the stack of firewood waiting to be cut.

The physical exertion felt good; Lucas knew that it wasn't in his best interest just to sit around the house. Swinging the ax had him using more muscles than he did in the average day, and while at first his body protested a little, it didn't take long for him to get into the swing of things (literally) and feel good. Even in the cold, he worked up a sweat, and once all the cutting was done, it was another chore to move all of the wood to the shed that was built onto the back of his house.

By five o'clock, Lucas felt a satisfied sense of exhaustion as he stepped back into the house, prepared to settle in for the night. The first flakes were already falling and it didn't take long for the weather to change and turn into a full-blown blizzard. As he built a fire in the main fireplace, a chill ran through his body and a sense of unease filled him. It wasn't like Lucas to feel restless. He'd grown accustomed to his isolation and found that he'd made peace with being alone.

His knee ached and his muscles were sore from exertion. He walked around the house searching for something—for what, he couldn't be sure. All he knew was that everything felt suddenly out of sorts. After checking all the rooms and seeing that nothing was out of place, he found himself back in front of the fireplace. It was completely quiet in the house with the exception of the occasional popping coming from the fire. When his phone rang, he jumped higher than a grown man should.

"H'lo," he answered gruffly, not even bothering to check his caller ID.

"Lucas? Are you okay?" His father. There were few things that Lucas could count on anymore but one of them was that his father would call him at least once a day just to make sure that he was doing okay and had a conversation with another human being. While at times it annoyed the hell out of him, other times, like now, the calls were a comfort.

"Fine, Dad. How about you?"

"Oh, your mother and I are up here by you. She is positively giddy about the snow."

Lucas laughed. As much as he hated being cold, he loved the way the snow looked. He clearly had gotten that fascination from his mother. "She always gets like that," he said with a laugh. "You just up here for the weekend or staying longer this time?"

"Depends on the storm," William said, his tone a little distracted.

"Dad? Are you okay?"

"What? Oh, um, yes, yes, just fine. How about you? Do you have everything you need in case we get snowed in?"

"Today was my day to stock up so I'm good for a while."

"This storm really came out of nowhere, didn't it?" William asked, worry now lacing his words.

"Not really," Lucas said. "It's been in the forecast

but it's just a little more intense than they originally thought. Nothing new for this area. What's going on, Dad? Sounds like you've got something on your mind. You're not worried about this storm, are you? We've lived through ones like this dozens of times before."

"I know, I know, it's just that…" His voice trailed off.

"No, I don't know. Are you sure you're okay?"

"I'll be fine," William lied. "What about you? Are you there by yourself?"

Lucas laughed. "That's an odd question. Of course I'm here by myself. Who else would be here with me?"

Nervous laughter escaped before William could stop it. "What was I thinking?" he said, trying to sound lighter. "As long as you have everything you need. You'll call if you have a problem, right?"

Lucas pulled the phone away from his ear and looked at it like it was a foreign object. Call if he needed anything? What in the world? "I'll be fine, Dad," he reassured. "In case you've forgotten, I prefer a good storm; it keeps me inside where I like to be."

"Lucas," his father began, "it's not good for you to be by yourself all the time. You need to get out of the house more, maybe come back to work or—"

"I appreciate the concern," Lucas said with frustration, "but I really don't feel like having this particular conversation right now. I just got done stocking the wood shed and I was just about to go and take a hot shower to ease some of the soreness out of my body."

"You know I only nag because I love you, Son, right?"

No words could have taken the wind out of his sails more than those. Pinching the bridge of his nose, Lucas closed his eyes and mentally counted to ten before answering. "I know you do, Dad. I honestly do. This is my decision, though, and I need everyone to back off, okay?"

His father made a sound like he was going to argue, but then changed course. "Fine. I promise to back off. Stay safe during this storm and we'll talk to you over the weekend, all right?"

"Thanks, Dad," Lucas replied as he hung up the phone. Shutting it down, he placed it on the counter, his shoulders feeling the tension from the conversation. Lucas couldn't understand why this was such a big deal for everyone. It wasn't as if he was asking all of them to stay shut in with him.

His knee was throbbing now. All he wanted was a hot shower, an even hotter dinner, and a chance to put a heating pad on his knee. It sounded like a good plan for the evening—so good that it sounded like what he did every evening. That thought made him frown as he walked into his bedroom. Sure it would be nice to get back into the land of the living again, but the life he wanted, the one that he'd worked so hard for, was long gone.

Some people would say he was lucky; he'd lived his dream for many years and he went out while he was still on top. The problem was that he hadn't wanted to leave; he'd been forced out. It was funny because when it had happened, promises were made to him left and right about how there would always be a place for him within the organization. Once his therapy proved that his injury was more severe than originally diagnosed and that he would be in treatment longer than anticipated, those offers came with less and less frequency, until the phone finally just stopped ringing. Lucas hated pity, and the fact that he was having a daily pity party for himself annoyed him even more.

Stripping down and stepping under the steaming shower spray, he let the hot water beat down on him as he sighed wearily. All of the tension eased from his body, and with it all thoughts of his previous life. An inner pep talk reminded Lucas that he enjoyed the life he had created since his football career ended. He finally had his privacy; reporters were no longer camping out, desperate for a picture or a quote from him. He could come and go as he pleased with little to no recognition. His time was his own.

In the last eighteen months, he'd agreed to work for the family organization, and while it was far from his dream job, at least he had the privilege of working from his own home, making his own hours while having something to keep him busy. When he wasn't taking care of Montgomerys business, Lucas had taken up photography, nature photography to be exact. The act of going out and walking around in the parks and the massive properties his family owned was therapeutic; at the same time, it allowed the creative side of him to come out. Both sides gave him a great sense of satisfaction that he hadn't felt in a long time.

Toweling dry and then dressing in a pair of faded, well-worn jeans and a sweatshirt, Lucas strolled into his kitchen and went about deciding what to make himself for dinner. That was the beauty of living alone: he could make whatever he felt like, whenever he felt like it, and then could eat in front of the television and have the remote to himself. It was some sweet bachelor living, and he was sure that the masses would be envious.

Reaching into the freezer, Lucas was about to pull out a steak to grill when the glare of headlights caught his attention. No one ever came out this way—he was set far back from the road—and in this snow at this time of day, clearly the person had to be lost. With a curse, he walked toward the window near the front door and watched in horror as the car skidded dangerously and then went off the narrow path of his driveway, down into the ravine below.

"Dammit," he muttered, running to grab his boots, coat, and phone before heading out the door. Once outside, he ran toward the spot where he saw the car go down. It was easily a ten-foot drop and he could hear the sound of the horn blaring as if someone was lying on it.

With another curse, he carefully made his way down and did his best not to slide and end up injuring himself too. "What kind of idiot drives around in a snowstorm after dark?" he muttered as he reached the car door. The windows were fogged and the sound of the horn was near deafening. He yanked the car door open and found the driver slumped over the steering wheel. Doing his best not to jar them too much, he reached into his pocket for the small flashlight that he always carried and jumped back in horror at the sight of blood coming from the driver's head.

"Emma…"

Meet the Montgomerys

---~~~---

Trust in Me

The Montgomery Brothers

Book #2

---~~~---

Jason

With a make-or-break business expansion in the works, Jason Montgomery needs an assistant he can trust, and Maggie Barrett seems perfect for the job. But when mutual respect turns into mutual attraction, how will Maggie explain that the only thing standing between them was just a little white lie?

---~~~---

From *Trust in Me*:

Jason had done a damn good job. Sitting on the private plane that was getting ready to take off, he looked over at Maggie and smiled. They had worked long hours for the last two weeks, and she was just as familiar with every aspect of this project as he was. She was smart, inquisitive, and well versed. He knew without a doubt that she was going to be an asset to him on this trip and that he wouldn't have to spend precious time explaining things to her, because she clearly understood exactly what it was he was trying to accomplish.

Not once during the previous weeks had there been

an issue with the long hours. At first Jason was sure that her husband was going to put up a fight; after all, Maggie had been working fairly regular hours for so many years that this was quite an adjustment. But just as there'd been no complaint from the husband, Maggie hadn't complained either.

They'd worked side by side from eight in the morning until sometimes as late as ten at night. Jason found that after their initial clashing during their interview, they both seemed to come to understand each other and had formed mutual respect for one another. Conversation flowed when it was needed and at the same time, they were both comfortable working in silence. For having worked together only two weeks, they were seemingly in sync. Jason wasn't used to that.

"If we don't hit any delays, we should be in Chicago by ten. I called and confirmed the town car, and since we'll have missed most of the morning traffic, we should be at the hotel by eleven," Maggie was saying as she glanced at their schedule on her tablet. "We're meeting the Claremont people at one, so once we're checked in, we can have lunch brought up to the rooms and be ready to go by twelve thirty." She looked up at him. "How does that sound?"

"Good," Jason said distractedly. Meetings like this didn't normally stress him out, but this plan for expansion that he had made him a little edgy. "Did we leave the evening free or did you pencil something in?"

"I left it free just in case they wanted to meet over dinner. I didn't want to overschedule us on our first day," she said lightly. "I've researched several restaurants in the area and the one at our hotel would actually be perfect for a meeting. I can call in a reservation now if you'd like, just in case?"

She was very efficient; that was what Jason admired most. Maggie was certainly making his life easier already. "Let's wait and see how the afternoon goes. For all we know, they can be exhausting and not people we want to work with. In which case, we'll just have a quiet dinner and discuss our next plan of attack."

Maggie laughed. "Sounds like a plan. I'll just mark these places for future reference."

While she was busy tapping away on her tablet screen, Jason studied her. With her blond hair pulled back into a severe ponytail and her brown eyes downcast, Maggie seemed to do her best not to stand out. Jason had to wonder a little at that. While he could appreciate her professional manner and her obvious desire not to draw attention to herself, he couldn't help but wonder why. Most of the women he knew, both in business and in his personal life, did things to make themselves look attractive. Maggie, on the other hand, wore little to no makeup, dressed ultraconservatively, and did her best to blend into the background. This was exactly what Jason had said that he wanted, but the more he got to know Maggie, the more he had a feeling that she wasn't presenting her true self.

Their captain announced their turn for takeoff and Jason watched Maggie's response. Her white-knuckled grip on the seat told him that flying was definitely not her thing. While most of their travels were going to require flying, there were going to be some shorter legs that he had planned a rental car for. He was sure that Maggie would be relieved on those days.

"Not a fan of flying, huh?" he asked, hoping to distract her.

"No, not really."

"It's not so bad," he said in a soothing tone. "The key is to just relax."

"Easy for you to say," she mumbled and heard Jason laugh.

"Look, don't focus on what you're feeling. Focus on me."

Maggie's eyes went wide. "Excuse me?" she said, indignant.

"I mean, talk to me about this meeting today. Talk to me about the weather. Talk to me about what you think of my tie," he suggested.

"Your tie?"

"Sure. Whatever you need to talk about, we'll talk about," he said, and smiled at her confused look. "So what do you think? Stripes? Is it a good look?"

He was teasing her and for that Maggie was relieved. In their time working together, they had gotten along much better than she had expected. They had always kept things on a business level; this light side of him was a pleasant surprise. His dark eyes twinkled and she felt herself relax. "I'm not normally a fan of stripes, but they aren't overly obnoxious."

"Stripes are obnoxious?" he asked.

"They can be. Think of prison stripes."

That made Jason laugh again. "Well, I can guarantee you I will not be going for the prison-stripe look. Ever."

"Good to know," Maggie said, and realized that her stomach no longer felt so queasy and that they were no longer climbing. She loosened her grip on her seat and looked out the window. "Is that it? We're done with takeoff?"

Jason smiled at her. "See? A little distraction always works." The next hour passed quickly, and soon they were in the car and heading for their hotel. Check in went like clockwork. Jason was glad they had adjoining rooms. They were only going to be in Chicago for two days, but it would make things easier if Maggie was close by when he needed her help.

No sooner were they settled in their rooms than lunch was being delivered. While Jason had been checking them in, Maggie had been taking care of ordering their food. Jason knocked on the door dividing their rooms and Maggie unlocked it and let him in.

"That was fast," she commented as she reached for her briefcase.

Jason stopped her. "Whoa, we're going to eat lunch like normal people and not talk business for the next fifteen minutes, okay?"

Maggie more than readily agreed. They had been talking business for weeks and she felt like if Jason were to fall ill, she would be able to handle any and all of his meetings because she knew the details so intimately. To be able to have a few minutes reprieve to eat and relax sounded like heaven.

Jason had set up their food at the table in his room and waited for Maggie to sit down before he joined her. "I hope you had enough time to get at least a little settled into your room."

Maggie waved him off. "I don't plan on getting too comfortable. It makes it easier when it's time to leave if I haven't taken everything out."

"That makes sense. Did you have time to call home?"

"What for?" she asked without thinking.

Jason arched a dark eyebrow at her. "I thought you would check in with your husband and let him know we arrived safely."

"Oh," Maggie said, forgetting for a moment that she was supposed to be married. "I texted him. He's at work so I just figured we'd talk later tonight."

It sounded believable enough, but Jason had to wonder how good a marriage she had if they spent so much time apart and didn't seem to mind it at all. If he was married, he'd certainly be uncomfortable with his wife traveling with another man! What was wrong with Maggie's husband?

Meet the Montgomerys

Stay with Me

The Montgomery Brothers

Book #3

Mac

Is a little peace and quiet too much to hope for? Mackenzie Montgomery is floored when he reluctantly agrees to help out an old childhood friend and finds she's grown into a gorgeous woman. After watching his father play matchmaker for his brothers, the last thing Mac wanted was to get married and settle down. But he hadn't counted on Gina Micelli.

From *Stay with Me*:

Mackenzie Montgomery was tired. Weary-to-the-bone exhausted. It wasn't the long hours at the office wearing him out; it was the incessant rounds of well-wishers with their "Congratulations" and "You all must be so happy" that were grating on his every last nerve.

"*Must* I be so happy?" he muttered under his breath. Deep down, Mac knew they all meant well; he shouldn't begrudge their pleasantries. Unfortunately, for the last two years, all he'd seemed to hear was how happy everyone was for his brothers, their wives, their lives...

Sure, it was great, but didn't anyone have anything else to think about? To focus on?

"Great news about Lucas and Emma, isn't it, Mac?"

Mac looked up, and there in the doorway stood one of his junior executives with an eager look and a wide smile on his young face. Mac tried to return the smile, but at this point in the day, it made his face hurt. "It sure is."

"Tell them I said congratulations!" the young man said before disappearing.

Mac slumped down into his plush leather chair and turned to face his wall of windows. The sun was starting to set and the view of downtown Charlotte was one of bustling activity. Glancing at his watch, he saw that it was just after five, and he knew he should head to the hospital, where the rest of his family had congregated to welcome the newest Montgomery.

A girl. Mac couldn't help but chuckle. His former NFL player brother, who had been so certain he was going to have a son to teach all of his moves to, now had a tiny baby girl. There was a joke in there somewhere, but right now Mac couldn't seem to find it. He'd go, meet the newest member of the family, pat Lucas on the back and hug Emma, and remember to smile at all of the excitement that was sure to be going on around him. But all he really wanted to do was go home, have a beer, and just relax.

The drive to the hospital was short, and he even remembered to stop and pick up a bouquet of flowers for his sister-in-law. As he headed toward Emma's room, the noise level told him his prediction was right on the money. He was greeted by his father first, then his brother Jason, finally making his way to shake the new father's hand before handing the flowers to Emma.

"Oh, Mac," Emma said as tears swam in her eyes. "They're perfect. Lilies for our Lily."

Right, the baby's name was Lily. Happy coincidence? Or maybe he had subconsciously remembered his father telling him that was what they had named her. Neither here nor there, the fact was he had done a good thing and now everyone was staring at him with sappy grins on their faces.

Great.

"Do you want to hold her?" Emma asked, nodding toward the bassinet next to her bed.

Mac was about to break out in a cold sweat. Hold her? *The baby?* Wasn't that against the rules or something? He wasn't the father! He could give her germs or drop her! Lucas must have seen the look of pure terror on his face because he chuckled and said, "I'm not ready to entrust my princess to him yet. He can't even catch a football!" The room erupted with laughter, but Mac took it all in stride since it got him out of infant holding.

"Were you planning on throwing her to me? Because I'm pretty sure the hospital has rules against that," he teased, and then smiled when his mother came over and looped her arm though his, pulling him close.

"You'll have to hold her eventually," she whispered with a sassy smile.

"Sure, when she's talking in complete sentences, I'm sure I'll be fine." He heard his father's cell phone ring in the distance and watched as William quickly exited the room. Mac quirked an eyebrow at his mom, but she simply shrugged and then walked over to gaze lovingly at her new granddaughter.

His brother Jason patted him on the back. "Nice side

step with the baby; for a minute there I thought you were going to cry."

Mac took the ribbing, but his mind was on his father. Was something wrong? "Is there a problem at the office I'm not aware of?" he asked his brother, ignoring his comment.

"Not that I know of," Jason said. "Why?"

"Probably nothing, but Dad got a call and sort of bolted from the room." Mac looked toward the doorway to see if his father had returned.

Before Jason could offer any input, Lily let out a small cry and all attention was on the newborn. Mac never understood the attraction of babies, particularly newborns. They were tiny and wrinkly, fragile and terrifying, and they cried a lot. He watched in amazement as Lucas walked over and picked up his daughter with such gentleness that Mac almost couldn't look away. He was used to seeing Lucas being rough and physical; after all, years of high school sports and a career in the NFL had toughened him. But watching him now? He seemed at ease handling the tiny pink bundle and handing her to his wife. A collective sigh went out as Emma took the baby and cuddled her. Even Mac got a little misty at the sight of mother and child.

What in the world?

Taking a step back, he saw his father walking back into the room. "Everything okay, Dad?" William's face was drawn and sad. "Dad?"

William reached out and touched Mac's arm and pulled him aside. "Son," he said, his voice cracking slightly, "I need you to do something for me."

Meet the Montgomerys

—⚡—

More of Me

The Montgomery Brothers

Bonus Novella

—⚡—

Ryder

Ryder Montgomery has returned to North Carolina to take a break from the corporate world and the first item on his agenda is to look up the woman he walked away from more than ten years ago. But Casey can't decide which burns hotter—her desire to be with Ryder or the pain he left her with.

—⚡—

From *More of Me*:

Being on the beach before sunrise was nothing new to Ryder Montgomery. He'd been living on the beaches of San Diego for more than ten years and taking an early-morning run along the coast was part of his routine. As he stood and inhaled the scents of the Atlantic Ocean, Ryder knew that for some reason, Wrightsville Beach would always be home.

He hadn't made a whole lot of time to come home since he'd left, but that didn't mean that everything wasn't still familiar, comforting. Stretching, Ryder tried to decide which direction to head in, and then, as if it had been yesterday and not years ago, he took off in the one direction that had always called to him.

The sun was just starting to make its debut as he made his way down the beach all by himself. No one else was privy to the start of this day, and that was the way he liked it. Soon the sand would be covered with residents and tourists alike, and Ryder knew that by that time, he'd be safely ensconced back in his home. Not that he was antisocial—far from it. It was just that right now, at this point in his life, he needed a little quality alone time. Work had been brutal for the last several years, and as the one heading up the West Coast branch of Montgomerys, a lot of heavy responsibility had been placed on his shoulders.

Right now, the only responsibility he wanted was deciding what to eat for breakfast and nothing more.

Up ahead, a flash of bright green caught his eye. Not breaking stride, Ryder did his best to focus on it. One more person out on the large expanse of coastline shouldn't have been an issue; it was the placement of that person that had his nerves more than a little on edge.

There was no way that it was possible.

It was both too much to hope for and everything that he dreaded all at once.

The closer he got to the house at the end of this particular section of the beach, Ryder knew that all of his hopes and fears were about to collide.

Casey Peterson.

Ryder slowed his pace as his mind raced to what he was supposed to do. She was standing out on the deck on the back of her house, looking out at the waves and the sunrise. The wind was blowing her wavy, brown hair out behind her, and his fingers actually twitched as he remembered how silky it was. Soon, his other senses jumped on board the memory train, and he could no longer smell the surf, only the scent of vanilla. Casey always smelled like warm vanilla, and he had enjoyed nothing more all those summers ago than tasting every inch of her.

This was so not the relaxing morning run that he was used to. Now, every inch of him was on alert, and Ryder considered doing a quick about-face back toward his home before she saw him. Who was he kidding? Chances were that Casey wouldn't even remember him, and if she did, she'd either ignore him or find something heavy to throw at his head.

He was hoping for option one but had a feeling that she'd definitely go for option two.

He'd been a royal jackass back then. Cocky to the point of being obnoxious. Even though he knew that she was too good for him, Ryder'd had no choice but to get involved with her.

And then to let her go.

Twelve years was a long time to hold a grudge though, he thought to himself. What would happen if he continued on his run, stopped at the base of the stairs that led up to her house, and said a quick hello? In business, Ryder was the poster boy for confidence, but suddenly, when faced with having to confront an ex-girlfriend from way too long ago, he felt as if every ounce of that confidence had been left back in San Diego.

How bad could it be? Wasn't it better just to rip the damn Band-Aid off all at once? Casey lived less than a mile from his family home; they were bound to run into one another eventually. Why not just get it over with so they could move on with their lives?

Because she may be pint-sized compared to you, but she has the ability to knock you on your butt.

Truer words had never been spoken—or thought.

When Ryder had told Casey that he was leaving right after graduation, the look on her face had nearly destroyed him. While the Montgomerys had money and a secure social status, Ryder had been determined to make a name for himself on his own, far away from where anyone knew who they were.

Even if it meant leaving Casey behind.

Hell, her blue eyes, so full of hurt and disappointment, still haunted him. Looking back, Ryder knew he had done the right thing. But now, as he got closer to the base of those steps, he found that he was more than a little afraid to face the woman who had been everything to him.

Never one to walk away from a challenge, Ryder jogged the last few yards to the foot of the stairs and looked up just as Casey was looking down. He knew the instant she recognized him because her face went from serene to wary to disgust in a matter of seconds.

"Hey, Casey," he said, hating the uncertainty in his voice. Where the hell was the cool confidence that was always with him?

"Wow," she said with barely concealed disapproval. "You certainly didn't waste any time."

Ryder looked at her with confusion. "Waste any time? What are you talking about?"

"Mac and Gina's wedding? Your uncle said he'd be calling you, but I figured you'd at least wait until I actually needed to involve you before showing up here. And even then I figured you'd just come to the office."

That did nothing to alleviate his confusion. "I'm afraid you've lost me, Case," he said, and saw her stiffen. Everyone used that nickname, but when he called her that, it had always made her melt.

"Didn't William call you?"

"No."

"How about Mac?"

Ryder shook his head.

"What are you doing here, Ryder?" Wariness laced her voice.

"I'm on sabbatical…"

Casey shook her head. "No, what are you doing *here*?"

Ryder took a deep breath and then just shook his head again. "I don't know. I came out to do my usual morning run and this is where I ended up."

She looked at him with disbelief. "So this is all just a weird coincidence?"

"I don't know," he admitted honestly, and before he knew what he was doing, Ryder found himself walking up the stairs toward her. When finally they were face-to-face, Ryder knew he was in deep trouble. The years simply faded away; Casey was just as beautiful as he remembered. Maybe even more so. Her big, blue eyes stared up at him. "Hey," he said softly, his own dark gaze captivating hers.

~~~

She was in trouble. Deep, deep trouble. One look at the man that Ryder had become and Casey was almost ready to melt into a puddle at his feet. He was taller than she remembered and much more muscular. Standing before her in a pair of black athletic shorts and a gray T-shirt, she knew without a doubt that he was in prime physical shape. But once her gaze settled on his face? His whiskey-colored eyes, his disheveled sandy-brown hair…and that dimple barely making an appearance in his right cheek made one thing abundantly clear.

Her perfectly organized world was about to be turned upside down.

Meet the Montgomerys

———

Return to You

The Montgomery Brothers

Book #4

———

James

James Montgomery has achieved everything he'd hoped for in life…except marrying the girl of his dreams. After a terrible accident, Selena Ainsley left ten years ago. She took his heart with her, and she's never coming back. But it's becoming harder and harder for him to forget their precious time together, and James can't help but wonder what he would do if they could ever meet again.

———

From *Return to You*:

James wasn't sure what to say. If what she was telling him was true, then he had wasted a large part of his life over a lie. But how was he ever going to be sure? How could he just blindly believe her? His mind was still reeling with all of this new information when Selena continued to speak.

"Coming back here was too painful. I knew that if I allowed myself the opportunity, no matter how many years had passed, I'd still look for you. I had no idea if it

would do me any good, but I…I just needed to see you."
She nearly choked on the admission.

"Do you know why I became a cop?" he asked suddenly. Selena shook her head. "It was because of what happened that night. I was put in a position that wasn't fair and it wasn't right, and I vowed that I would never let that happen again. I left town the next morning, stayed with some other relatives in upstate New York. I worked my ass off to get my GED and joined the academy. I had to struggle and fight my way to get a job back in this area. Because, like you, I felt if I stayed here in the area, I'd be able to find you and prove you and your family wrong."

She ignored the last part of that statement. "What about your plans for college? Your landscaping business?"

"What was the point?" he said. "I had to make sure I never felt like I did that night ever again."

"So you gave up your dream?" Disbelief laced her tone.

James shrugged. "It was worth it. I have a job where I am respected, and now *I* have the authority." His voice was hard, and Selena cringed. She had never seen this side of him. "I used to wish that I'd run into your father, that I'd pull him over for something and threaten him like he threatened me. The idea of seeing the look of fear on his face was something that kept me going through a lot of hard times."

"And now?" she asked quietly.

"Now, he doesn't matter. What's done is done, and if you're not willing to make him admit that he lied, then we're at an impasse here."

Selena balled her fists. "Seriously? You still think

I'm the one who's lying? Why? Why would I even do that? Did this morning mean nothing to you? Do you think I'm the type of woman who just sleeps around? I have never given myself to another man the way I have to you! I could never!"

The thought of any man with his hands on Selena had James seeing red. "No," he said through clenched teeth. "I don't think that, but maybe this was all about closure or maybe just passing the time while you're here. Or maybe, just maybe, you thought it would be fun to play with my head a little bit more for old time's sake."

Shock hit Selena as if he had physically thrown a punch. "If that's what you think of me, then I guess you never really knew me at all. Maybe everything that happened back then was for the best, because if you think so little of me that I would do all of those horrible things, then you're not the man I believed you to be." Tears began to form again, and she quickly swiped them away. Straightening her spine and doing her best to keep her voice steady, she faced him. "I think we're done here, and you should go." Looking around the room, Selena found where his keys had landed earlier and went to pick them up. Walking over to James, she faced him and held them out for him.

They stared one another down for several minutes. The only sound in the room was their breathing. Finally James broke the silence. "It's not supposed to end like this." His voice broke with emotion. "Not now."

"It didn't," she said with equal sadness. "It ended ten years ago, and it was so much worse."

He stepped forward and winced when Selena took a step back. Stopping where he was, James dropped his hands to his sides in defeat. "I just don't know how I'm supposed to believe you." But James was filling up with a sense of self-loathing; if she were right, then he had nothing else to hold on to. All of the anger, all of the years of self-discipline, were for nothing.

"I never lied to you, James, not once. I can apologize for the things my father said and did, but it won't change anything. Even if I picked up the phone right now and called him, would it change anything? Our baby is gone; ten years of our lives are gone." She wiped away the last of her tears. "I can't keep living in the past; I've been there for too long."

"I have too," he admitted. "I don't know how to live any other way anymore." This time when he took a step forward, she didn't move. He kept walking until he stood right in front of her. "If I don't have my anger, I don't know what I have."

You have me.

The words were on the tip of her tongue, and yet Selena wasn't sure if she should say them. "I'm angry too," she said quietly.

James knew that he couldn't hold back any longer; the need to reach out and touch her was too great. His hand came up and caressed her cheek. "Where do we go from here?"

"I can't force you to believe me; I can only tell you the truth. I've only ever told you the truth. Only you can decide whether you're going to believe me."

"I want to, Selena; I really do. I just don't know how. For so long, I've believed the things your father said to me. It's hard to believe that someone, even a distraught father, would make up such a hateful story."

She snorted with disbelief. "Then you never really knew my father either."

And that's when it hit him: he didn't. Selena's parents had formed their opinion of him right from the start, and James had done his best to steer clear of them while he and Selena had been dating. They'd made their feelings perfectly clear, and at the time, James hadn't been interested in trying to change their minds.

In the heat of the moment, at a specific point in time when emotions were running high, James had chosen to believe the words of a man who had never shown him anything but hatred. Why? How could he have let himself do that? At the time, he knew why he couldn't have fought the man; Jerry Ainsley held all the cards, and James knew without a doubt that the man wouldn't think twice about having him arrested. James had worked too hard to let that happen.

So he ran.

Back then, he didn't have a choice, but he could have come back when things settled down. He should have come back and at least confronted Selena then. He dropped his chin to his chest. He should have listened to his heart instead of being so damn stubborn and full of pride. Hadn't his own parents told him that it was his worst trait and that it would likely be the ruin of him? They were right, and it had.

It was a bitter pill to swallow.

"Don't make me leave," he finally said over the lump in his throat as he raised his head, his brown eyes shining with unshed tears of his own.

It was more than Selena could bear. "I don't really want you to." The last was a mere whisper as she wrapped her arms around him and pulled him close. Together they wept for all they'd had and lost, grieving together like they were denied so long ago.

Minutes passed before they reluctantly pulled apart. Before she moved too far away, James put his arm around Selena and tucked her into his side as they walked over to the sofa and sat back down. When he was sure she was comfortable, he poured them each a glass of water.

"I'm so sorry," she began, but James placed a finger over her lips to silence her.

"I'm the one who's sorry. I should have been there for you."

"But you couldn't…"

"Maybe not right then and there, but I should have come back. I was so angry and hell-bent on proving everyone wrong that I completely lost sight of what was most important. And that was you." Shoulder to shoulder with her, he leaned in and rested his head against hers.

Meet the Montgomerys

—⁓—

Meant for You

The Montgomery Brothers

Book #5

—⁓—

Summer

Ethan Reed would like nothing more than to live by his own rules. Not wanting to disappoint his best friend Zach, or any of the Montgomerys, Ethan's had to push aside his long-denied feelings for Summer Montgomery. But it only takes one night away from watchful eyes to make impossible dreams come true…

—⁓—

From *Meant for You*:

"It's quiet; it's too damn quiet."

"No, it's peaceful. For the first time in over a month, I can hear myself think."

Zach Montgomery looked over at his friend Ethan and grimaced. "That's the problem. When Summer is in town, no one should be able to hear themselves think. I'm telling you, something is up."

"Why are you looking for trouble?" Ethan asked wearily. "For weeks you've been practically begging for a little peace and quiet, and now that you have it, you're bitching about it. Just be thankful, and long may it last."

While Zach knew Ethan had a point, it just wasn't sitting right with him. When his father had warned him his little sister was coming to Oregon to try her hand at the family business, Zach had been less than enthusiastic. It wasn't that there was anything wrong with Summer, per se; it was just that she was like a force of nature.

And not in a good way.

"Why would she go silent now?" Zach said as he paced his office. "Besides trying to work in every department we have here at Montgomerys and making everyone her new best friend—she's baked cookies for every department she's interned with, when she was in accounting she organized Sheila's baby shower, in human resources she taught Margaret's daughter how to tap dance, and in legal she dog-sat for Mark—and in the midst of it all, she has been particularly vocal about this whole Denali thing. I leave in less than thirty-six hours and she goes missing? She's up to something." He looked to his best friend and company vice president and waited for his agreement. "Right? She has to be up to something."

Ethan shrugged. "Personally, I'm just enjoying the quiet." The truth, however, was that Ethan was worried about Summer's whereabouts, maybe even more so than Zach. Summer had been a distraction since she'd arrived on the West Coast. The first time he had seen her step off the elevator, Ethan was lost. When had Zach's little sister grown up into such a vibrant and sexy woman? It had been a shock for him to see that the girl he had grown up with wasn't a little girl anymore. She wasn't a nuisance anymore, and the more time he spent with her and got to know her, the more intrigued he became. He had come to expect to see her around, talk to her. Hear her laugh.

See her smile.

Oh man, he had it bad. A quick glance at Zach and he was relieved his friend was too busy staring out at the city skyline to notice what was probably a goofy look on Ethan's face. He'd gotten pretty damn good at hiding his feelings for Summer; hell, he had to. If Zach or any of the multitude of Montgomery males found out Ethan had a serious thing for Summer, he'd be screwed.

And beaten to a bloody pulp for sure.

Not something he was looking to see happen.

So he hid his feelings, brushed her off, and generally tried to make her feel like she was just a friend, a coworker. She was far from it. Summer had a light about her, an energy that was impossible to ignore. Sometimes all she had to do was walk into a room for him to feel it. He wanted to embrace it and engage in conversation with her. Unfortunately, there was always one of her brothers or cousins or uncles around waiting with the stink eye whenever he let his guard down. It was pretty exhausting to keep up with them all.

So right now? Yeah, he was happy to have a little peace and quiet and a chance just to be himself without having to watch how he spoke or looked or hovered whenever Summer Montgomery was in the room. He'd take whatever he could get in that department until she moved on to whatever adventure she wanted to take on next.

"Why won't she answer her phone?" Zach snapped, effectively pulling Ethan out of his own introspection.

"Maybe you just finally succeeded in pissing her off." Ethan sighed. Honestly, dealing with this family was enough to make him thankful to be an only child. One minute Zach was complaining about having his sister around, and the next he was complaining because she wasn't around.

"What's that supposed to mean?"

Ethan stood and walked toward the large picture window to stand beside Zach. "Listen," he began, placing a hand on his friend's shoulder. "You have been less than hospitable since your sister got here. You've let her know on a daily basis that you're not taking her interest in the company seriously because you think she's just going to move on whenever the mood strikes."

"Well?" Zach said with a hint of annoyance. "It's true! She's been…what? She's been a photographer, a yoga instructor, a New York City tour guide…then there was her whole dog-walking business. I mean, Summer has a short attention span, Ethan. She's wasting my time and the company's time by coming here and trying to play in the business world like some sort of corporate Barbie."

"That's just cold, Zach, even for you."

"Look, you've known my sister almost as long as you've known me. Am I exaggerating any of this?" Ethan shook his head. "Summer is a free spirit; hell, my mother must have known it at birth because she gave her the perfect name for her nature. She's an amazingly talented and creative woman; she just needs to channel her energy someplace else and leave me the hell alone."

"Isn't that what she's doing?" Ethan reminded.

"No. She's being a pain in my ass right now. I

wouldn't listen to her constant harping on me about the climb and how I am being irresponsible and—"

"Well, she kind of has a point there."

Zach rolled his eyes. "Not you too," he said, sighing irritably. "We've been over this. I got the doctor's clearance."

"And that doesn't mean squat and you know it," Ethan replied. "I've known you for far too long, man. I know when you're not one hundred percent on your game, and you're not. You're still limping from the last trip."

"It was a broken leg, Ethan. It wasn't a big deal."

"It is when it's not fully healed. You need to be thinking a little more responsibly. This isn't an easy trip. You need to be in top physical condition, and you're not."

"It's a limp and it's not going to be a problem."

"Zach…"

"Can we get back to the subject at hand? Summer and how she's off pouting somewhere and probably hoping I'll cancel my plans because I'll have to look for her. Well, it won't work; I'm not buying into it."

"You can't have it both ways," Ethan muttered as he turned to walk away.

"Excuse me?" Zach said, his gaze honing in on his friend.

Throwing up his hands in frustration, Ethan turned back around. "I can't keep saying it; you say you don't want her here, so she's not here and now you're ticked off. Make up your damn mind, Zach!"

Ethan was right; Zach knew it and yet it didn't help to put his mind at ease. Stepping away from the window, he went and sat back down at his desk, resting his head in his hands. "I swear she's like a miniature hurricane;

she swoops in, wreaks havoc, and then moves on. I just wish she'd answer my damn calls so at least I'd know she's all right before I leave for Denali."

"Have you asked around the office? Maybe she mentioned to someone she was going someplace."

Zach looked up and considered Ethan's words. "I hadn't thought of that. She's so chatty that I'm sure she had to say something to someone." He immediately reached for his phone and called his assistant into the room. While he waited, he returned his attention to Ethan. "Gabriella knows everything that goes on in this building; if she doesn't know where Summer is, we're screwed."

"We?" Ethan said with a laugh. "Sorry, bro, your sister, your problem."

"Don't give me that," Zach said dismissively. "You and I both know you're practically family and I'm sure that, deep down, you're a little bit worried about her yourself."

More than you know.

Luckily he didn't have to respond because Zach's assistant came into the room. Gabriella Martine looked like she'd stepped right off the pages of Italian *Vogue*. She was tall and slim with just enough curves to grab a man's attention. Ethan had always admired her beauty, but not in a way that made him want to act on it. Gabriella had jet-black hair, crystal-blue eyes, and a cool, distant disposition.

Ethan seemed to prefer the type with blond hair, dark eyes, fair skin, and a chatty nature.

Summer Montgomery.

He was so screwed.

Meet the Montgomerys

—◆◆◆—

I'll Be There

The Montgomery Brothers

Book #6

—◆◆◆—

Zach

Zach Montgomery's perfect world is turned upside down when a climbing accident leaves him broken, angry, and maddeningly dependent. In his slow quest for recovery, Gabriella Martine is always there to help…but Zach is being forced to reevaluate what it means to be a man worthy of her love.

—◆◆◆—

From *I'll Be There*:

"What?!"

"You heard me. I know you banged your head pretty hard when you fell off that mountain, but your hearing is just fine."

Zach Montgomery looked at his father and felt nothing but rage. With everything he had been through, this was what he got? "So you're firing me?"

Robert shrugged, trying to seem indifferent to his son and the situation at hand. "I'm not saying fired; it's an ugly word. I'm just saying with everything you have going on, maybe it's best for you to have one fewer responsibility."

"I made this office what it is!" Zach yelled. "You and Uncle William didn't want to branch out to the West Coast. You were more than happy with things as they were. I took the chance and started things out here, and I've made millions for the company! How can you just forget that?"

"I'm not forgetting anything, Zach," Robert said wearily. "We all know what you did and how hard you've worked. But with things the way they are right now, we need someone at the helm and that's not you. We need a full executive staff. I need to get back home and so does William. Ethan can't handle everything by himself, and you're not willing to pitch in and help out."

"So I'm out and Ethan's in?" he sneered. "Who's going to take Ethan's position?"

"We've approached Summer about it."

That felt like a slap in the face. A couple of months ago, Zach had found the idea of his sister working in his office to be laughable. She was more like a damn camp counselor than a business executive and now— after one massive deal—everyone saw her as vice-president material? Maybe he had hit his head harder than he thought. "This is the most ridiculous thing I've ever heard. Summer isn't ready to take on that kind of responsibility. Besides, doesn't she have a wedding to plan or something?"

"She did," Robert said, rising to get himself something to drink. There was no way he could look at his son with a straight face right now. The look of sheer

shock on Zach's face at the mention of Summer stepping up into his league had been comical. He almost
felt bad about it.

"What do you mean, *did*? Has something happened?
Is Summer all right?"

"Yes. But you had an accident, Ethan's been running
the company, and Summer has really stepped up. They
haven't had time to talk about wedding plans or see how
their house back east is coming along. You are their main
concern right now. Their lives are on hold right now *for
you*. I know Summer was hoping to have her engage-
ment party back home, but she won't plan anything until
you're better. She wants you there. We all do."

It didn't sound like it to Zach. It sounded like everyone was gearing up to wash their hands of him. "That's
not fair, Dad," he said. "There's no timeline for when
I'll be better, or even *if* I'll be better."

"There would be if you'd do the therapy your doctor
prescribed and make an attempt to help yourself."

"You don't think I've tried?" he snapped. "Do you
have any idea how freaking much I've been through
already? They tell me I'll walk again and be just like
I was before, but I don't see it happening. I still have
spells where I can't feel a damn thing, and when I *can*
feel, it hurts like hell! So until you've had your entire
body broken, don't think you can preach to me about
hurrying up and healing. It's not that easy!"

"And when have you ever walked away from a challenge?" Robert yelled back. "For crying out loud, Zach,
ever since you were a kid, you've refused to be told you
couldn't do something. You challenged your mother and
me in every aspect of your damn life! But now? Now

that it really counts and it's really hard, you're going to sit here and quit?"

"I'm not quitting! I'm just—"

"I think," Robert interrupted, "that up until now, everything in your life has come easily to you. You were a naturally gifted athlete. School and academics required very little effort from you. Starting this office and getting it off the ground, while challenging, still seemed to go according to your plans. But this injury? This accident? It's messed with your psyche. When you didn't see immediate results, you gave up and quit. It's not happening fast enough for you. Well, news flash, Son, no one said it was going to."

"You have no idea how painful it is," Zach said through clenched teeth.

"I don't," Robert said solemnly, "and I hate more than anything that you have to go through it. If I could, Zach, I'd do it for you; I'd take the pain on myself. But I can't. This is something only you can do. You have to decide if you're going to fight for it or if you're going to let it defeat you."

Zach stared defiantly at his father for a solid minute. Seriously, did the old man have any idea the level of pain he was dealing with? Did he even know most days it took a Herculean effort just to get out of bed and move to a chair? Or the humiliation of needing someone to help him get dressed or take a shower?

"I think by taking the responsibility of the company off your shoulders, you can put your focus on your physical therapy," Robert said to break the silence.

"This branch of Montgomerys is *mine*," he growled. "I know Ethan was there with me from the beginning and I appreciate everything he's doing, but you have no right to put him in charge. It wasn't your decision to make."

"What choice did I have?" Robert said with frustration. "We can keep going around and around in circles on this. You can't have your cake and eat it too, Zach! You don't want to work and there's a company to run! Enough now! The decision is made!"

Zach tried to stand up, but his legs wouldn't support him and he fell right back down into his seat. He yelled out a curse of frustration and wanted to scream at the unfairness of it all. Thankfully, his father hadn't rushed to his side to offer his help. He hated when people took pity on him and fussed around him like he was an invalid. Taking a minute to calm himself down, he flexed his legs until he had the feeling back in them completely before turning his attention back to his father.

"Please," he said as calmly as possible. "I'm really trying to find a balance here. I don't like asking for help. I don't like *needing* help. What…what can I do to prove to you that I'm trying?"

Robert's expression remained neutral. "For starters, you have to stop firing the therapists. You're not going to get better on your own, Zach. You need them."

"But they're idiots."

"No, they're not. They know what they're doing and you need to listen to them. In this situation, they're the experts, not you."

"Fine," he murmured. "So if I do the therapy, you'll back off firing me?"

"No."

"What the *hell*, Dad? I just asked you what I had to do and you said therapy and I agreed!"

"That's only part of it."

If you love the Montgomerys, wait until you meet The Shaughnessy Brothers

Made for Us

Aidan

Book #1

—◁ܓ▷—

The Shaughnessy brothers have spent the years since their mother's untimely death taking care of one another and trying to make their father proud. Oldest son Aidan is hardworking, handsome, successful—and still single. Sure, he'd like to have his own family someday, but who has the time?

Zoe Dalton, a stunning designer Aidan meets on one of his construction jobs, has the beauty and heart to make Aidan realize how much he's been missing. But it's not easy to break down walls you've spent years building up. Now there's a major storm bearing down on the North Carolina coast, and it could be catalyst enough to force Aidan and Zoe into some major decisions of the heart.

Love Walks In

Hugh

Book #2

—⁓—

Aubrey Burke is on the run from an about-to-be-disastrous mistake when resort owner Hugh Shaughnessy catches her climbing through his office window. Until Aubrey tumbled into his life, Hugh had relied on work and discipline to safeguard a heart damaged by family tragedy. Now his careful world will never be the same.

Hugh's approach to life and love is the opposite of Aubrey's, but she soon finds herself falling hard for the handsome hotel mogul. There's a darker reason behind her "live for today" attitude than Hugh could possibly know, but for the first time Aubrey dares to hope this man's love might make it worth taking a chance on the future.

Always My Girl

Quinn

Book #3

—◦◦◦—

Quinn Shaughnessy's two older brothers have found their true loves…but Quinn's not about to join that parade. Nope, as he tells his best friend Anna, there's a lot more to life than getting tied down to one person. He's positive tomboy Anna will be on his side—except she's inexplicably developing other interests—even dating! Suddenly Quinn is seeing Anna in a very different light.

Quinn has been Anna's buddy since they were both five years old. She can tell him anything—except the one big secret she's been hiding for years—that she's fallen in love with him. Now Anna is determined to make a life for herself that doesn't include pining for Quinn. Falling in love with your best friend? Easy. Telling them how you really feel? Impossible.

About the Author

New York Times and *USA Today* bestseller/contemporary romance writer Samantha Chase released her debut novel, *Jordan's Return*, in November 2011. Although she waited until she was in her forties to publish for the first time, writing has been a lifelong passion. Her motivation to take that step was her students: teaching creative writing to elementary-age students all the way up through high school and encouraging those students to follow their writing dreams gave Samantha the confidence to do so as well.

When she's not working on a new story, she spends her time reading contemporary romances, playing way too many games of Scrabble or solitaire on Facebook, and spending time with her husband of twenty-five years and their two sons in North Carolina.